SELDOM GOES

SELDOM GOES

VANESSA GRAY BARTAL

Dry Creek Press

Author's Note

In aiming for historical accuracy, one character uses words that our society no longer deems appropriate to describe other ethnicities. Another character points out the hurtfulness of the words, and he doesn't use them again. The usage in this context is merely to denote how much things have changed and should not be taken as an endorsement of the words.

I

"Your peanut butter buttercream is to die for."

Seldom heard some version of that comment multiple times a day and never grew weary of it. This was, after all, why she'd opened a bakery. It certainly wasn't for the long hours, the early mornings, the thin profit margins, the supply and employee headaches, the governmental tax bureaucracy. It was, in a nutshell, to bring people pleasure through food. And so far she was succeeding, at least in that. How long she'd be able to survive in the city's tough and competitive economy was anybody's guess. *You should have done a food truck,* the cynical little voice in her head was always ready to chime in with criticism. It would have made more financial sense to at least begin with a truck, but Seldom wasn't known for doing the safe thing, nor the popular thing. She had always been singular. With a name like Seldom, was it any wonder? Nonconformity had been a foregone conclusion the moment her mother signed the birth certificate.

And now, three years into the running of Seldom Sweet, her eponymously named bakery, and she was beginning to breathe a little easier. Not that she was thriving by any means. Every day was still an uphill climb for survival and likely always would be. But the myriad little things required of her were starting to wane. The shop was finding a groove, and so was Seldom. That was why she went on the date in the first place, and that was when her life went haywire.

"Thank you so much," Seldom said, packaging the cupcakes with extra care. The bakery did everything but wedding cakes, but the cupcakes were the best sellers by far, along with the frosted cut out cookies. She could probably make a go of it by selling those two things, but it wasn't the vision she had for her bakery. She wanted it to be an old fashioned, full service bakery. The kind full of oatmeal bars and chocolate chip cookies and brioche doughnuts on the weekends.

"I think that about wraps it up, boss," her employee, Josh, said as the last customer made his way outside, fully loaded box in hand.

"That it does, Joshua. Flip the sign." Josh was 21, only seven years younger than her 28, but so guileless he reminded her of a baby bird, freshly pushed from the nest. Meanwhile Seldom had been absent the nest so long she was beginning to wonder if she'd ever been in it. He dutifully flipped the sign and they began the closing routine. She handled the money while he cleaned the dishes. When she was finished with her portion, she washed the windows and floors. It was a soothing ritual, a preparation that would ensure everything was perfect tomorrow when she opened. Beginning her day fresh with no mistakes made the possibilities seem endless. Somehow survival had made her an optimist, a badge she wore with honor.

They finished their cleanup and stared at each other, reluctant to say goodnight. It was always this way at the end of the day. There was something cozy about the bakery, something that made people want to linger. That, more than anything else, made Seldom feel good, the fact that maybe she had created the sort of environment that made people feel cozy. Or maybe Josh's life was as messed up as hers and they clung to each other like monkeys. Either way, he'd become a real friend to her, the little brother she never had, the only one of her employees who felt like family.

"Tonight's the night," he announced unnecessarily.

"Yes." She agreed, nodding decisively.

"I can't believe my little Seldom has a date," he said, shaking his head.

"I'm turning into a real girl, Joshy," she replied, rifling his hair. He dashed her hand away, annoyed at the disturbance to his artfully gelled mane.

"Don't mess up my locks, man. I have a date, too."

"That's not a very deferential attitude to use on your boss," she chided.

He put her in a headlock and bussed her cheek. "Have fun on your first date in a decade, loser. How's that?"

"Better," she said, returning his affection with a hug around his waist. "And it hasn't been a decade. More like three years." She had been far too busy building her business to concern herself with a social life. When she first began to open the bakery, she had a boyfriend. But relationships took a back seat when twenty-hour days became routine. Lately she had been able to dial it back to fourteen-hour days, giving her hope of a social life again. Still, she was nervous. Her taste in men had always been sketchy at best.

"Can't wait to hear all about it, boss," Josh said, looping his elbow with hers as they walked outside. He paused beside her as she locked up and then, with a final pat to her head, walked away. She watched him go a minute, feeling preemptively melancholy. Josh would not stay at the shop forever. He was young and sharp and enthusiastic. At some point he would grow up and find his way in life, as he should. But it would also mean that she would lose him as an employee and likely also as a friend. She wasn't idealistic enough to believe their friendship would last when they no longer saw each other every day.

Seldom sighed and made herself turn away. It was often like this for her. She seemed to always live both in the present and the future, with a near-omniscient understanding of what was about to take place. For instance, she already knew that her shop wouldn't last forever, that businesses such as hers rarely survived past a decade, that at some point she would have to find something else to do with her life. She thought these things even as she was working a hundred hours a week to make a go of it. She had always been dichotomous in nature, a cynical optimist, an outgoing introvert, a sure-footed dreamer, a lazy go-getter. She used to wonder if she was crazy for being two people at once, but now she accepted it for the gift it was. Her chameleon nature made her adaptable and resilient. And her intuition was off the charts.

Except when it came to men. It was as if she had a mental block about them, an inability to heed the red flags. For that reason she usually avoided dating altogether, but crippling loneliness was a painful burden to bear. And so she'd signed up for online dating. At first it had seemed tacky, almost desperate. But how else was it done these days? Work was her life. When men came into her shop, they were usually there to buy treats for someone already in their lives. No one came to a bakery in search of romance. No one but Seldom, maybe.

Tonight's date had been online flirting with her for months. On paper he was perfect, professional, handsome, established, witty. Of course it was possible she'd been catfished, that in reality he was a six hundred pound gamer who lived in his mother's basement. Maybe he wasn't even a man. On the internet, people could be anyone. Even Seldom had found the most flattering picture possible to post on the site, one that showed her curvy figure at its best, hiding her tummy pooch and the dusting of flour that always covered her apron. Her hair had been down though usually, as now, it was worn up for work. How honest was honest enough? Should she have warned him that the picture made her look like a size six but in reality she was a solid size ten? Weight was a tricky thing. Seldom had found that though men often said they wanted a woman with curves, in reality they tended to go for the Hollywood size zero types.

Thoughts of her appearance caused her to pause, reach into her bag, and touch up her makeup. She had been blessed with good skin, naturally smooth and blemish-free. Her lashes were a bit skimpy. She added another dose of mascara and reapplied her lip gloss. Satisfied, she snapped the mirror closed and continued on her way to her destination.

The restaurant was five blocks from the bakery, and Seldom walked, as she did most places. She had sold her car to help pay for the bakery; she didn't miss it.

They had chosen to meet at the restaurant for safety's sake. It had been his suggestion, and Seldom appreciated it, though she cynically wondered if he merely wanted to give himself an out in case she turned out to be less than promised. A valet opened the door for her. She nodded, smiling, and stepped inside.

The interior of the place was dark and trendy. Seldom glanced helplessly around for her date but didn't immediately see him.

"May I help you?" the hostess asked.

"I'm supposed to meet someone. I'm not sure..." Seldom trailed off, not sure how to finish. I'm not sure if he's here? I'm not sure what he looks like? I'm not sure I'm doing the right thing by meeting a guy I hooked up with on the internet?

The hostess smiled. "He's waiting for you."

"How did you know?"

"He described you and told me to keep an eye out." There was something in the hostess's manner that made Seldom's stomach stir. Envy, maybe? But why would she be envious of...oh. They reached the table and stopped short. Seldom's first thought was that she hadn't been catfished. Her second was that maybe he had because he was way, way, *way* out of her league. It wasn't merely that he was devastatingly handsome, although he was. It was his air—suave, confident, assured. If one didn't know better, one might assume he owned the restaurant. He had certainly commanded center stage. Everyone was staring at them as she made her approach. She had the mad desire to curtsy and the thought had to be stifled before it made her giggle.

"Seldom," he said, standing. "Thank you, Maria," he added to the hostess who actually blushed and stumbled as she backed away.

"Christian," Seldom said, extending her hand. He took it and brought it to his lips, kissing the back of it.

"Please, have a seat," he said as he came around to hold the chair for her. Something prickled within her. Whether it was a silent alarm warning her away from him or merely the comparison of him to everyone else she'd ever dated she had no idea. No one had ever kissed her hand or held her chair for her. But that was what she wanted, wasn't it? Someone different than the others? Someone with a job and future and self-possession? No more Peter Pan imitators, afraid of life and success and maturity.

"I have to tell you I am pleasantly surprised," he said. He picked up his napkin, flicked it open, and laid it in his lap.

"Oh?" she asked.

"You'd be shocked how few people live up to their photos."

"I could say the same about you, but this is actually my first date on this app."

"Really? I find it's the most expedient way to meet people these days. Everyone is so busy, myself included. Maybe it's cynical, but online dating feels like cutting through a few layers of red tape."

"I don't disagree, but I tend to think the red tape is where the fun is—the thrill of the hunt, you know? That back and forth dance in the beginning, the does he or doesn't he like me, the will we or won't we fall in love? It's as enchanting as it is nerve wracking and disheartening. And therein lies the magic, I think."

He regarded her with an amused half-smile. "That speech was enchanting. So far, you're a delight, Seldom. From your name to your dress to that French twist in your hair. A real throwback."

She glanced down at her swing dress self-consciously. "I try to keep up the image for my business. It's my hope that the retro look will make customers feel welcome and nostalgic."

"It's definitely working on me, and I'm not even a customer," he said. He smiled at her. She felt the prickle again and glanced down quickly at her menu to hide her reaction. There was no rational reason for it to be there. Christian was perfectly handsome and polite. And yet... The waiter arrived soon after to take their orders. His name was Charlie. Seldom remembered because Christian used it three times while he was taking their order.

"You're big into names," she observed when Charlie left.

Christian gave a light shrug. "I like to make people feel valued, to know that they're seen, no matter who they are or what they do."

Again it was one of those things that should have made him more likeable, but behind the words Seldom wondered if she sensed some hidden pretension. Humility or condescension? She couldn't tell, and she wasn't certain she had ever encountered anyone who caused her to confuse the two before. If nothing else, Christian was a fascinating study in character.

He was adept at small talk too, keeping up such a string of innocuous questions that Seldom found herself opening up to him much more than she usually did, especially for a first date. In contrast, he said very little at all.

"I'm sorry, I'm monopolizing the conversation here. Let's talk about you. Where are you from?" she asked.

"I'm from all over. My family traveled a lot for my father's job. You were born and raised here, is that correct?"

And then she was off again, being lulled into talking about herself while she ate. Soon her meal was finished and she flushed with embarrassment, realizing she'd talked the whole time.

"I never talk that much, honestly," she apologized when she finally took a breath.

"I always enjoy hearing a beautiful lady expound," he said with the smile again. Was the smile supposed to be charming? That wasn't the word Seldom would use for it. *Chilling* would be better, except of course that was crazy. She was being paranoid because it had been so long since she had a date. Maybe this was how it was done now. Everything old was new again. Maybe manners had made a comeback. If so, Christian seemed to possess them in spades. It was as if he was reading from a manual, and maybe *that* was the problem. Everything felt a bit too practiced. Whatever the problem, Seldom realized there wouldn't be a second date. Despite his perfection, or maybe because of it, he was pinging on her meter in a bad way. Despite all logical evidence to the contrary, her instincts were warning her away from him. She was old enough now to be selective and wise enough to listen to her gut.

They walked outside together. The night air brought a much needed sting of mental clarity, enforcing her vow to have done with him. Something was wrong with him, even if she couldn't put her finger on it.

"Would you care for a nightcap?" Christian asked, smiling down at her in that way that should have been enticing but instead made goose-flesh stand on her arms.

"Thank you, that's such a tempting offer, but bakers have early mornings. I'm afraid I'm not much of a night owl anymore." She held out her hand for him to shake. "Thank you so much for supper. I wish you'd let me pay my share. It was so nice to meet you."

She tried to withdraw her hand. He held onto it a beat too long, bringing it to his lips again. "The pleasure was all mine, Seldom."

Seldom swallowed hard and tugged her hand away, wishing for her car for the first time in a long while. It would have been comforting to slide behind the wheel and lock the door. As it was, she had to make the long walk to the subway alone. At first she feared Christian would offer her a ride, but he didn't. He remained on the street, staring at her as she walked away. Somehow that was almost creepier. She could feel his eyes burning into the back of her.

Her phone beeped with a text from Josh.

How was the date? You're not kidnapped or dead in a ditch somewhere, are you?

Yes. I bequeath you the bakery.

Hard pass, boss. I'm too young to devote that much of my life to flour and sugar. By your ready answer I take it there won't be a repeat.

Nah. He was polite and charming and handsome, but...

But?

Creepy like a vampire, not the sparkly ones, but the old-school ones who sneak up in a dark alley and drain you of blood.

Sorry. FYI the sparkly ones are creepy, too. XO

Seldom smiled and tucked her phone away. What would she do without Josh? He was such a sweetie.

There was no sound to alert her to the presence beside her. One moment she was alone, and the next Christian was there, smiling down at her. *Wolfishly,* she thought. Maybe he was a vampire.

"I don't like the idea of you walking alone at night. It seems best if I see you to your destination," he explained.

"Oh," Seldom said, caught off guard and trying not to show it. It wasn't in her nature to let other people take care of her, and certainly not a stranger she didn't trust. "That's kind, but I don't want to trouble you."

"It's no trouble. What are we, a few blocks from the station?"

"Yes," she said. Her voice came out in a scared little squeak. His smile widened as if her fear amused him.

"We're so close to your store. Maybe we could stop in for a personal tour," he suggested.

"Oh." Her mind scrambled. How did he know where her store was when she'd never told him? Of course it bore her name, so it wasn't exactly hard to figure out. "Everything is cleaned and put away for the night. I kind of hate to disturb it." *And I don't want you there because you scare me.* Assigning words to her feelings made them more real and she quickened her pace. Christian did as well. They reached the crosswalk and he put out a hand as if to hold her back, even though she made no attempt to step off the curb.

Annoyed by his presumptive touch, she turned to face him. "What are you...?" She stopped short, blinking. His face was swimming in and out of focus, and now her arm stung. "What?" she tried to speak again, but her tongue felt thick and foreign, too big for her mouth.

"You're so lovely, Seldom," Christian murmured and everything went black as the sidewalk rose up to meet her in a rush.

2

Apparently the stages of grief are also applicable to captivity. That was Seldom's thought when she reached the depression portion of things.

First came the shock. When she woke, sitting up, arm chained to a pipe, she could not believe it had happened to her. That despite her attempt to get away from him, Christian had drugged and kidnapped her. She knew it was him, of course. Who else? No wonder he had made her gut churn; he was psychotic. She wasn't in denial that he had taken her, merely that she had been naïve enough to let it happen. She'd lived in the city all her life. How had she been stupid enough to end up in this predicament? She was no better than a tourist.

Denial burned off quickly, to be rapidly replaced by anger. How dare he? *How dare he?* He had no right to assume control over her person, to put whatever cocktail he had put into her body, to take her wherever this was and chain her up like an unwanted dog. When he returned, she would kick him, hit him, scratch him, bite him, do whatever it took to get away.

But when he returned, she did none of those things. Because he was carrying a tray of medical instruments that made it clear his interest in her was even more nefarious than she first realized. To her chagrin, she whimpered.

Christian smiled, the weird smile that pulled his handsome face taut. "It didn't have to be like this, Seldom."

"How could it have been any different?" she whispered. Her throat felt parched and dry, her lips cracked and swollen.

"If you had come willingly, I would have made it hurt less. But you rejected me, Seldom. And you're going to pay for that." She shrank away from him, trying not to shiver and failing mightily. The building was damp and cold, but she shivered from fear. She could smell it on herself, dank and sour.

His smile widened. He liked her afraid. That should have made her be unafraid, out of stubbornness or pride. But when she needed those things the most, they left her. In their wake was only terror. This man was going to kill her. And he would do it in the worst possible way—slowly, with pain and total enjoyment.

"Oh, not now," he said easily. "I have some other things to see to, some arrangements to make. But I'll be back soon, Seldom. I'll be back very soon." He leaned in and kissed her softly on the lips. *Head butt him, bite him, kick him,* she commanded herself. But her body refused to co-operate. She froze, going stock still while his lips played with hers, part-ing them slightly, his tongue smoothing over her bottom lip. Before she could try to marshal herself and take control of her failing limbs, he was gone, leaving her alone with her terror and revulsion.

That was when the tears arrived. They ran in a river down her face, smacking with audible plops onto the dirty ground beneath her. If not for her horror, the sound would have been soothing, like rain on a metal rooftop. When was the last time she had cried, let alone wept aloud? She couldn't remember, but she did so now, sobbing as her body shook and shuddered. *Please don't let me die; please help me.* Whether a prayer to God or a silent plea for help, she had no idea, but the next moment someone was beside her as if in answer to her request.

"Hey now, what's this?"

Seldom blinked up at the newcomer in surprise, not sure if she was hallucinating. A man stood before her dressed in a suit and tie, a fedora perched jauntily on his head.

"Uh," she stammered, her mouth hanging open. Did Christian have an accomplice? Possibly, but this man was far less scary than Christian.

Despite his impressive height as he towered over her, his face was open, questioning, *gentle*. "Are...are you real?"

He knelt beside her, reached into his inside jacket pocket, withdrew a cloth handkerchief, and began wiping her face. "I'm as real as you are, sweetheart. What's the fuss here?"

After quickly deciding he was a much better option than Christian, no matter who he was, she decided to trust him. Really, what choice did she have? She yanked on the handcuffs, making them rattle. Her companion's eyes narrowed on them, as if noticing them for the first time. "What happened here?" The gentleness was gone from his tone. Now it was menacing, though not directed at her.

"He handcuffed me. He's going to kill me," she said, her words tremulous with shock and fear.

"Your husband?"

"No. Some man I met for a date."

"Let's get you out of here." He reached into his pocket, removed a small key, and inserted it into the cuffs. Seldom was free, but her wariness was back.

"Why do you have a handcuff key in your pocket?" she whispered. *Was* he working with Christian? Was this some elaborate setup, to send in another guy? Would she be taken to another place and tied up again?

Far from being angry, the guy now seemed amused. "Good question." He tossed her a little wink and reached into his inner pocket again. "I'm a cop, sweetheart." He showed her his badge before tucking it away again.

She studied him, from the top of his fedora to the end of his leather wingtip shoes. "With the fashion precinct?"

His smile widened. "I take it that means you think I'm a snappy dresser, thanks, doll. You ready to get out of here?"

She nodded. He grasped her elbow and offered assistance while she toddled shakily to her feet. Christian must have removed her shoes. She saw them lying together a few feet away and reached for them, holding the arm of her companion as she slipped them back on. He stared down at her legs, speculatively.

"What happened to your stockings?"

"My...what?" she asked.

"Your stockings," he pointed to her legs.

"I'm not wearing stockings," she replied.

"Did he take them from you?"

"No, I don't..." she started to say she didn't own stockings, but that wasn't true. She'd bought a couple of retro pairs with seams running up the backs to go with dresses on the occasions she felt like wearing them. Retro was her calling card, after all. "I didn't wear them today."

The man beside her gave her an odd look. "I've never known a dame to leave the house without them."

There were a lot of ways Seldom could have replied. She might have told him she'd never heard anyone call a woman a dame before, let alone the absurd stocking comment. But she was too weak and shaky to do anything more than nod. How long had she been unconscious? Minutes? Hours? Days? The guy slipped his arm around her, and she clung to him as she wobbled outside.

It was still dark when they emerged from the building, a warehouse she didn't recognize.

"What day is it?" she croaked.

"Wednesday, June seventh," he said. His voice was soft and pleasant, almost melodic. Seldom nodded, relieved. It had only been hours, then, since Christian took her captive. "Now." He faced her and ran his hands up and down her arms, whether to try and reassure her or chafe warmth back into them, she had no idea. The effect was the same, either way. The touch was both bracing and warming. "What happened?"

"I had a first date with this man."

"What's the man's name?"

"Christian Renaldo, or so he said. We met at the restaurant."

"He didn't pick you up?" he asked and, once again, his tone was an indictment of some sort.

She shook her head. "That's not safe. It was our first meeting. We met at the restaurant. He was polite and friendly, but I got a bad feeling. So I ended the date and walked away. He followed and must have drugged me. Next thing I knew, I woke up there." She pointed to the building and shuddered.

"You're safe, Miss..."

"Murphy, Seldom Murphy."

One side of his mouth turned up in a smile. "An Irish girl?"

"I suppose." Her family roots were so watered down she was basically a mutt at this point. "Is that a problem?"

He reached into his pocket, withdrew a wallet, and flipped it open to his police ID. She squinted in the darkness of the street lamp to read his name. *Callum J. O'Rourke.*

"Perhaps we're cousins," she suggested.

"Pretty sure I woulda remembered a cousin like you," he said, snapping his wallet closed and stuffing it back into his pocket. "Ready?"

"Where are we going?" she asked.

"To the station. I'll fill out a report and maybe have you look at some mug shots, see if you can find the guy." He clasped her elbow, urging her toward the street, keeping an easy pace so she didn't have to trot. They reached the car and Seldom stopped short. The car was massive, metal, clearly a vintage edition.

"I didn't know they were doing this," she said.

"What's that?" he asked, opening the passenger door for her.

"The throwback thing. You'd think that would have been in the news." It was cute, but was it practical? Was he a real cop, with his fedora and oversized old car? Or was he a fake cop, someone they trotted out for festivals and goodwill events? He waited until she was fully inside before closing the door and walking around to his side. Seldom was entranced by the car until she reached for her belt.

"Where's the seatbelt in this thing?"

He glanced at her. "What?"

"The seatbelt." She tapped the spot behind her where it should have been. "You know, the law."

"Yes, I know the law, but I have no idea what you're yapping about. Would you care to inform me, Miss Murphy?"

"Would you care to inform me, Officer O'Rourke, why you're

dressed like a gangster from a black and white movie and drive this behemoth monster with no seatbelt? Are you really a cop?"

"Dollface, I'm really a cop, and I can assure you from firsthand experience that gangsters dress way better than this," he said, tapping his suit.

"Okay," she drawled, turning her attention out the window. "Where are we?"

"24th and 8th."

She sat up. "What? No we're not."

He stopped and pointed to the street sign.

"This is my neighborhood, but this is not my neighborhood." Everything was different. She clutched the door, pressing her face nearly to the glass. "Can you go to 27th and 7th?"

"Sure thing," he said, but his tone was warier now, the earlier friendliness bordering on suspicion.

"Stop," Seldom shouted, barely waiting until he did so before springing from the car. She bolted onto the sidewalk and stared at her building, her bakery. Only it wasn't her bakery. It was a beautiful old brownstone, cheerful red geraniums lining the stoop. "This...this..."

"What is it, sweetheart?" he asked, coming to stand beside her.

She clutched his arm for support and peered up into his face. He was staring down at her with a mix of concern and suspicion. "What year is it?"

He blinked before answering. "1946."

"Uh. Oh." Her knees buckled, and she would have fallen if not for Callum's strong arm that shot out and caught her.

"What's the story, doll?" he asked, his voice softer, now fully concerned.

She clutched at his arm, trying to swallow down the hysteria. "I think...I think maybe I'm dead."

He smiled and swept a stray hair off her face. "Well, you're some kind of angel."

"No, I'm serious here. Either I'm dead or dreaming or hallucinating."

She squinted up at him. "Though I must be dead. I couldn't conjure anything like you. I didn't even know men looked like this then."

He grinned. "Why, Miss Murphy, is that a compliment?"

"You look so real," she said, standing on her toes to let her fingers skim over his face. He blinked at her again, frozen, not sure what to make of her. "One way to know for sure, I guess." She pressed her palms to his chest, leaned in, and kissed him. Soundly. And he kissed her back, with equal alacrity. After a moment, or possibly two or three, she pulled away and stared up at him. "That felt real."

"It certainly did to me," he agreed. "Are you ready to go to the station, or would you like to keep necking? And you should know I'm fine with either answer."

She puffed a shaky little laugh. "I don't suppose it much matters at this point."

"Well, then," he tipped her face and gave her a soft and lingering little kiss before letting her go and opening her car door once again.

She slid inside and stared at him. He was a decidedly handsome man, tall and broad shouldered, though that might have been the suit. He was dark, dark hair, dark eyes. *Swarthy.* The word popped into her head unbidden and refused to be dislodged. In another time and another place, he would have made an excellent pirate. "Callum," she said, resting her hand gently on his forearm.

"Yes, Miss Murphy?"

"Please call me Seldom."

"Seldom," he dutifully repeated, letting the word roll around on his tongue, testing it.

Seldom leaned closer. "If I'm dead, it's not so bad."

He eased his hand back to clasp hers. "Sweetheart, if I'm dead, it means I wasted a full year back from the war, just waiting for you to show up." He brought her hand to his lips and kissed it. Unlike with Christian, the gesture had its intended consequence, filling her midsection with flutters.

3

If she hadn't been in the midst of a full-blown mental break, Seldom would have enjoyed her glimpse of the city in vintage form. The precinct, Callum's precinct, was so much like she had imagined police stations to be from that era she began to once again believe it sprang from her mind. It was filled with men, white men. Since it was the middle of the night, no women were present. The only people of color anywhere about were doing menial jobs—cleaning, opening doors, serving coffee. It was a jolt for Seldom. Most of the cops she knew in her neighborhood were black or women or black women. It was less crowded, less hectic than her modern precinct, and no computers in sight. Instead there were solid oak desks, a typewriter at each one.

"Come along, Seldom," Callum urged, jogging her out of her gaping trance. She tagged behind him to his desk at the far side of the room and sat down in the proffered chair. More than a few curious eyes turned in her direction before flicking to Callum with a coy smile.

"Stuff it, Seamus," he said to one such onlooker, cuffing him on the ear as they passed.

He seated himself behind his typewriter and put in a fresh sheet of paper. "What's your full name, doll?"

"Seldom Murphy."

He paused to regard her over the top of the typewriter. "No middle?"

"There's a middle. I don't like to give it."

"Why not?"

"Because it's embarrassing."

He smiled in anticipation. "Try me."

She cleared her throat. "Suffragette."

He pressed his lips together. She could see him biting the inside of his cheek to keep from laughing. "I'll put S, mostly 'cause I have no idea how to spell what you just said. That work for you?"

"That works for me quite well, Officer O'Rourke," she replied and then glanced down demurely when she realized she was likely flirting with an object of her imagination.

"Address," he said.

"Um." Seldom looked around the station. She could give her address of course; it was a real place. But who knew what that place might be in 1946? The less said about the reality of her life, the better. "Next question, please."

He glanced at her again. "No place of residence, dollface?"

She gave her head a little shake.

"Date of birth?" he tried.

She shook her head again.

He reached around the desk, grabbed her chair with both hands, and scooted it close to his. He leaned forward earnestly, resting his elbows on his knees. "What gives, sweetness? You pulling the wool over my eyes?"

She shook her head. The shock and confusion was beginning to wear away, leaving only horror. Christian. The kidnap. Her unexpected rescue by Callum. The possibility that he might not be real, that none of this was real, that maybe she was already dead. How else to explain it?

He reached into his pocket again, pulled out his handkerchief, and used it to dab her eyes.

"Thank you," she whispered. He took her hands in his big, warm ones and held them loosely, comfortingly.

"Tell old Callum the truth about what happened, all right?"

"I already did. I went on a date with a man who drugged me, kidnapped me, and chained me to that pipe. I was crying, and then you showed up." She glanced into his face. It was a nice face, trustworthy and honest. He had taken off his hat when they entered the building. It rested on his desk now. His hair was mashed and disheveled from the band. She had the sudden urge to smooth it. *Why not? One or both of us isn't real right now.* Tentatively, her hand reached out and rifled through it, dislodging the pieces that were molded to his head. He watched her warily.

"You're a pretty, well-kept girl, kid. How do you not have a home?" he asked softly.

She couldn't tell him the truth. He wouldn't believe her. *She* didn't believe her. So she went with an approximation, somewhere between a truth and a lie. "My father ran off when I was a kid, and my mother kicked me out." Both of those things were true. She had been eighteen when her mother made her leave, however. In the ten years since, she'd made a home for herself, a life. But those were somewhere else now, somewhere unreachable. He blinked at her, clearly disturbed by her story.

"Surely you've been staying somewhere," he said, but not unkindly. "I mean, look at you, you cleaned up nice somehow."

"I got ready at work." Another truth. She kept all her necessities at work so she wouldn't have to go home first if she decided to go out.

"Where's work?"

"A bakery," she said, her voice tremulous. What would happen to her store? It was everything to her, everything she had worked for, the full measure of her success and independence in the world, a tangible reminder of how far she'd come.

"You've got no one?" he asked, incredulous.

Who would miss her if she didn't show up tomorrow? *Josh.* Josh would worry if she wasn't there, would likely be frantic at her absence. But Josh wasn't here in this time, in this dream. She shook her head, smiling sadly now. Callum let go of one of her hands and swiped it tiredly over his face. "How'd you meet the bum, the one that tied you to the pipe?"

How could she possibly explain internet dating to someone who had likely never seen a computer? "It was a kind of fix up, a friend of a friend of a friend type thing. Someone thought we'd hit it off." That "someone" being an algorithm.

"I'm going to ask you this once, and I need an honest answer: Are you a gang moll?"

"No," she said, properly affronted. She might not have mid-century sensibilities, but she wasn't so far gone that she didn't recognize the insult in a cop thinking she was a gangland hooker. "I didn't do anything to deserve being kidnapped and chained to a pipe. And I didn't know that man, hadn't met him before this night. Furthermore, I haven't had a date in three years." She sat back with a frown, yanked her hands out of his grasp, and crossed her arms over her chest.

"Don't give me guff. I see a lot in this racket. You'd be surprised. Even pretty girls who look sweet are into bad things sometimes."

"I am not one of them, I assure you. I spend my days baking cupcakes and cookies and my nights getting ready to do more of the same."

"Sounds like you need a new job, dollface," he said appraisingly.

"Yes, well, it looks like I'll have to find one. I can't go back to the bakery." Mostly because it didn't exist yet. For that matter, neither did she.

"Answer me this. You say you didn't do anything wrong, but you have no one to look out for you, no place to live, no job to go back to. So what gives?"

She knew what he was really asking: what did she do to end up so completely alone? In this world that was an easy answer because it wasn't her fault. But her life wasn't so different in her own time, and how did she explain that? The closest thing she had to a best friend was an employee, seven years her junior. Her family had cast her out, and she poured every drop of energy, time, and effort into a business that couldn't love her back.

"Callum."

"Hmm."

"May I have your handkerchief again, please?"

He fished into his pocket and handed it over. She waited until she had it pressed to her eyes and then burst into pitiful sobs. Her shoulders shook with the effort of crying, and then Callum's arm slid around her, drawing her against his chest in a comforting hug. "Aw, kid, cut it out. You're making me look like a monster here."

"I'm sorry," she whispered when she had herself under some semblance of control.

"You're all right," he said, chafing his hand up and down her arm. "Whatever led you to this point, it's going to be okay. You're safe, I promise." He peeled back from her and grasped her biceps, smiling encouragingly.

How she wished she could believe him. Maybe at this moment, it was true. But eventually she'd have to go home again, if she wasn't dead already. And then what? Seldom had never had a protector. Not even her father had stuck around to offer that service. Anything she'd done in her life she'd done for herself. "You're very kind," she said.

"Don't tell the crooks that. I've got a reputation to maintain," he said.

"Maybe you're only nice to women with a hard luck story," she suggested.

"Not usually," he said, a little furrow working between his brows. "I don't like people who play me for a fool."

"I promise you I'm not," she said.

"I never said I didn't like *you*, did I?" he asked, his thumbs making soothing little passes on her shoulder. "Come on, kid." He stood and held out his hand to her. She clasped it and allowed him to lead her back through the maze of desks until they were once again outside. He continued leading her until they reached the car and opened the door for her, once again tucking her safely inside. Suddenly she was exhausted. Even blinking felt like too much effort.

Callum slid behind the wheel and the monstrous vehicle roared to life.

"Where are you taking me?" her words felt leaden. The act of opening her mouth and using her vocal chords felt like too much.

"Somewhere you can get some rest," he said. "Somewhere safe."

Seldom glanced out the window and bit her lip worriedly. Where did homeless women go in 1946? "The YWCA?" she guessed.

He snorted a laugh and tossed her a speculative glance. "What? No. I'm taking you home, to my home."

She should probably be alarmed by that. He was, after all, a stranger. And it was 1946. Men didn't take strange women to their houses in the middle of the night for any good reason, even eighty years ago. But somehow Seldom wasn't alarmed. She studied his profile, noting his strong features, his lips now set in a grim line of determination.

"Okay," she murmured, and the next minute she was asleep.

4

She woke in the morning to the sound of birds chirping outside the window. Her mind was in a muddle over the strange noise. Birds? What happened to traffic? The most she'd ever heard from birds was the coo of pigeons on the sill, but even that was usually drowned by honking, beeping, revving, and zooming.

Gingerly, she sat up, feeling sore for no reason in particular. She still wore last night's dress, but that was all that was familiar. She was in a strange bed in a strange room. Stranger still, the place smelled like food, something other than the reek of stale oil from the Chinese restaurant below her apartment.

The door was slightly cracked. A hand reached in and pushed it open and suddenly Callum was there, bearing a tray heaping with food. He set it down beside her and perched on the edge of the bed, eyeing her with a smile. "How's it going, sweetness?"

"Oh," she said, making a lame attempt to push at the hair that had come half loose from its French knot. "I'm still here." Where was here? She had no idea.

"You slept twelve hours, kid. When's the last time you had a good night's sleep?"

She had to think about that one. "When I was eight." That was when her father left, when she first became aware that her mother's boyfriends were a danger to be avoided. She reached for the cup of coffee and took a sip. "Thank you for this. It's very sweet."

"Don't give me too much credit. It was my mother's idea. I'm the delivery mule."

Her eyebrows rose. "Your mother?"

His smile turned wry. "Come now, Miss Murphy, you didn't believe I brought an unaccompanied lady back to my bachelor apartment, did you?" He tsk'd. "Like all good unmarried Catholic sons, I live with my mother."

"Is she here now?" Seldom glanced nervously at the door. As a rule, she did well with old ladies. But customers at her store were a far cry from her rescuer's mother.

"No. She went to visit my brother."

"Does he live nearby?"

"Yes. He's in an institution. She visits every Thursday."

"Oh. I'm sorry."

"Why?"

"Because your brother is in an institution."

"That's the way of it." He shrugged one shoulder and tapped his temple. "Tetched. He was born okay, but went mute, curled up in a little ball, and rocked himself all day."

"Is he autistic?"

"I've never seen him draw. They aren't allowed pens or paintbrushes."

"No, I mean..." She didn't know the timeline on autism diagnostics and therefore gave up. Instead she began nibbling at the hearty breakfast—eggs, toast, juice, oatmeal, and coffee. The coffee tasted like instant. Seldom wasn't sure if it would have been a new and marvelous invention or post-war necessity. How long had rationing lasted?

"Can I ask you a question?" she said after a moment of strangely comfortable silence where he watched her eat.

"Yes."

"How is a good Catholic boy like you still a bachelor?"

He smiled easily and shrugged one shoulder again. "Before the war, everybody was pairing up like the world was ending, you know? At the time it seemed like it was. When I came back, all the good girls were gone. Seems I missed my window. What about you? How's a girl who looks like you end up on a date with a stranger? Were you married and your fella died in the war?"

How could she possibly explain the difficulty of 21st century dating to him? "I suppose sometimes when you see the worst that people have to offer, it makes you in no rush to attach yourself to one."

He blinked at her and shook his head like a dog emerging from a pond. "You're too pretty to end up a spinster." He clasped her hand and gave it a squeeze. "What's that smile for?"

"I'm twenty eight, Callum. By your standards, I'd guess I'm already a spinster." In her time, most people hadn't even begun pairing up for life yet. Here she was already past her prime. In this way, their generations were quite different, indeed.

"I guess we're in the same boat," he mused.

"Maybe we should marry each other, solve both our problems," she suggested. To her it was an obvious joke, delivered with a smile.

"Believe me, I've considered it," he said, deadpan. "But I don't think I could take a bride without the benefit of knowing where she came from."

She set down her coffee with a sigh. He picked it up and drained it, staring at her over the brim. "I'm happy to tell you, but when I do, you're going to want to put me in the asylum with your brother."

"Try me."

"Last night, when I went on my date, it was June 7th."

"Yes," he nodded encouragingly.

"2020."

His eyes narrowed on her, clearly disbelieving. He didn't comment, though, so she kept talking. "Everything I've told you is true. My name is Seldom Suffragette Murphy. I was born in New York on May twenty seventh, 1992. I own a bakery called Seldom Sweet. I have no idea what I'm doing here. Last night when I said I might be dead, I wasn't joking because I have no other rational explanation for my presence in 1946."

"I don't suppose you have any proof," Callum said, his tone carefully neutral.

"My date took my purse and my phone."

He blinked at that. "You carry your phone around with you?"

She smiled. "My phone is this big." She held up her hands in a small rectangle. "And an entire computer. It runs on cellular technology. Wireless. I carry it everywhere. It functions as my phone, my calendar, my camera, my source for information. I'm never without it. No one is."

He blinked at her again. "So without this 'phone,'" he actually used air quotes, "you have no proof?"

"Well, there's one thing that *might* help. Close your eyes."

"Sweetheart, you just told me you're from eighty years in the future. No thank you."

"Futuristic or crazy, I'm fairly certain you can take me in hand-to-hand combat. Now close your eyes, Officer O'Rourke." She reached out and pressed her hand over his eyes, covering them. He dutifully complied while she reached back and shimmied out of her dress. When the fabric touched his fingers, he opened his eyes and stared at the dress in dismay.

"How is your dress supposed to help me? It looks like every other dress I've seen," he said.

"Look at the tag."

He did so and then looked up with a helpless shrug. "What am I looking at here?"

"Spandex. It hasn't been invented yet, not until the fifties."

"How do I know that? This is New York, the fashion capital. Could be something new from the textile mills. The garment district comes out with crazy stuff all the time."

"So take it to one of them and ask," she directed. "Oh, hold on. Close your eyes again." He did so with easier grace this time, but when he opened his eyes and saw her bra dangling from her fingers, his jaw dropped and he stammered.

"Take them this. I guarantee it will get a reaction," she promised.

"It's definitely getting a reaction from me," he agreed, taking it tentatively with the tips of his fingers. She had drawn the blanket up to her neck. He glanced at it and quickly away, his cheeks flushing. "Would you like to take a bath?"

Now it was her turn for shocked stammering.

He motioned around the room. "My sister, Rose, left a few things. I imagine you'll find enough to scrape together an outfit. Help yourself to the soap or whatever's in there."

Her heart came back down out of her throat. So it hadn't been an invitation, then. Merely an offer to clean herself up. "I would appreciate that very much, thank you, Callum."

He smiled. The flush had left his cheeks by now when he looked at her, but still he made a concerted effort to keep his eyes on her face. "Get yourself cleaned up, kid, and we'll talk some more."

"Can I ask you one more question?" she asked.

"I thought I was going to be the one asking the questions, but go ahead."

"How did you find me last night?"

"I heard you crying."

"Were you already in the building?" she asked.

"No, I was driving in my car and I..." he trailed off, staring hard at a spot on the wall over her shoulder. "My windows were up and you were in the bowels of that building. How *did* I find you? I don't know, Seldom. You're a mystery in all the ways." He picked up her free hand, the one that wasn't holding the blanket to her throat, and kissed it.

"How old are you?" she asked.

"Twenty six."

"I'm older, and yet you call me kid."

He grinned at her. "If what you say is true, I'm seventy two years older. You're definitely a kid." He kissed her hand again, picked up the tray, and eased from the room, closing the door in his wake.

5

The mystery sister had left plenty behind. Seldom hoped she wasn't dead as she searched through her wardrobe and assembled what she hoped was a day dress. It seemed dressy to her, but she was coming from a world where yoga pants were the norm. Remembering Callum's comment about stockings from the previous night, she made an especial search for those and came up empty. There were no shoes left behind, but Seldom's own shoes were vintage-looking high-heeled Mary Janes that would suffice with anything.

She emerged from the bedroom with more than a little trepidation. Would Callum find it triggering if he saw her wearing his dead sister's clothing? Then she realized he had survived five years of combat and the word "triggering" likely wasn't in his vocabulary. And if it was, it had a completely different connotation. She should have been nervous about the reappearance of his mother, something that had apparently occurred while Seldom was getting ready. She looked up at Seldom with a smile of welcome.

"You must be Seldom," she said.

"Hello," Seldom said, feeling suddenly shy. The woman's hair was gray, but her face was wrinkle-free. Seldom guessed her to be in her late forties, at the most. She was much more youthful and vigorous than expected, and somehow that increased Seldom's nerves. Old ladies she could work with. Middle-aged ladies were an unknown quantity.

"Callum said you've had a bad turn. He also said you're as pretty as a picture. Looks like he was right, at least on the second count."

"Thank you so much for welcoming me into your home. I know it's...unusual." She had no idea how much Callum might have told her.

"You're most welcome," she replied. "I see Callum directed you to Rose's leftovers. It's a good fit, and a good color for you." She tipped her head appraisingly. "You look a bit like my Rose, same dark hair, bright eyes, and rosy cheeks. Maybe that explains Callum's strange reaction to you."

Was bluntness a family trait or a generational thing? Seldom had no idea. "His reaction to me was strange?"

"Callum doesn't warm up to people easily these days. Trust comes hard."

"Something we have in common," Seldom mused, though she had readily trusted him, too. She had blamed it on the dire straights she'd been in, but had it been something more?

"He also told me your story about where you're, uh, from. And he showed me your clothing. I have to admit my doubts about such outrageous claims, but I know those items did not come from here." She paused, considering. "Is the, er, brazier, more comfortable than the ones we wear now?"

"I've never worn the kind you're wearing now, but I'd have to say no. In eighty years, still no one has managed to create a comfortable bra."

"What about girdles? Please tell me at least those have gotten better?"

Seldom smiled. "Those have gotten obsolete. Now everyone wears something called Spanx, sort of like a stretchy sock around the midsection. I don't, though. What you see is what you get." She patted her slightly paunchy midsection.

"Good for you, dear. Callum said you're a baker? Is that what girls do in the future?"

"No," Seldom said, laughing. "Women aren't as much into the culinary arts. They pretty much do whatever they want—doctor, lawyer, policeman, firefighter, politician, pilot. There aren't a lot of limits any-more."

"Like during the war," Mrs. O'Rourke mused. "I must admit it was fun to get out there and work a man's job, for a switch. To bring home a paycheck and feel we were contributing to society. To be in charge of ourselves, for once. But then the night would come. There would be some sound, and I would long for my husband or Callum to be here to check it out. I missed the warmth, the security, the protection and pro-vision. Do girls have that still, being so independent all the time?"

Seldom hesitated before shaking her head. "It's been a bit of a trade-off. With equality came a certain forfeiture of things like that. Not for everyone, I'm sure. But I've never had anything like that in my life." She paused. "Your husband, was he...did the war..." She trailed off, not sure how to finish the question tactfully.

"No, he never made it long enough to see us join the war. He was killed by a bomb at the World's Fair in '39. Patrick was a copper, too, like his father before him. He and another officer were killed by the blast. Callum had just joined up then. They never found who did it. It's eaten at him, I think, the inability to solve the case." She sighed. "His life has been...not what I would have wished it to be."

"He still has plenty of time left," Seldom encouraged.

"What if there's another war?" Mrs. O'Rourke asked, twisting her fingers nervously together.

Seldom shook her head. "Not until Korea in the fifties. I don't think they drafted men who served in World War II."

Mrs. O'Rourke blinked at her. "Oh. And what of after? Has there been a big war in your time?"

"Yes, but not the same kind. In the sixties and seventies there will be a war in Vietnam, not our war, but we're still involved. I never figured out how, honestly. And then there are a bunch of wars in the Middle East, starting in the eighties and lasting off and on through the present day."

"The Middle East? What do the Arabs have against us?"

"It's kind of a religious thing. They have a resurgence of the orthodox Muslim and...it's complex."

"Isn't it always?" Mrs. O'Rourke mused, sighing.

"There will be a Cold War, starting in the late sixties and lasting until the eighties. That one has to do with this one, with the East and the West having a war of words and an arms race. It will seem like it's going to escalate into a nuclear war, but thankfully it doesn't."

"My lands," Mrs. O'Rourke said, leaning against the counter as if for support.

Seldom offered her a smile. "It's a lot to take in. The good news is that right now is the beginning of a massive economic boom that will last for decades. Not just in America, but worldwide. Wealth and stability begin to skyrocket. My generation, we're very spoiled, very wealthy. We have every conceivable gadget and technological advance."

"So, there's no more poverty, then? No more hunger?"

"No, those things are still present. It's a complex issue, not always as simple as giving someone a meal or a job," Seldom said, frowning slightly.

"That's true enough in any age, I suppose," Mrs. O'Rourke said, also frowning.

"Callum's generation, those who fought in the war, will be respected for as long as they live, will be revered as heroes for what they did for the world."

"As well they should be," Mrs. O'Rourke said, nodding her approval. Seldom didn't disagree, but she thought it unfair that Mrs. O'Rourke's generation had been overlooked. Not only had they spawned the heroes, but they had survived the first World War, the Great Depression, the Spanish Influenza.

"I'm never going to complain again when I go home," Seldom muttered.

Mrs. O'Rourke's smile turned wry. "Hold onto that thought, dear. What if you never go home?"

Seldom shuddered, trying not to view the words as foreshadowing or foreboding. Of course she would go home. This delusion had to end sometime, didn't it?

"There she is," Callum announced as he entered the house, his hands loaded down. "Picked up your things while I was out, Ma."

"Thank you, dear. Oh, my, that's a load. I'd best get started." She eased away and began sorting through the stack of clothes.

"Ma does tailoring and repair work," Callum explained. "Fastest needle in Manhattan, right, Ma?" he asked.

"Well, I don't know about that," she said, but she was clearly pleased.

"I could go for a cup of coffee," he said and sat down at the table. Seldom watched, somewhere between amused and disturbed, as his mother left her work, jumped to attention and set about preparing one for him.

"What's that face for, doll?" Callum asked.

"Where I'm from, when a man wants coffee, he makes it himself," she explained. She tried to say it without censure. This wasn't her time, after all. The women's equality movement wouldn't gain a foothold for another twenty years. "It's very unusual for a woman to serve a man that way."

"I don't think I like that," Callum said, frowning.

She laughed and took a seat at the table opposite him. "No, I don't imagine you would. The sixties are not going to go well for you, I think."

"Do I want to know what happens in the sixties?" he asked.

"Probably not. Just remember when your children are teenagers and young adults during that decade that you've likely already lost the battle. It'll go best for you if you concede defeat and let them get on with it."

"With what?" he asked.

"Upending the world as you know it."

He laughed. "Sweetheart, if a World War didn't do it, I doubt a group of teenagers will."

"You've been warned, Callum O'Rourke," she said, her tone portentous.

"Have I now?" he asked, his tone flirtatious. He reached across the table and clasped her hand, brushing his thumb on her knuckles. Cheeks aflame, her gaze darted to his mother who kept her back studiously to them, a half-smile on her face. Callum squeezed her hand and let it go with a laugh. "At least girls in the future are still modest."

Seldom couldn't help it, she laughed out loud and slapped both hands over her mouth.

"No?" Callum guessed.

She shook her head. "Not even a little."

"Give me an example," he demanded.

She glanced at his mother's back and shook her head. No way she was going to talk about life post-sexual revolution while his prim mother was in the room. And maybe not even with her gone. Some things had to be seen to be believed. She doubted he would believe how different life was in her time. More than that, she felt no desire to disillusion him, to shatter his innocence. It was, after all, why she dressed the way she did. Because she *liked* those throwback virtues she categorized as quaint.

"You seem awfully modest," he said. Mrs. O'Rourke finished making coffee and set a mug before her son, as well as one before Seldom.

"Thank you," she said to the older woman before answering Callum's unspoken question. "People tell me I was born out of time because I do the things I do and look the way I look."

"I don't follow. You look good to me," he said.

"Thank you for that," she said. "But that's what I'm talking about. I shouldn't look good to you; I should look different and foreign. But I've always enjoyed this era, so I wear swing dresses and listen to Big Band music. I style my hair in intricate twists and bake old fashioned treats. It's kind of my thing, my calling card. I'm vintage."

"What do other women look like?" he asked, resting his chin in his hand as he regarded her with curiosity.

"There's no set style. It's sort of anything goes, whatever makes you feel good. Some women have short hair, long hair, medium length hair. You can make it whatever color you want. Tattoos are really big right now."

Mrs. O'Rourke gasped. "Tattoos on a woman? On purpose?"

"Yes, ma'am," Seldom replied.

"But you don't have one," Callum said. By his mocking smile, she knew he thought she was making the whole thing up.

"Don't I?" she asked, sipping her coffee with a coy smile.

His cheeks flamed. He pressed his lips together and looked away.

"But what do women wear if they don't wear dresses?" Mrs. O'Rourke asked. She sat at the table between them, her work temporarily forgotten in light of her fascination.

"Some women wear dresses. Dresses are much shorter. To here." She pointed mid-thigh. Mrs. O'Rourke gasped again. "Or ankle-length. Those are called maxi-dresses. Casual style is very, very big. Lots of jeans and yoga pants."

"Jeans? Yoga pants?" Mrs. O'Rourke repeated. Callum apparently had little interest in fashion, though he was still staring hard at her, probably wondering if she'd been serious about the tattoo.

"They don't call them jeans now? Denim. Heavy blue fabric, worn by workers now, maybe?"

"Overalls," Callum supplied. "You're trying to tell us that women wear overalls all the time, in public and on dates?"

She nodded.

"I don't like that," he added, frowning.

"I could have guessed that you wouldn't," she said, tossing him an amused smile.

"What about the other thing? Yo-ga," Mrs. O'Rourke interjected, sounding it out with elongated syllables

"Yoga is a kind of exercise from India, with stretching and deep breathing."

"You need special pants for that?" Callum asked.

"No, but leisure wear becomes very popular."

"Leisure wear? Like housecoats? People wear their housecoats in public?" Mrs. O'Rourke said. It was clear she was insatiably curious about the fashion side of things.

"No, more like clothes people wear to exercise in," Seldom replied.

They both blinked at her, confused. "You expect us to believe people wear special clothes to exercise in? And why are they exercising so much?" Callum asked.

"Because obesity is a big problem," Seldom replied.

"We all get fat?" Mrs. O'Rourke said, eyebrows aloft.

"But you're not fat," Callum remarked. "You're per..." he paused and cleared his throat. "You're pretty okay."

"Thank you for that, but I exercise, too, because I own a bakery and eat a lot of treats. There's a lot of processed food."

"Processed food, what does that mean?" Mrs. O'Rourke asked. Callum was busy tipping his head, scanning any of Seldom's exposed pieces for signs of a tattoo.

"Pre-made, pre-packaged, frozen."

Callum grimaced. "Like K-rations?"

"No, better than that. But they have a lot of fat and calories."

"And that's bad?" Mrs. O'Rourke asked.

"Well, when you combine it with so much salt and preservatives, yes."

"Do you do yo-ga?" Mrs. O'Rourke asked, returning to the earlier subject.

"Yes. I mean, I'm not an expert, but I've taken a few classes."

"Can you show us, then?" she urged. "Can you do it without the special pants?"

Seldom chuckled. "Yes, but it's not, uh, exactly what you'd call ladylike or modest behavior, I'd say."

"Then we definitely need a demonstration," Callum urged.

Seldom glanced at Mrs. O'Rourke, but her eyes were alight with interest. She stood and stepped away from the table. "This is called a sun salutation," she said and began the series of stretches while they watched in rapt fascination. When she finished, Callum was the first to speak.

"Reminds me of the moves the Jap soldiers used to do."

Seldom flinched and covered her ears.

"What?" he asked, looking to his mother to see if she had any clue about the odd action.

"You said...you called them...we don't say words like that," Seldom explained.

"Like what?" he asked, clueless.

"About Japanese people," she explained softly.

"What did I say?" he asked. She shook her head, lips pressed together. "Japs?" he guessed.

"Don't say it again," she implored, plugging her ears once more.

He laughed, but it was more from frustration than amusement. "What's wrong with calling them what they are?"

"It's a derogatory term, and the Japanese are our friends now."

"What?" he all but shouted, smacking his palm on the table. "Are you trying to tell me people forget about Pearl Harbor? About what they did to us? To our POW's?"

"Of course not. But it's been eighty years. It's all water under the bridge," she said.

He regarded her in silence a moment, stood, and walked out of the room. Heart fluttering, she looked at Mrs. O'Rourke. "That didn't go well."

Mrs. O'Rourke gave her a sympathetic smile. "It may have been eighty years for you, dear. But for him it's only been one."

"Yes, of course you're right," Seldom said, swallowing hard. "I'm sorry, should I...do you think I should go after him?"

"That's a question only you can answer," Mrs. O'Rourke replied, returning her attention to her mending.

After a moment to pluck up her courage, Seldom took a deep breath and went to find Callum.

6

She found him in the living room, facing the street, his gaze distant and unblinking. "I'm so sorry, Callum. I was only thinking about it from my point of view, from my generation. And I wasn't trying to chastise you. I was merely explaining my reaction. We're pretty big on not saying words that might hurt or castigate others."

He blew out a breath but didn't remove his eyes from the window. "Do you really like them?"

"Who?" she asked. She came closer and peered outside, hoping to gain some clue as to what he was talking about.

"The Japs," he said impatiently, turning to frown down at her.

"Well, yes, actually. I do. They apologize, eventually. They keep to themselves for a long time, and then in the eighties their technology begins to soar. We become allies. They're good friends."

"And the Krauts?" he asked.

She flinched and tried to hide it. "Yes. When the country was divided, we were friends with the West, not the East. And then the Iron Curtain fell, and the country was reunited. We've been allies with them ever since."

"What about the Italians?"

"I think we became friends with them right away, not a lot of left-over anger with them. Italy is a big tourist destination. And of course the food." She kissed her fingers and released them. The side of his mouth ticked up in a half smile.

"I was in Italy for a while. You're right about the food." His eyes were still far away and filled with private horrors. She tried to see things from his perspective, but how could she? He had seen things she wouldn't have dreamed possible, if she hadn't read about them in history books. She touched her fingers to his forearm.

"I'm very sorry," she said. She was sorry not only for her careless words, but for all he'd had to endure. With effort, he looked down at her.

"I still don't know if I believe you. What if you're a spy? An anti-war sympathizer?"

"I'm most assuredly not. You were on the winning side, and you saved the world. I'll believe that to my dying day, even if the people you fought against are our allies now."

He studied her, considering. "I took your clothes to the garment district. They flipped, never seen anything like it."

"What did you tell them?"

"That it came from some scientist who was implicated in a crime," he said easily. "They wanted to keep them; I wouldn't allow it." His hand reached out, resting on her neck. His thumb brushed against her pulse, making it jump.

"Probably for the best. You might have caused a rip in the space-time continuum or something." She closed her eyes and leaned in to his touch.

"What's that mean?" he asked.

"I have no idea. Something they say on television," she said.

"You have a television?" he asked, sounding impressed.

"Actually, no. I stream everything on my laptop."

"I have no idea what that means," he whispered.

"I can't imagine you would."

"It's not possible, what you say. And yet I can't think how else to explain you," he said.

She opened her eyes and smiled up at him. "Want me to show you my tattoo?"

He swallowed hard, his eyes darting to the kitchen to check the whereabouts of his mother. Satisfied that she was still engaged there, he nodded.

Slowly, she pushed his hand away and eased aside the shoulder of her dress, revealing the small heart tattoo she kept hidden there. Hands shaking now, he reached out to touch it with his thumb, attempting to smudge it away.

"Huh," he remarked. "I've only ever seen one on a sailor."

"I've never been on a boat, I assure you," she told him, realigning the sleeve of her dress.

Callum licked his lips, his eyes still fixed on the spot. "I, um, liked it better than I thought I might."

"But you still don't believe me," she guessed.

His glance slid to her face, locking on her eyes. "You're getting warmer every minute, kid."

She touched her fingers to his flushed cheeks. "So are you, Copper."

A few hours later, Callum went to work. Seldom sat with his mother, making surprisingly comfortable and pleasant small talk as they worked on her sewing. Seldom had volunteered to help, if only the small jobs like replacing buttons and hemming seams.

"Everyone must still know how to sew," Mrs. O'Rourke commented after inspecting Seldom's first repair job.

"No, I'm afraid that's another way I'm peculiar. I taught myself to sew by watching tutorials on YouTube. It seemed like a handy skill, and I wanted to learn to upcycle."

"What's upcycle?" Mrs. O'Rourke asked, pausing in her work to regard Seldom with fascinated curiosity, a thing she'd been doing all day. It seemed she couldn't get enough of learning about twenty first century life. It was so unexpected that Seldom couldn't stop staring at her in equal measure. She had expected to find skepticism, fear, disbelief, accusation, to be labeled a modern-day witch. Instead she had been welcomed with open arms and questioned like a much beloved visitor from a far away land.

"It's when you take an old dress and remake it in a new way," Seldom explained. "I go to thrift stores, search for usable things, and remake them. It was a handy skill when times were hard."

"What's a thrift store?"

"A place where people donate used goods," Seldom amended.

"You mean a junk shop, a charity bin?" Mrs. O'Rourke said, pausing again, needle held aloft. "Are you quite poor, then?"

Seldom laughed. "No, I'm not. I used to be, when my mother threw me out. I couch surfed, that is to say I slept on the couches of various friends for as long as they'd have me, taking whatever job I could land, working my way up to better and better pay until eventually I landed a job at a swanky restaurant with good enough tips to make a living."

"But you didn't stay a waitress," Mrs. O'Rourke said.

Seldom shook her head. "That would have been the wise thing to do, but I've never been accused of being wise. I wanted to be a pastry chef, but at those kinds of places they only hire trained pastry chefs from the Culinary Institute or somewhere equally prestigious. I didn't have the money or the inclination to go to pastry school, but I had persistence. I kept bugging the head pastry chef until she relented and allowed me to be her assistant."

"Let me guess, you worked your way up to the head position," Mrs. O'Rourke said, smiling in anticipation.

"That would have been a much better ending to the story. No, I've never much cared to do things the right way, the ordinary way. I wanted the experience and knowledge I gained working as her assistant, but in the end I wanted to be my own boss, and I didn't want to make the sort of fancy, overpriced cuisine at the restaurant where I worked. I quit, took my meager savings, acquired a massive loan, and opened my own bakery. Eventually. No one told me about the ridiculous amount of bureaucracy involved in opening a restaurant in the city. So many permits and inspections. I spent nine months begging and pleading for my final inspection, working as a waitress once again to try and make ends meet." She stared into space, remembering. "In my off hours, I would dream and plan my menu. That became my escape, the best part of my day."

"Your family must be worried about you," Mrs. O'Rourke said, her tone a combination of sympathetic and nosy.

"No," was all Seldom said. She couldn't try to explain to this loving, caring mother that her own mother wanted nothing to do with her and neither did her absentee father.

"Is there no one in your life who will note your absence?"

"My employee, Josh," Seldom said with a fair amount of worry and regret.

"Is he your fella, then?"

"No, I don't have one of those. Josh is just a kid, a good, sweet kid who has been with me since day one, when he was only eighteen."

She was quiet a few minutes before she piped up again. "Tell me more about this microwave. Can it really cook food in an instant?"

"Yes. You put in a frozen entrée, push a button, and a minute later you have hot food," Seldom said.

"That sounds like a dream," Mrs. O'Rourke replied, her tone dreamy. "No more cooking."

"It has its merits, but there's nothing like a home cooked meal," Seldom said.

"Unless you're the one who always has to cook it," Mrs. O'Rourke returned.

"Touché," Seldom agreed, and they continued to sew in companionable silence.

7

Mrs. O'Rourke and Seldom both went to bed at nine. It was Seldom's usual time, but then she woke at two, ready to go to work. Worried about the bakery, she tossed and turned until her ears lighted on a sound, a soft footfall, the creak of a floorboard outside her door.

Someone's in the house. She remembered Mrs. O'Rourke's words about how her independence during the daytime gave way to fear in the night. Seldom had never had anyone besides herself to depend on. And yet her first thought was that she wished for Callum. Whether because he was a cop or because he was a man she didn't know and didn't want to delve too closely into. *Suffragette indeed,* she thought with a humph.

Plucking up her courage, she eased from the bed, stole to the door, and opened it a crack. The streetlights outside were dimmer and fewer than in her time, meaning she couldn't see much of anything.

There. Another step, this one in the kitchen. She eased in that direction, rounded the corner, and was tossed against the wall, a heavy body pinning her, arms outstretched.

"Where are you sneaking off to, kid?" Callum whispered.

"I thought you were a burglar," she replied, heart thudding.

One corner of his mouth tipped. "What were you going to do, if I was?"

"Fashion a weapon and drop you," she said.

He tsk'd. "What do they teach you ladies in 2020?"

"A whole lot of self-actualization," she said.

"I have no idea what that means," he said.

"I know. That's probably why everyone likes your generation better than mine," she said.

"What's wrong with your generation?" he asked.

"We're spoiled, entitled, self-involved, and shallow, or so the saying goes," she said.

"That can't be. You're nothing like that," he said.

"You've never seen me in a temper," she countered.

"Same goes for me. I'm a beast."

"I believe it completely," she said. They regarded each other in silence, hearts thumping in sync.

"I'm starving," he said at last.

"Your mom left food for you."

"Come with me into the kitchen," he said, a command, not a request. He eased away, clasped her hand, and led her beside him. When they reached the table, he sat. She remained standing.

"Are you suggesting I serve you?" she asked.

He grinned. "My century, my rules, doll."

"I would love to introduce you to 2020," she said, striding forward to arrange his plate and stick it in the oven to heat. She sank to the chair beside him. "How was work?"

He stared at her a minute before speaking. "It's like a fist to the gut to see you in Rose's clothes."

"I'm sorry," she apologized. "Is she...did she die in the war?"

"She might as well have. She signed up to be a nurse, went overseas, and married a Brit, lives in England now."

"And you miss her," she guessed.

"As much as any fellow misses his sister, I guess."

"But you said it's like a fist," she reminded him.

"Because seeing Rose in that nightgown was another matter entirely. Definitely not the same effect."

She returned his frank and admiring gaze. "You're not so bad yourself, Copper."

He wiped a hand over his eyes. "You're knocking me off kilter, sweetness."

"Because I'm not a shrinking violet?" she guessed.

"No, because I usually don't like the type that's not. Bold girls, brash girls, worldly girls. But you," he drew in a breath, held it, and let it out slowly. "You're something altogether different, Seldom."

She stood and retrieved his plate from the oven, setting it before him with a fork and a glass of buttermilk. She'd had buttermilk with her meal, too, at his mother's insistence. *Good for digestion,* she'd commented as she set the glass before Seldom.

"What happened at work?" she asked as he wolfed down his food.

"How do you know something happened?" he asked.

"Because you didn't answer me when I asked you the first time," she said.

He paused eating to regard her with a slight frown, finished his food, wiped his mouth with the cloth napkin from his lap, and sat back. She stood to clear his plate and take it to the sink, but sat back down with a thud when he spoke.

"I found another girl."

"Another girl like me?"

"Another girl cuffed to a pipe," he said.

"Was she from the future?"

"I didn't get a chance to ask her. Somebody carved her up like she'd been to the butcher. Drained the blood right out of her."

She swallowed hard. "The...the man, Christian, he had a whole tray of medical instruments. I think he intended the same for me."

They stared at each other. "If you're really from where you say you're from, how do you explain that?"

"What if..." she paused and cleared her throat, "What if he's from my time, too? What if he followed me here? Or what if he's from this time and was visiting my time?"

"Do you understand how bonkers that is?" he said.

"Yes, but I'm here, aren't I? And you know I'm not lying to you, Callum. You *know*." She rested her hand on his forearm. "Christian, he was like you."

He scowled. "What's that supposed to mean? You think I'm some kind of cuckoo butcher?"

"Of course not. I meant he had manners, he was courteous. He held my door and kissed my hand, observed all the social graces."

"How is that different from any other man?" he asked.

She gave his arm a squeeze. "You're adorable. Please believe me when I tell you it's not the same in my generation. Men are...it's not the same."

He picked up her hand and began toying with her fingers. "I might be willing to accept your arrival here without explanation, but I can't do the same for a suspect. I deal in the here and now, the solid and concrete. A phantom, time-traveling killer isn't on my radar."

"I understand that but..."

"But what, sweetness?"

"What if he's here?" she whispered and couldn't repress a shudder. What if it was Christian? What if he knew she was here? What if he'd followed her, was stalking her, even as they spoke? Her eyes scanned the windows, searching for signs of life outside.

"Seldom. Hey," he touched his finger to her chin, drawing her attention to him. "You're safe. As long as you're with me, you're safe. I won't let anybody hurt you, I swear it."

She nodded, believing him completely. There was something about him, whether it was because she knew he was a man of his word or knew he was capable of doing whatever it took to keep her safe, up to and including taking another man's life. Hadn't he already proved himself worthy on the battlefield? She thought of all the things he must have seen, including the victim tonight. Her palm skimmed his stubbly cheek.

"You've seen too much death for a twenty six year old man," she mused.

"You'll get no argument from me on that," he agreed, but his matter of fact tone didn't change.

So stoic, she thought. "It's okay to feel things, to talk about them sometimes."

"What difference would that make?" he asked. He turned his head and kissed her palm. "Wouldn't change anything. Things are what they are. You do your duty, and then you do it again and again."

"See, this is why everyone calls you the Greatest Generation."

"Really? I thought it was because of this," he said as he leaned forward and kissed her.

"I'm definitely going to add that to the list," she said when the kiss was finished. They rested their foreheads together, trying to steady their breathing.

"How did you know where I lived?" he asked.

"I don't. I have no idea where I am," she said.

"Last night, you told me to take you to 27th and 7th."

"So?"

"So that's where we are, that's this house."

She jerked upright. "I told you to take me there because it's the address of my bakery."

"Your bakery is in my house?"

"No, they tore it down at some point. My shop was built in the year 2000."

"They tore down our house?" he scanned the interior of the brownstone. "Where was I, I wonder?"

She didn't answer because the answer was obvious. He was already twenty six. Sixty years from now, the chances weren't great that he'd still be alive. "I guess we found our connection," she said.

He turned his attention back to her. "How so?"

"We share this plot of land. That's quite a coincidence, don't you think?"

"Sweetness, I've been a cop for four years and a soldier for five. I try never to think at all anymore," he said. He kissed her again and broke away almost as abruptly, resting his forehead on hers once more. "There's a dance tomorrow night. How's about you come with me for a little R and R?"

Seldom bit her lip and glanced out the window again. As long as she stayed in the house, she was safe. Safe from what, she had no idea. But the thought of leaving was scary. Then again, hiding had never been her nature. "What will you tell people about me?" New York may be a massive city, but each neighborhood was small, a village in and of itself. If she went to a dance with Callum, there would be talk.

"I'll tell them you're from Canada," he said, and she snickered. "What?"

"It's what you tell people when you have a fake relationship and someone asks about it. You say they're in Canada."

"Taking you in public will definitely answer the question of whether you're real or imaginary," he said.

"If we're figments of each other's imaginations, then what?" she asked.

"Pray we never wake up," he said. He might have kissed her again, but his mother turned on the light in the bathroom. They froze until she was safely back in her room, then Callum walked Seldom to her door and bade her goodnight.

8

Callum solved the problem of no stockings by buying her some from the department store at the end of his block.

"I thought I'd feel embarrassed, but it turns out a lot of men buy these things. Must be for their girl, right? It's not like a man's going to wear them," he explained.

"Actually," Seldom began and then changed her mind. No need to explain her generation's issues with gender identity to him. Judging by his fixed ideals of the sexes' assigned places, it was likely he wouldn't believe her anyway.

Rose must have fled with only the clothes on her back, if what she left behind was any indication. Since she'd been gone four years, it was likely the clothes were now slightly dated, but Seldom had no idea, nor did she care. To her they were iconic from the time, and she had never been much of a slave to fashion anyway. Mrs. O'Rourke consulted on the night's wardrobe choice, settling on a pretty pink dress with a pair of white gloves.

"Why did Rose leave so many things behind?" Seldom asked as Callum led her to the car.

"Because she knew I'd skin her alive if I found out she ran away."

"What could you have done from overseas?" she asked.

"Sicced the priest on her," he said. "What are you doing?"

She hadn't realized she was repeatedly reaching for the nonexistent seatbelt until he pointed it out. "Looking for the belt."

"People really truss themselves every time they get in the car?" he asked, incredulous.

"I've never ridden in a car without one," she said.

"Why?"

"Cars go a lot faster," she said. "And they're made of plastic. They don't fare too well in crashes."

"How fast?"

"Sixty, seventy miles per hour," she said.

He stared off into the distance, a quixotic expression on his face. "Man, I'd like that. I can imagine cruising on Route 66 that fast."

"No one uses Route 66 anymore."

He glanced at her, horrified. "Why not? What happened to it?"

"Interstates. I don't know when they came about, but they connect the whole country, kind of like railroads. That's why you can go so fast, because there aren't any stops along the way."

"What's the point of that? Half the fun of driving is getting out to look at stuff," he said.

"I wouldn't know. I've never left the city," she said.

"No, you're from Canada," he reminded her, pinching her bicep.

"Right. What's our cover, exactly? How did we meet, if I'm all the way up in Canada?"

"A buddy in the army showed me your picture, and I asked if I could meet you. We wrote back and forth for a while and fell in love. And here you are."

"Sounds plausible, more plausible than that I'm from the future and we met two days ago when you rescued me from a madman," she agreed, though she was still twisting her fingers nervously together. "Is there anything I shouldn't do or say that would give me away?"

"Definitely don't show anyone else your tattoo," he said.

"Which one?" she asked and he had to jerk the wheel to correct his drift.

He cleared his throat. "There's more than one?"

She gave him the coy smile, and he jerked the wheel again before reaching to roll down his window.

"Are you sick?" she asked with feigned innocence.

"A bit warm, is all," he said. When she turned to her window to laugh, he pinched her again.

Callum found parking a block from the dance hall. "What are you doing?" he asked when she reached for her door.

"Getting out," she said, but it came out like a question.

"In 1946, you stay there until I come for you," he said.

"Why, though?" she asked.

He sat back, thinking. She was fairly certain no one had ever questioned him on it. "It's like this, Seldom. I spent five years surrounded by men and death, dodging bullets, sleeping in foxholes because I wanted to preserve the things I believed in, the traditions and values that were important to me. So if I don't have those traditions anymore, then what was I fighting for?"

"And you lump holding doors for women as part of those values?" she asked. She wasn't being accusatory, merely curious. They were in the same place physically, but the eighty years between them had changed everything.

"I believe that women are to be cared for and protected in all the ways, but how else do you show that except by doing all the things you're supposed to do?" he asked.

"You could say the words," she said.

"Words are meaningless without actions to back them up," he said. "You can say anything to anyone, but you only do for the people you care about."

"I think you just summed up the problem with my entire dating history," she said. She was too susceptible to words, to listening to the pretty things men told her. It took her much too long to realize their actions instead.

"I'm glad I could be of service, Miss Murphy. Now stay there," he wagged a finger at her in mock sternness. She nodded, pressing her palms together in a pose of reverent submission. He opened her door for her, took her hand to help her out, and kept it, linking his fingers through hers as they made their way to the hall. He opened the door for her again. She took a step inside and stopped short, her eyes watering. A thick haze of smoke hung over the entire establishment, made worse by the dozens of men and some women who were currently smoking. To her further dismay, Callum reached in his pocket, pulled out a pack, tapped one out, and stuck it between his lips. He was reaching for his lighter when he caught sight of her expression.

"What's that face for, sweetness?"

"You smoke," she said.

"Don't tell me there are no cigarettes in the future," he said.

"There are, but everyone knows the risks. They'll give you cancer of the lungs for sure, the throat, lips, and stomach maybe."

He lit his cigarette and waved his hand dismissively. "Some people say that now. I think it's a lot of bunk. The doctor in the army is the one who gave me my first smoke."

"Then the doctor in the army is a moron," she said, and he laughed.

"No argument there. I gotta say, life in your time doesn't sound like much fun. You have to wear a belt every time you get in the car, you can't say certain words for fear they'll hurt someone's feelings, you have to use a computer to tell you who to date, and you're not allowed to smoke."

"On the other hand, we've added a decade to our life expectancy," she said, her tone turning smug and condescending.

His answering smile was wry. "Dollface, I've been almost killed more times than you have fingers. Believe me when I tell you that life's not worth living if you're not living it well."

She made no reply because she had none. He mistook her silence for censure. "You can't tell me not to smoke," he added, annoyed. "My mother never let my father smoke. Drove me nuts."

"I wouldn't begin to presume to tell you not to do anything, Callum O'Rourke. But I've never kissed a man who tastes like an ashtray, and I don't plan to start tonight." She sauntered ahead of him into the room. He followed behind her with a heavy sigh, but when he reached her, the cigarette was gone.

9

"Well, well, well, the old man shows up." A man approached them, a woman on his arm. Callum and the man were intent on greeting each other, but the woman's eyes were fixed appraisingly on Seldom.

"Bob, whad'ya know, he brought a girl," the woman said, tugging Bob's sleeve.

"I didn't know he knew any girls," he said, cuffing Callum in the shoulder.

"I don't. I only know ladies," Callum said, bringing Seldom's hand to his lips and bestowing a kiss and a look that, to her chagrin, had the intended effect of making her blush.

"Boy, that's a smooth operation. How come you never do that?" the woman said, patting Bob's shoulder.

"Cause I don't know no ladies," he replied, but put his arm around her shoulders and gave them a squeeze.

"Seldom Murphy, this is Bob Kelly and his wife, Susan. Bob, Susan, this is Seldom."

"How-di-do, Seldom. Where did you come from?" Bob asked, taking her hand and shaking it politely.

"Canada," Seldom said.

"Yeah? What's it like in Canada?" Susan asked.

"Cold," Seldom replied as more people began to gather around them and clamor for an introduction.

They were all friends from Callum's neighborhood or from his work,

"

all of them Irish, and all of them married. "You're the last of a dying breed," she whispered when they found a moment alone.

"Not for lack of trying on their parts, believe me. I got all the left-over unmarriageable girls foisted on me when I came back home," he said, shuddering.

She knew the feeling because she'd lived it. Seemingly all the good men were taken and she had only dated the stragglers. "You should have checked in Canada sooner," she said.

"If I knew there were girls like you in Canada, I would have moved there and set up shop," he said. "Become an Eskimo or something."

"What are you going to tell them if I disappear back to Canada?" she asked.

He stared off into space, thinking. "I suppose we'll cross the bridge if it gets here. In the meantime," he took her hand and gave it a squeeze, "there's dancing."

There was certainly dancing. Callum was an excellent dancer, much better than Seldom who only had a cursory acquaintance with the dances he knew by heart. It was obvious he'd spent a lot of time doing so, had probably filled his pre-war evenings with careless nights spinning a hundred different girls around the floor. She wondered why none of them had ever stuck. Was he so choosy? Or had he been waiting for her in whatever unknown way had brought her to him? Or, as she had previously believed, was she dead and none of this real? It *felt* real. For the moment that was all she had to go on.

"You're going to have to excuse us, Callum. We're taking your girl to the ladies'," Susan said as she came up alongside Seldom, linked elbows, and began dragging her away. Seldom gave Callum a pleading glance, but he tossed her a wink in return. *Good luck*, he mouthed.

"So, tell us how you landed the big fish, Jonah," a woman named Margaret instructed as she, Seldom, Susan, and a handful of other women closeted themselves in the club's expansive and glamorous ladies' room.

"I don't know that I have," Seldom said.

"Oh, you have all right," Susan said, nodding sagely. "Most of us grew up with Callum, remember. This is the first time we've ever seen him head over heels for anyone."

"When's the wedding?" Margaret prodded, dead serious.

"He hasn't proposed. I only got here two days ago," Seldom said, pressing her palms to her cheeks to try and push down the sudden panic.

"Then you got to make him, dummy," a woman named Edwina interjected. "You gotta hit him while he's too blindsided to know what's going on. That's how I got my Earl." For emphasis, she ground her fist into her open palm.

"I don't think Callum could be blindsided by anything," Seldom replied for lack of a better answer.

"I bet his mother would help you. Mrs. O'Rourke's a hoot," Susan said.

"No, no, no, I couldn't do anything like that. Callum and I, it's, I mean, we're just friends," Seldom stuttered. When they all stopped talking to stare at her in silence, she realized she had somehow said the wrong thing. "I mean, you know, weren't you ever friends with men before you were married?"

"Sure, I used to play baseball with my brother and his stupid friends, but I was eleven at the time," Edwina piped up.

"So, maybe the rumors about Callum are true," Margaret said, and Susan hissed in disapproval.

"What rumors?" Seldom asked. Was he abusive? A cheater? A drug addict? Latent alcoholic? Dirty cop on the take? At this point in her dating career, she wouldn't be surprised by anything.

"That he's a, you know, *confirmed bachelor*," a woman named Jane added while the other women studiously avoided eye contact with each other.

Seldom almost agreed that this was the case, that Callum was in no rush to get married, that he seemed happy being single. But before she could say the words, she paused and considered their connotation. Why would they say it like that unless...did they mean...? "You think Callum, that he..." Did people use the term "gay" in the forties? No, that still meant happy, she was almost certain. No matter. She remembered the way Callum had reacted to her tattoo, the way he'd pressed her against the wall in the night, the way he'd kissed her and made her turn to mush from the top of her head to the tip of her toes. And instead of trying to find the right word, she burst into laughter, so loud and sudden that she clapped her hand over her mouth. "Let me assure you ladies, he's definitely not," she said. "Definitely."

"Oh, yeah? Do tell," Margaret urged, elbowing her.

"No," Seldom replied, elbowing her back. "Loose lips sink ships."

"Just how loose are Callum's lips?" Susan asked, one eyebrow cocked in pure orneriness.

"The perfect amount," Seldom said primly. "And that's all I have to say about that."

The women laughed at her discomfort. Seldom couldn't believe she was the one from a century of free love, and *she* was the one who was embarrassed by the current conversation.

"But you are going to stay, right?" Edwina said as they made their way back to the men.

"I really don't know yet," Seldom said. "For the time being, yes, and I need to find a job."

Susan spoke from her other side. "How are you with kids?"

"I have no idea," Seldom said.

"No matter, the guy is desperate. I'll give him your number," Susan said.

"For what?" Seldom asked, but they reached the men. Callum reclaimed her, and she never got an answer to her question.

"How was the interrogation?" he asked during a slow song on the dance floor.

"I survived," she said. "It seemed fairly widely assumed that we're engaged. Is that how things go here? You're seen in public with a girl and you're as good as married?"

"Pretty much," he said. "That's not how it goes for you?"

"No. Marriage isn't as big of a deal."

"Why?"

"There's a lot of cohabitation."

"You mean people living together without the benefit of marriage?" he clarified.

"A lot of people would argue there is no benefit to marriage," she said.

"Are you one of those people?" he asked.

"I've never lived with anyone, not even close," she said.

"But if the opportunity presented itself," he urged.

She was quiet, thinking about it. "I guess I'm old fashioned in all the ways. I'd prefer marriage. But there's no guarantee marriage will work, so I've never done it."

"Sure there's a guarantee," he said.

Her eyebrows rose, waiting for him to elaborate.

He leaned in closer, touching his nose to hers. "Don't get divorced."

"You're a charmer, Mr. O'Rourke," she accused.

"Is that was the girls told you about me?" he asked. His tone was light, but she could hear the weight behind it, the worry that maybe they told her something bad.

"They seemed to think you're a catch. Either that or you're purposely uncatchable."

"What's that mean?" he asked.

"They hinted that maybe you're a confirmed bachelor," she said.

"I hope you set them straight on that," he said.

"Why would I? I mean you are, aren't you? A man who enjoys his freedom, someone who'd rather be happily single than unhappily married?"

"No, that's not...that's not what that means in this day and age," he said, exasperated.

"Oh," she drawled. "Does 'I'm teasing you,' have the same connotation?"

He eased her decidedly closer. "You're kind of impossible, Seldom Murphy."

"Maybe, but I also hold your reputation in my hands, so you'd better make a good impression before I start some rumors of my own."

"Maybe we'd best go so I can get a jump on things," he suggested. "It's better to keep ahead of these things."

"One more song," she pled. She hadn't danced with someone like this since her prom, and not even then because her date had been so busy trying to put his hands on her that the entire night had felt like a fist-fight with a squid.

"I'll Be Seeing You," began to play as they danced their last dance together.

"I remember hearing this at a USO concert when I was in France one time," Callum mused. "All around me guys were pretending they got dirt in their eyes, you know? Thinking of some girl back home. And I was so cocky, so unaffected and dry-eyed. But I think if I'd known you then, I might have discovered a whole lot of dust in my eyes. So I guess it's good I met you now instead of then because I don't like to think how it would have felt to be over there, knowing you were here."

"Probably the same as it will feel if I ever get back home," Seldom said softly.

The song came to an end. Quiet now, he led her to the car.

I O

"I don't like this. It's a bad idea."

"So you said." Seldom and Callum sat in his car, staring at the massive brick mansion. Susan's contact had come through, scoring Seldom a job interview for a governess to the people behind the bricks.

"These people, they're not like us," Callum warned.

"Are we the same?" Seldom asked, turning to survey him.

"Aren't we?" he asked, reaching for her hand.

"What's different about them?" she dodged.

"Rich people, they have different values. To them we're nothing more than the servant class. Especially the Irish."

"That's still a thing? I mean, people care if you're Irish?" she said. "I thought that was a *Gangs of New York* thing, a nineteenth century thing.

"Not as much as with my Pop or my grandparents, but it's still there a bit," he said. "People say we're poor, dirty, drunken rabblers with too many kids, only good for police or fire patrol. No one cares that you're Irish?"

"Only on St. Patrick's Day. Lots of kisses for me," she said. "The middle class is much bigger and more prevalent, something that begins to happen in response to the war you just won. There's not a lot of old money, like this," she motioned to the manse in front of them. "Celebrities and athletes are the closest we come. As for racism, I can only hope that another eighty years after my time we'll finally get it all figured out."

"The negroes have it pretty rough nowadays. Harlem's a mess, ever since that race riot in '43," he agreed, sighing.

"Yeah, we never really get away from that one. Except the word you used as a descriptor."

"Don't do this," he said, changing the subject entirely.

"Callum," she began, but he interrupted her.

"Stay with us. Why are you trying to get away? Has it been so bad?"

"Of course it hasn't. You and your mother have been wonderful, and I've enjoyed my time with you so much. But if I'm going to stay here, and for the time being it looks like I am, then I have to get a job, to support myself, to find my own place to live."

"Why?"

"Because that's what I do," she said.

"I make plenty enough to support you," he said.

"But you shouldn't have to," she said.

"Why not?" he asked.

"Because I'm not your responsibility," she said.

"Why aren't you? I found you. I brought you here. By all rights, I should get to keep you," he said, reaching over to touch her cheek.

"That's not how it works in my world. Women are independent as much as men."

He pressed his thumb between his eyes. "What happened in your generation that made you believe you can't depend on anyone?"

"What happened in your generation that made you believe you have to take care of everyone?" she countered.

They sat in silence a few beats. "I should go. I don't want to be late."

"Very well," he said and reached for his door.

"What are you doing?" she asked.

"I'm going with you," he said, confused.

"You can't go with me," she said.

"Why not?"

"Because it's a job interview, not preschool. You can't accompany me to my job interview."

"I have no plans to, but I am going to be there to introduce you," he said. He left the car. She waited until he came to get her, out of aggravation this time.

"Callum, that's a very nice thought, I suppose, but you cannot go with me into this interview. I'm fully capable of introducing myself, thank you very much. I've been on my own the last decade."

He put his hands on her shoulders. "It's 1946, dollface. *1946*. Right now it's my time, and this is how it's done. I introduce you to this man so he knows that you are very much *not* on your own. You are under my protection and will be for as long as you remain here. Believe me, he would think it more strange if you showed up unaccompanied, a girl with no connection to anyone."

She bit her lip and glanced at the mansion again.

"You're not going to win this one, Seldom," he warned.

"Am I going to win any of them, ever?" she asked, peering up into his handsome face.

"You don't see me smoking right now, do you? And I really, really want to," he said in a conspiratorial whisper that made her smile.

"All right, Greatest Generation. Make your introduction, but then please leave me on my own so I can have my job interview like a grownup, competent woman."

"Why, Miss Murphy, your wish is my command." He took her hand and placed it on his arm in a courtly fashion, escorting her not to the front door, but to the servant's entrance in the back. For that piece of knowledge, she was grateful. Until that moment she wouldn't have thought of such a thing, wasn't aware of the separate entrance.

A maid answered Callum's knock. Seldom knew it was the maid because she was dressed like one, with a black dress and a white starched pinafore. Seldom opened her mouth, but Callum squeezed her hand and spoke for her.

"Miss Seldom Murphy to interview for the job of governess," he said.

The maid nodded to Callum and closed the door in their faces.

"Why did she go away?" Seldom whispered.

"To retrieve the house manager. It will be his decision if you're allowed in or not," he explained. All of a sudden she was thankful for his presence. Apparently things *were* different when it came to getting a job here. The maid returned.

"Come along." Without waiting for a response, she turned and walked away.

Seldom caught Callum's eye. *She seems nice,* she mouthed.

Told you, he replied. They were led to a small room off the kitchen where a man sat wearing a white starched shirt and pinstriped pants. He looked Seldom up and down, clearly assessing her by her appearance, before turning to survey Callum. His eyes narrowed speculatively on Callum as if he's sensed something unpleasant about him. Callum's face remained impassively neutral, but Seldom tensed.

"Please be seated," the man said. He waited to speak again until they sat down. "My name is Arthur Madigan. I'm the head of household here."

Seldom opened her mouth, but Callum squeezed her hand again. "I'm Callum O'Rourke. This is Seldom Murphy; she's new to the city."

"And you're a police officer," Arthur said, and this time there was no mistaking his disdain.

"Yes," Callum said, his chin rising slightly.

"Hmm," Arthur said, finally turning his attention on Seldom. "Have you any experience caring for children?"

"No," Seldom said. It was highly likely her chin was tilted at the same angle as Callum's. Definitively so, if his amused smile was any indication.

"How much education have you?" Arthur continued.

"A high school diploma," she said.

"No finishing school?"

"No."

"How many languages do you speak?"

"English." *Unless you count Pig Latin,* she wanted to say. The man's snobbery was getting on her nerves. Only Callum's presence stopped her from saying the words. She didn't want to risk doing anything that would hinder her chances for getting the job. She couldn't be dependent on him anymore. "But I speak it *quite* well," she couldn't help adding, making her tone haughty enough to match his.

A male voice chuckled, but it wasn't Callum, and it certainly wasn't Arthur. Seldom's head swiveled to the doorway where she saw a man leaning against the frame.

"Mr. Pierce, sir," Arthur said, jolting to his feet. "I didn't think you would be home today, sir."

"And yet here I am," Mr. Pierce replied, his relaxed tone a sharp contrast to Arthur's snappish one. "Who do we have here, Arthur?"

"This is Miss Seldom Murphy, sir, and her companion, a police officer."

Callum stood and held out his hand to the newcomer. "Callum O'Rourke, sir. Pleased to make your acquaintance."

"And yours, O'Rourke." He turned his piercing blue eyes on Seldom. "Do you come to us from another placement, Miss Murphy?"

"No, sir. I was a baker before this."

"Where?"

"Canada," she said.

He blinked at her. "Canada, you say? *Parlez-vous français?*"

"Croissant, baguette, éclair," Seldom replied.

He blinked at her again. "Yes, well, it was lovely to meet you. Arthur."

The two men made eye contact over Seldom's head and Pierce disappeared. Seldom's heart sank. She hadn't factored French into her Canadian scheme. Of course she would speak French if she were from Canada. Of course the man knew she was lying. There was no way she was going to get the job now. Worse, she'd have to suffer the humiliation of rejection and failure in front of Callum. He probably already sensed as much because he was tense and stiff beside her.

"Shall we," Arthur said, indicating the chairs again. They sat. Seldom took a breath and braced herself.

Spit it out so I can slink away in shame, she silently pled.

Arthur made a show of adjusting the papers before him. He cleared his throat. At that moment, Seldom thought maybe she hated him. Was he taking perverse pleasure in her humiliation? "So, Miss Murphy, it would appear you have the job."

"I...what?"

"You will begin immediately," Arthur continued as if she hadn't spoken. "Tomorrow, if possible. Arrangements can be made to help you move your belongings."

"I'm going to live here?" Seldom said.

Arthur gave her a look that let her know exactly what he thought of her IQ. "It's a governess position. Obviously you'll need to be available to the children at all times."

Seldom swallowed down her panic. Children. At all times. She had no idea what to do with children for ten minutes, let alone all day and all night. "Yes, of course. Tomorrow should be fine."

Arthur droned on for a while longer, but she tuned him out. A few minutes later, Callum stood and held the door for her. She followed him silently to the car.

"You were right, Callum," she said as soon as they were in the car.

He patted his pockets. "I feel like I should be writing this down. Pray tell, how was I correct, kid?"

"I was out of my element in there. It was a 1946 thing, for sure. I have no idea how I got that job."

He laughed and swiped his hand over his eyes. "Sweetness, that had nothing to do with the year."

"What are you talking about?"

"It means some things are universal," he said.

"Such as?"

"Such as Andrew Pierce took one look at you and told his house manager to hire you," he said.

Now it was her turn to laugh. "No."

"Yes."

"Callum, that man saw me for all of thirty seconds," she said.

"That's apparently all it takes with you," he said.

"No. You know how I know? Because I've been me for twenty-eight years, and things like that don't happen to me. I'm not that girl."

"As you said, you were born out of time. Maybe all you needed was to find the right decade," he said.

"But I don't fit here at all," she argued.

"Don't you?" He didn't give her a chance to answer before he started the car and eased into traffic.

11

"Don't you ever sleep, kid?" Callum asked when he walked into the house at one in the morning and saw Seldom sitting at the table. His plate of supper was warmed and waiting for him. He bent to kiss her cheek before sinking into the chair beside her.

"Sometimes," she said. "How was work?"

He gave her a look but otherwise didn't answer. He couldn't talk about work over food if he had any hope of swallowing. Tactfully, she let the subject drop. Instead she sat in silence, watching him eat. Her eyes looked big and worried. For all her bravado about being independent, he thought she had no idea how often she wore that expression.

He finished his food. Seldom stood and set his plate in the sink. Before she could return to the table, he stood and led her into the living room. He sat on the couch. To his extreme amazement, Seldom sat in his lap, curling into a ball, her head pressed to his shoulder. It was not a gesture for unmarried people, at least none that he knew. He covered his shock by reaching for the afghan and drawing it around her. Despite his astonishment, it's not like he was complaining. She was soft and warm, smelled good, and felt even better. His hand made passes over her head, seemingly without his knowledge or permission.

"So tell me," she murmured.

He took another breath and dove in. "We found another girl, like the one before, cuffed, butchered, drained of blood."

"Oh," was all she said, but now her hand was making soothing passes over his chest, and it helped, that little bit of comfort. He took a deep breath, maybe the first one in hours. He would never understand people who killed on purpose. He'd killed because he'd had to, but it had brought him no pleasure, merely bad memories he worked so hard to push away they could only find release in his nightmares.

"I think we're looking at a mass murderer," he said, resting his head on hers. It was incongruous, holding this soft sweet girl and talking about such a thing.

"In my day we call them serial killers," she said.

"Huh, that's a pretty good phrase."

"Better not use it," she said.

"Because of the space time continuum?" he guessed.

"Exactly," she said.

He could feel her lips turn up in a smile against his chest, and he smiled in response.

"This isn't a subject for women," he said, trying to draw himself back to some sense of propriety.

"I'm fairly shock-proof," she told him.

"Have you seen a lot of death?" he asked.

"On TV and in movies."

He thought of the movies he'd seen, where death was portrayed so gently, so nobly, the victim falling silently to the ground while the camera slowly panned away. "The reality is different."

She pulled back to look at his face, studying him a moment. She seemed to have the ability to see into his mind, to read the thoughts he usually kept hidden. "I'm sure it is," she said softly, her fingers skimming gently along his cheek. He had the unbidden desire to tell her everything, to spew the burning memories and lay them at her feet. Before he could unman himself completely, he took a deep breath and pressed them back in again. They were his burden to bear, not hers.

"Do you know what they call my generation?" she asked.

He shook his head.

"Millennials, because we come of age in the new millennium. We're confident, probably overly, compassionate, but highly cynical because we've been lied to by every previous generation. We can spot a lie and a lack of authenticity from a mile away. There is nothing you can tell me that will shock me or horrify me or push me away, unless it's a lie. Don't tell me your secrets, if you don't want to. But don't try to tell me you're doing okay." She tapped his heart and lay back against his chest, resting her head on his shoulder.

"In 1946, we don't talk about things," he said.

"In 2020, we talk about everything," she said.

"Does it help?" he asked.

"Sometimes," she said after a moment's hesitation. "But I suppose you're right, too. Action has its merits."

"Maybe the trick lies in knowing the right time for each," he said.

"You probably solved all the world's problems with that one sentence," she said.

"I've got to earn that Greatest Generation tag somehow," he said, and she laughed. Of all the things that had surprised her about her journey back in time, laughter amazed her the most. They had just survived a massive world war. Compared to her time, they were still almost living in poverty. Illness was rampant; polio was on the rise and about to strike harder than ever. And yet everyone seemingly found the humor in everything. She'd laughed more since she'd been here than she ever had before. Mrs. O'Rourke was especially funny, she a widow whose only daughter lived overseas, whose youngest son was in an institution, whose oldest child had survived five years in a brutal war. Her eyes were always dancing, looking for the laughter in everything. It was a powerful lesson for Seldom who had always believed that hard times called for moroseness and lament. Here she was finding something different, that there could still be a light in the darkness, that the light could come from within, regardless of the circumstances without.

"Why don't you take a page from your own book and tell me what's eating you?" he said, rubbing a soothing circle on her back.

"I suppose I'm a little nervous about the new job," she admitted. Given her aforementioned confidence, it was a hard admission. She was used to feeling capable and in charge. But she had no idea what to do with children, and children from another century, no less.

"You'll do fine, sweetness. I can't imagine any kid not loving you," he said, his hand continuing its soothing trek around her back.

She slid her arms around his waist and pressed her face to his chest. "I don't actually want to go," she whispered.

"I know," he said.

"I have to," she continued.

"I know that, too." If he were in her shoes, he would likely feel the same way, the desperate need to stand on her own, to make her own way, to not feel beholden to anyone. "Listen." He eased away from her and cupped her face, forcing her to look him in the eye. "If it gets bad, you can always come back. There are other jobs, plenty of them. You don't have to stay if it's a misery. You have a place with us for as long as you want it."

Seldom's eyes welled with a painful mist of tears. She had never had a place with anyone. For all her brave talk of independence, all she'd ever really wanted was an anchor. How was it possible that she'd found it here, with this man who might not even exist?

"Can I ask you something?" she whispered.

He tensed, not certain he was ready to delve into anything she might say. "Yes."

"What is finishing school?"

"A place rich people send their daughters to teach them how to nab husbands," he said.

She grimaced. "Gross."

"I told you they're crazy," he said. "Their rules are different. Stay out of their way, or they'll eat you alive."

"They're just people; they can't be that bad."

He sighed. "Sweetness, you have no idea. Promise me you'll let me know if you get in a pickle."

"How will I let you know?" she asked.

"We have this thing called a telephone," he said.

"Oh, right. I think of it as being so primitive here, but of course you have the phone." She stared at it, a massive hulk of a thing, so important it had been afforded its own stand. "Quick question, how do you use it?"

"Are you asking this primitive individual to teach you how to use the telephone, Miss Millennial?" he said.

"My phone doesn't look like that. And there are no words in our phone numbers. My phone is…"

"A magical computer, right, right," he said. It wasn't that he didn't believe her, just that he didn't altogether believe her, either. She wasn't lying, of that he was certain. And yet her tale was so fantastical that it couldn't be real. The clothes weren't any kind of fabric he'd seen before, but the style was current. Maybe she was one of those people who'd been raised by wolves or savages, except her speech and dialect were better than his, no modern slang for Miss Murphy. She acted so certain about the future, and yet how could it be possible? It couldn't, and that was why his mind refused to accept it completely. He dealt in rational facts; there was nothing rational about Seldom Murphy, nor his over the top reaction to her presence.

He reached for a piece of paper and pencil from the phone stand, wrote down his number for her, both home and the precinct, and then showed her how to dial, starting with which end of the phone to speak into and which end to hold to her ear. She stared at the receiver, testing the weight of it in her hand as if she'd never seen the like.

"Ah, kid, you make me feel like I'm sending a lamb to slaughter here," he muttered.

"I'm fine, Callum. I take care of myself, and I always land on my feet."

He stared at her, disbelieving. She thought she was so sophisticated, a woman of the world. But she had never left Manhattan, and she had no idea how to use the telephone. She viewed him as some kind of backwards Rube for using words she found offensive to describe his enemies, but what did she know about it? She'd likely never had an enemy in her life, never been hunted and pursued by an entire country intent on destroying everything she knew and loved.

"Listen to me," he said, gripping her biceps with some ferocity.

"You've got to stop thinking you know everything about everything when you actually know nothing about anything. It's going to get you in trouble."

He braced himself for her angry reaction. Instead she pressed her palms to his cheeks and said, "Seriously, Callum, you're adorbs."

"I have no idea what that means, but I'll take it," he said.

They stared at each other, their faces an inch apart. "I have another question," she whispered.

"What? You want me to teach you to use the radio?" he whispered, his eyes on her lips.

"Why do they call it necking?" she asked.

His eyes flicked over her shoulder, checking to make sure his mother's door was still closed. "Allow me to demonstrate."

And she did.

<h1 style="text-align:center">12</h1>

The Pierce mansion wasn't exactly like *Downton Abby*, but close. Seldom had assumed Arthur was the butler. He was not. The butler's name was Charles. There were three maids, Mary, Kathleen, and Janet, along with a gardener, Walter, a chauffer, Stephen, a laundress, Bonny, and a cook, Mrs. Walsh. Adding a governess into the mix seemed like overkill to Seldom, but what did she know? There were only two children; how much trouble could they be? Surely one of the maids could keep an eye out, but apparently not.

There were two children—six-year-old Matthew and four year old Daisy. So far Seldom thought they dressed a lot like Prince William's kids—lots of short pants with suit jackets, starched white shirts, and smocked embroidery on the bodice of Daisy's dresses. Their father, Andrew Pierce, was a widower. That was all she knew about him, and all she cared to. Callum thought she was naïve, but of course she wasn't. She understood that Andrew had found her attractive, though why she had no idea. Kathleen and Janet, two of the maids, were both very pretty. He should try for one of them, though maybe he already had. Maybe it was a thing with him, collecting attractive young women into his keep. What Callum failed to take into account, however, was that Seldom was not desperate for marriage or money. She'd always been alone, and she'd always taken care of herself, financially and otherwise. She was not of this generation where women were born and bred for

77

the sole purpose to marry and breed. She had a career, a life outside the realm of men. And if she stayed here, she'd have it again or die trying.

It was no surprise to Seldom that Andrew apparently had very little to do with the rearing of his children. According to the schedule she'd received from Arthur, he saw them once a day, first thing in the morning. During this time they gave him a five-minute rundown of their lives, sort of like a book report, while he listened with half an ear, reading the paper with the better part of his attention.

"Marvelous," he said, nodding as Daisy detailed for him her favorite doll's latest ill. Seldom stood beside her, reading *The Wall Street Journal* over Andrew's shoulder. He was a stockbroker, she'd learned, though he also came from old family money. Previously she had never had any desire to invest, but now... Was it cheating to use the things she knew about the future? Unethical, maybe, but who actually would she hurt if she played the market? Could she play the market? Were women allowed to do that in this era?

She realized, all of a sudden, that Andrew had asked her a question. "I'm sorry, what?" she said.

"I said how goes it, Miss Murphy? Are you getting along okay? Is there anything you need?"

"No, we're doing fine," she said and meant it. She might not be a Pinterest-worthy governess with a constant stream of creative entertainment worthy of Mary Poppins, but the kids were still alive and they seemed to like her okay. Mostly they just wanted attention, no surprise since they got so little of it from anyone else. "Are women allowed to play the stock market?" she blurted, pointing to the paper. It was perfectly flat and crisp, owning to the morning's ironing.

"Yes, of course," he said, both surprised and amused by the question. "I'd be happy to invest something for you, if you'd like."

"Thank you, but I don't have any money." She was thinking instead of Callum and his mother. What if she helped them play the game? What if she made them rich?

"Say you did. What would you select?" Andrew asked. He opened the paper to the stocks and handed it to her, still clearly amused. Seldom scanned the list and called out the first three familiar names she recognized.

"Boeing, Pfizer, and 3M," she said.

He blinked at her, no longer amused. "Why those?"

"Commercial flight is about to take off, obviously. Pharmaceuticals are always a good idea. And 3M..." she had no idea what they did, outside of post-its, but she knew they were definitely a huge company. "I just have a feeling about them."

"I already own stock in Pfizer and Boeing, but on your recommendation, I'll be sure and add some 3M. And when you're ready to invest, do let me know, and I'll buy some for you, too," he said, smiling.

"Thank you," she said, smiling in return. Callum had spent so long warning her away from him that she was sure he'd be an ogre. But Callum was wrong; Andrew Pierce was just a man, and a possibly kind one at that. She remembered her charges and clapped her hands together. "All right, guys, say goodbye to Daddy."

Mathew and Daisy glanced at her sharply. "We call him Father," Mathew informed her, ever ready to correct her and take charge.

"Yes, right, my mistake. Say goodbye to Father and we'll be on our way," Seldom said. They dutifully complied. She picked up the picnic lunch she'd ordered, and they set off.

The children had never ridden the subway before. Seldom didn't know if she was supposed to allow them to or not, but she decided to take a page from Princess Diana's book and get them in touch with the common folk. Maybe it would have the desired effect of making them more compassionate capitalists in the future. Though these kids would come of age in the sixties. Maybe they'd rebel completely.

"You guys are Baby Boomers," she mused to no one in particular.

Mathew gave her another sharp look. "We're not babies."

"No, of course. My mistake again. How are you at flying kites?" she asked.

"Pretty good," Mathew said. His expression aimed for nonchalance, but his eyes were alight with excitement.

"You've never flown a kite before, have you?" she guessed.

"No, but I know I'm good at it," Mathew replied.

Seldom laughed and hugged him, squeezing him impossibly tighter when he squirmed to get away. "You sound just like me," she told him.

"No I don't because I'm a boy and you're a girl," he said, giving her a final shove to gain his freedom. Daisy took his place, snuggling close to Seldom's body as if starving for affection, which she undoubtedly was. Seldom picked her up and smothered kisses on her face while she giggled and squirmed. Unlike her brother, she was aiming to get closer and not farther away.

They took the subway to Woolworth where Seldom used the money Arthur had given her for the children's expenditures to purchase a kite. She had never actually flown a kite before either but, like Mathew, she was certain she could do it.

They got back on the subway and continued to Central Park where Seldom spread out their picnic on the grass. The kids barely ate, so excited were they to play with the kite. Giving up on lunch, Seldom repacked her basket and unfurled the kite. It took a few tries before they got it off the ground, but eventually they did. They spent a long time playing, until Daisy and even Mathew grew weary and began rubbing their eyes. Seldom, realizing she'd never be able to wrangle them on two subway transfers in their current condition, instead gave up and hailed a cab. They were asleep almost as soon as the car pulled away from the curb, tucked up against her like baby chicks. She kissed the tops of each of their heads, feeling suddenly warm and oozing with love. This, then, was why people had children, for these moments of tenderness that shot straight to the heart.

Her gooey thoughts were startled by the appearance of Andrew Pierce standing on the sidewalk to her right. They were at a stoplight, giving Seldom plenty of time to make sure it was him. She had to do a double and then triple take because the neighborhood was far from Wall Street. In fact, it was so seedy that the cabby reached over and locked the doors. And yet there stood Andrew Pierce, millionaire, stealing furtive glances before opening an unmarked door and dodging inside. *What on earth is he doing, and why does he look so secretive about it?*

Seldom wondered. *Probably a mistress,* she answered herself. But if that were the case, why was he there in the middle of the afternoon? And why did he look around like he was about to do something illegal?

Her curiosity was piqued, and at least she knew there was more to the man than money. Callum's warning voice rang in her ears. *Rich people aren't like us; they're crazy. Keep out of their way or they'll eat you alive, sweetness.*

She glanced down at Daisy and Mathew, still fully asleep. Maybe Callum was correct and rich people were insane, but their children were as innocent and sweet as the driven snow.

13

The next morning during the children's visit with their father, he once again seemed more interested in Seldom than his progeny.

"See anything that looks good to you today?" he asked, handing her the paper.

She skimmed it, keeping an eye out for familiar names. "The oil companies, obviously."

"Obviously," he agreed, fully sarcastic.

"Pepsi. Merck. AT&T, Coke, Proctor and Gamble, General Motors, Johnson and Johnson."

He snatched the paper back, frowning. "Johnson and Johnson is new, not on the Dow yet."

"Trust me, they're golden," Seldom said.

"Well, if one can't take investment advice from one's governess, then who is there, really?"

"One can't imagine," she said, her sarcasm matching his.

"When is the last time you were in Canada?" he asked.

"It feels like forever," she said.

"I'll bet it does," he agreed and surprised her by drawing his kids close for a hug before kissing each of them on top of the head. "Be good. Listen to Miss Murphy, unless she tells you to sell low and buy high."

"That would be a rookie governess mistake," she said, securing each of the children's hands in her own.

"Where are we going today, Seldom?" Daisy asked her. They were passing by one of the maids who tsk'd at the familiarity.

"To the library," Seldom replied, and the maid tsk'd again.

"What's a library?" Daisy asked.

"It's a magic place where they have all the books in the world," Seldom replied. Her own mother had never taken her to the library, of course. She didn't learn of its existence until she started school and became a voracious reader. Then it had felt magical to her, a transport to other, happier worlds. History had been her favorite genre, an irony since she was now living it.

They took the subway again. Seldom applied for a library card and let the kids check out as many books as she could carry, which turned out to be a lot. When they were finished with that, she took them to visit Callum and Mrs. O'Rourke. Seldom hadn't seen him since she started her new job. His hours made visits tricky. After the children went to bed, her evenings were free, but Callum worked second shift.

"What's this place?" Mathew asked, sounding suspicious as they stood on the O'Rourke's doorstep.

"This is my friend's house," Seldom explained after she knocked. Mrs. O'Rourke answered the door, as Seldom knew she would. Answering doors was a woman's job, apparently.

"Seldom," Mrs. O'Rourke said, pulling her into an all-encompassing hug. It felt so good, Seldom never wanted to let go. "And who do we have here?" she asked, surveying Mathew and Daisy.

"Mathew and Daisy Pierce, this is Mrs. O'Rourke."

"How do you do?" Mathew asked, extending his hand like a proper gentleman.

"I do very well, thank you," Mrs. O'Rourke said, returning his shake. "And I just pulled an apple cake from the oven. Would you like to come and have a piece?"

"Yes, please," Mathew and Daisy echoed together, trailing after Mrs. O'Rourke as she led them through the house.

Callum sat at the kitchen table, reading the paper. He set it aside and stood when they entered the room. "Heya, dollface. I thought that was you." He leaned in and gave her a peck on the cheek.

"She doesn't have a doll face," Mathew said, ever literal.

"You'd have to see what it looks like from up here," Callum replied seriously.

Mathew stood on his toes, trying to peer at Seldom's face from a higher angle.

"C'mere," Callum said, lifting him high to look. "See how big her eyes are, the way her little nose tips up on the end just so, her big, pretty lips, how smooth and fair her skin is? Like porcelain."

"Oh, yeah," Mathew said, nodding, "right, okay."

Callum set him down and rifled his hair. "You have to see it the right way is all."

Mrs. O'Rourke served them pieces of cake, and everyone sat at the table. "How's life on the Upper East, Snow White?" Callum asked Seldom.

"Predictably posh, Copper. How are the little people I left behind?" Seldom countered.

"Wasting away for lack of your presence," he said. His tone was flippant but his expression was anything but. She suddenly wished that they were alone so she could curl into his embrace and tell him everything that had happened since they'd been apart and hear everything of his. Had they found any more dead girls? Did he have any leads?

Sensing they needed alone time, or maybe because she wanted to, Mrs. O'Rourke took the children into the living room so they could show her the books they'd selected while they ate their cake.

"How's it going, really?" Callum asked, reaching for her hand.

"It's different, as you said. In the eyes of my coworkers, I'm doing everything wrong. I get the feeling they think I should be much more formal, both with the kids and their education. But I'm doing the things I wish someone would have done with me when I was a kid, spending time with them, playing, and reading books. We've gone on lots of adventures. It's been fun, seeing the city anew through their eyes. Apparently there are different rules for rich people, such as not riding the subway or going to the library."

"Those are for the unwashed masses," Callum said. "Like me."

She leaned closer and sniffed. "You smell freshly washed to me."

"You caught me on a good day." He leaned closer and pressed his lips to her neck, making her lose focus for a minute.

"What about you?" she whispered at last, albeit shakily.

"What about me?" he asked, his lips still moving against her neck.

"Your cases. Any leads?"

He sat back. "No, no leads, and it's a ticking time bomb before the papers get ahold of it. How we've been able to keep it under wraps this long is a mystery."

"If TV has taught me anything about serial killers, it's that he wants it to be publicized, he wants people to know what he's done."

"How do you figure?" Callum asked, tilting his head at her in question.

"Serial killers, they leave signatures behind. It's why all the murders are the same. And they want credit for those murders. I bet after it hits the papers, he'll contact you to brag, to rub your face in your inability to find him."

"You got that all from television?"

"And books and movies," she said. "Eventually the FBI will have profilers who specialize in serial killers. At least I think that's true. Again, it's in all the books and movies, and they had to get it from somewhere, right?"

"What do you mean by a profiler?" he asked.

"They make a psychological composition of the killer, based on his signature, based on his style, his handwriting, everything. After they put it all together, they can make suppositions, like a man in his forties with a stern mother who was kicked out of the military or something like that."

"That's an interesting thought," he said, leaning in, warming to the subject. "I guess I never thought about it that way, linking everything together, seeing what the big picture can tell us. I've been looking at the individual pieces." He stared hard at her, but he wasn't seeing her. He was seeing the crime scenes, trying to link them in his mind.

"If he's doing it here, he might be doing it elsewhere, in other precincts, maybe even other states. Letting it go public might get you that kind of information. On TV they release only as much information as they want the public to know. They always hold something back, some secret only the killer would know. That way when he makes contact, they know it's him. And lot of times serial killers either take a memento or leave something behind, like a calling card. Was there anything unusual left behind or was something taken from the women, a chunk of hair, a piece of a dress, a shoe?"

"I don't know. I'm going to look at the photos, make some comparisons, go over everything with new eyes." He shook his head as if to clear it and then smiled at her. "I never thought I'd be able to talk to a dame about work and, what's more, that I'd find it helpful."

"We're more than pretty faces and kissable lips," Seldom said.

"But with a face like that and lips like these, why would you have to be?" he wondered, leaning in to kiss her again.

The kiss was cut short by the appearance of Mrs. O'Rourke and the children. "Sorry to interrupt, but I believe your charges are growing sleepy."

Daisy was rubbing her eyes in a way that was becoming familiar and Mathew, though insistent that he was *not sleepy at all*, was blinking almost twice as much as normal.

"Thank you, Mrs. O'Rourke. We should definitely be going. What do we say to Mrs. O'Rourke and Callum?" Seldom prompted.

"Thank you, Mrs. O'Rourke and Callum," the children chorused. Seldom stood and put her arms around them, herding them toward the door. Callum stood behind her.

"I'll drive you."

"Thanks," she said, smiling up at him in relief. The subway was all well and good when the children were bright eyed and full of vigor, but it was something else entirely when they were tired and clinging to her skirt. And if she took a cab every day, she'd have to ask for more money from Arthur, something she definitely didn't want to have to do unless it became necessary.

She tucked the children into the back seat, cringing at the lack of seatbelts or car seats. On the other hand, they were able to spread out and lie down. Daisy was out before Callum pulled away from the curb and Mathew wouldn't be far behind.

"They seem like nice kids," Callum commented.

"They are," Seldom agreed, tossing them a fond look over the seat.

"Must take after the mother," Callum said.

"What are you talking about?" Seldom asked.

Callum darted her a look. "I take it you aren't acquainted with Andrew Pierce's reputation."

"No, but he seems nice enough."

He rolled his eyes. "Nice looking doesn't equal nice, dollface. He's ruthless. Rumors about his business dealings are rampant. Cross him, and he'll end you in this town. And he has more money than Moses."

"To me he seems like a lonely widower."

"Don't let appearances deceive you. And keep your distance. Guy's a shark," Callum said.

"No worries. I see him for approximately five minutes a day. Hey, I wanted to ask you something." She turned to face him. He darted her a smile, amused by her sudden enthusiasm.

"Have at it."

"I was thinking of taking the kids to a baseball game tomorrow. Want to tag along?"

His smile fled. "Are you...are you asking me for a date?"

"Yes, and I take it by your tone I've done something you deem inappropriate."

"The man asks the woman for a date," he said.

"What does the woman do?"

"Wait to be asked."

"How could you ask if you didn't know I wanted to go to the game?"

"You wait until I suggest it," he said.

"What if you never suggest it?"

"Then you don't go," he said.

"That's ridiculously stupid," she huffed.

"That's how it is," he said. "How it's always been."

"That's not how it's going to remain," she said.

"And how's that working out for you, Miss Independent? Because the last guy you made a date with tried to kill you," he said.

She gasped. "Callum, low blow."

"All I'm saying is that you can't have it both ways. You can't want to be the one in charge and then be disappointed by the results. Seek out weak men, and weak men you will find."

"Okay, and how have your results been, with all the sweet, flowery girls you've pursued? Have they met your expectations, or have they bored you senseless?"

He opened his mouth and closed it again. They sat in tense silence a moment before he spoke once more. "It's how it is, how it's always been. If you're going to stay here, you're going to have to accept it."

"Why?"

"Because."

"Because why?"

"Because it's biblical," he said with a satisfied nod, as if that decided matters once and for all.

"No it isn't," she argued.

"Yes, it is. The man has dominion over the woman. We're the ones in charge, God said so."

"Show me where," she demanded.

He rolled his eyes. "I don't have the whole bible memorized, Sister Mary Seldom. But women are commanded to submit to men."

"No, Father Callum, women are commanded to submit to their *husbands*, not all mankind. You have no power over me, and neither does any other man. If I want to go to a baseball game, I'll go to a baseball game. Whether or not you tag along is up to you."

"You cannot trek out to the Bronx by yourself with two kids in tow," he roared.

"Why not?" she snapped back.

"Because it's not safe," he said, dashing his hand on the steering wheel.

"So come with me, you stubborn Irish mule."

"I'm not going to be kneecapped into a date by my own girl," he said.

"Then I hope you enjoy your evening tomorrow. You'll have plenty of time to enjoy your vast power and authority, " she said. "*Alone.*"

They finished the ride in silence. Seldom stared out the window, arms crossed, while Callum white knuckled the steering wheel. He pulled up in front of the mansion. She reached for her door, but he held her back.

"Would you like to go to a game with me tomorrow?" he asked. His tone pleasantly soft and gentle, his fingers trailing lightly on her arm.

She pressed her lips together to push back her smile and faced him. "What a wonderful suggestion. I'd love to."

He put his arms around her and pulled her to him, sliding her easily across the seat.

"The no seatbelt thing has definite advantages," she said, easing her arms around his neck.

"You may have a point there, that a single lady doesn't have to take direction from a man," he conceded.

"Boy, howdy," she agreed, making him smile. She had no idea which generation the saying came from, but it sounded like something he might say so she went with it.

"I gave you something, and now you have to give me something," he said.

"What's that?"

"The assurance that if we were married, you'd listen to a blasted word I said," he said.

She considered it a minute and leaned up to whisper in his ear. "I'd definitely take it under advisement." She bit his earlobe and slid back to her position by the door.

"You're leaving me on that note?" he said, dismayed.

She thumbed toward the back seat. Callum jumped slightly. "They were so quiet, I forgot they were there."

"I guess I'd better wake them," she said reluctantly. They were so peaceful and beautiful when they were sleeping.

"Nah, I'll help you carry them in." He hefted Mathew easily into his arms. Seldom struggled under the weight of the much smaller Daisy. Kathleen opened the servant's entrance for them with a doubly disapproving glower, one that encompassed both Seldom and Callum. They tucked the children into their beds and paused in the hallway outside Seldom's room, conveniently located between the children's bedrooms.

"What did you do to the maid to make her look at you like that?" Callum whispered, pushing a stray strand of hair off Seldom's face.

"I told you the staff doesn't like me. I think they sense I'm an outsider and don't fit," she said.

"It's fairly obvious, but in a good way," he said.

"My charms must only work on you," she said.

"I'm more than okay with that." He leaned in to kiss her cheek. "Watch your back, sweetness. These people play for keeps."

"Only if you're a threat, which I most assuredly am not," she said.

"Not yet, maybe, but give it time." He leaned in for another kiss, on the forehead this time, and sauntered down the hall.

14

Seldom had seemingly just fallen asleep that night when she was awakened by an earth-shattering clap of thunder. She bolted upright, confused by her unfamiliar location, heartbeat thumping in her ears. Eventually her mind reoriented itself and her adrenaline began to recede. She was in her bedroom in the Pierce mansion. It was only a bit of thunder. Everything was fine.

A minute later the door on the left side of her room opened and Daisy trundled in, weeping.

"It's only thunder," Seldom said, gathering the girl close and tucking her beside her in bed. Almost as soon as she got her settled, the other door opened and Mathew poked his head in, his face a mask of false bravado. He dithered at the edge of the room, clearly frightened but not wanting to show it.

"Daisy and I are having a sleepover. Want to come be our protector?" Seldom offered, patting the bed on her other side. Relieved, he rushed forward and climbed into bed, burrowing as far under the covers as his sister.

The storm was nowhere near over. It raged and thrashed outside while the kids cowered and whimpered. Eventually Mathew gave up the pretense of bravery and wept along with his sister. The scene was so reminiscent from *The Sound of Music* that Seldom could only replicate Maria's actions and hope for the best.

"Do you know what makes me feel better when I'm afraid?" she asked. Neither of the kids answered, but she went on undaunted. "I sing." And she began to sing, "My Favorite Things," or as much of it as she could remember, which wasn't much, as it turned out.

"Raindrops on posies and whiskey for kittens, something and something and something from *Frozen*. These are a few of my favorite things!" That line she definitely remembered, and sang it with vigor. At the very least it worked to distract the kids, and when she pulled them out of bed and started to dance with them, they began to giggle, hard.

"This one is called the twist. It's going to be mad famous when you're teenagers," she said, demonstrating the dance for them and leading Daisy in a twirl as she continued to sing her made up lyrics to a song that wouldn't be released for another twenty years.

The storm had died completely by the time she was finished. The kids might not sleep now, but for a different reason. They were laughing and dancing, twisting and twirling around her room, when a voice spoke from the doorway.

"What an interesting song," Andrew Pierce said.

Seldom jumped and faced him, hand on her heart. "Filet mignon! What on earth are you doing here?"

"I came to check on the children. Sometimes they become frightened by storms. I see now they were in good hands. Where did that song come from? I've never heard it before."

"My Austrian ancestors made it up," she said.

"Austrian, eh? *Sprichst du Deutsch*?"

"What, do you know every language in the universe?" she asked, still a bit snappish from the fright. The children were subdued, looking between the two grownups as if not sure if they were in trouble.

"Boarding school in Switzerland," Andrew explained.

"Really? That's fascinating," Seldom said and meant it. She had always wanted to go to Switzerland. Or anywhere, really. She'd been far too busy with survival. Travel remained the stuff of dreams.

"It's nice you think so," Andrew said. He opened his arms and his children ran into them, clinging each to a leg. He kissed the tops of their heads and gave them a squeeze. "Back to bed, Moppets. Let's let Miss Murphy get her beauty sleep."

"Dolls don't need beauty sleep," Mathew said, glancing at Seldom in an uncanny imitation of Callum.

"That they don't, and yet governesses do, even the pretty ones."

"Do you want me to put them to bed?" Seldom offered.

"I think I can handle it, thank you. Rest well, Miss Murphy," he said, giving her a nod. She gave him a curtsy in reply. He shook his head, "Doesn't suit at all."

"I'll work on it," she promised. She waited until he was gone before switching off the lamp beside her bed and crawling between the sheets. She was certain she wouldn't be able to sleep after the interruption, but she was out in minutes.

The next morning the children woke no worse for their interrupted sleep. Seldom, on the other hand, felt groggy, but she knew coffee would help. Breakfast was a grand affair at the manse as was every meal, with multiple options served in silver and crystal containers. They had fresh squeezed orange juice and freshly ground strong coffee with cream fresh from the milk truck. It was a delightful sensory experience, even if it was partaken in the kitchen with the children.

As soon as they were finished, it was time for their morning visit with Andrew who, Seldom was learning, genuinely loved his children. It made her sad that societal constraints kept him from having a genuine relationship with them. She had dreams and visions of breaking the barriers, but realistically that wasn't bound to happen. Nor did she know how to bring it about. So she did the best she could within the limits that had been set for her, trying to make the most of her time with the children, as well as their moments with their father. She had started coaching them on what topics to cover with him each day in order to limit the dead space and awkward pauses. Now the kids had almost as much fun practicing their responses with her as they did relaying them to their father.

The morning was gray and rainy, no good for outdoor play. Seldom had high hopes the clouds would clear before the game that evening.

In the mean time, she intended to find something indoors to do. As she scanned the massive kitchen, she found it. She would bake. Baking soothed her like nothing else and she had missed it since she'd been here. Mrs. O'Rourke wouldn't have minded if Seldom baked in her kitchen, but the items Seldom made used a lot of expensive ingredients. Seldom hadn't felt comfortable enough imposing in that way. But here, at the mansion, everything was overflowing. Money was no object, and it was like a fantasyland.

"How would you two like to help me make cookies today?" Seldom asked Mathew and Daisy as soon as they'd finished their visit with their father.

Daisy clapped her hands excitedly, but Mathew regarded her with suspicion, as usual. "You want us to cook?"

One of the maids was passing by them and tsk'd in disapproval.

"Something in your throat, Janet?" Seldom asked.

"Mrs. Walsh ain't going to be happy," she whispered.

"Mrs. Walsh is at the market. We'll be finished by the time she gets home, probably," Seldom said, tossing a nervous glance toward the door. Mrs. Walsh was a formidable woman who wouldn't like to have her kitchen messed with. On the other hand, Daisy and Mathew were technically her bosses, in a manner of speaking. If they wanted to bake, they could bake.

Janet scurried away. Seldom finished setting out ingredients when Arthur entered. "What do you think you're doing?" he snapped. He was an overbearing man, mad with power, Seldom thought, and she didn't much like him. The way he watched her every move was creepy and foreboding. More than once she had caught him peeking around corners, spying on her. She had taken to locking her door whenever she was in her room, not trusting him not to barge in and spy on her there.

"Mathematics lesson," she said with a smile, and that gave him pause.

"I think there are much better ways of teaching mathematics than to have the young master and mistress in the servants' space."

"I don't," Seldom said, continuing her prep.

Short of physically removing her, what could he do? Nothing, apparently. "We'll see about this," he huffed before storming off.

"Is Mr. Madigan mad at us?" Mathew asked.

"Of course not. He's just sad because he doesn't get to help. Now, I need someone strong who can stir this dough," Seldom said, which wasn't a lie. She was used to using mixers, and professional ones at that. Mixing by hand was a whole other matter. If she stayed in this century much longer, she'd have Popeye arms.

At last the dough was ready. She dusted the counter with flour and set it out, allowing the children to take turns rolling it. She had developed a sugar cookie recipe that didn't need to be chilled before it was rolled, had made it so many times she had the recipe memorized. Both those facts served her well today.

Her bakery's signature shapes were teacups and butterflies. Today she used a glass and let the kids cut circles. They helped her clean the kitchen while the cookies baked. Daisy thought standing on a chair to wash dishes was the most amazing experience ever. Seldom cynically thought it was likely the only time in her life she would ever touch dishwater, unless her adolescent rebellion someday extended to firing the household staff.

Seldom made the buttercream herself; it was a boiled meringue, definitely not safe for preschoolers. And once again she had to beat in the butter by hand, making her long for her oversized mixer. Or even Josh who occasionally did the heavy lifting required in the bakery. *Josh.* Would she ever see him again? He was so young, so innocent, so sweet. Losing her would be the first blemish on his innocence, a dawning reality that life was hard and might someday hurt. *Josh, I'm okay.* Maybe if she thought it hard enough and long enough, he would sense it. She made a piping bag from parchment paper and helped the children pipe the frosting. They had just finished the last one when Mrs. Walsh entered the kitchen, eyes narrowed in speculation as she took in the sight of three interlopers in her space.

"And what might ye three be doing in here?" Her speech pattern was a strange mishmash of several dialects and accents. Was she American? Irish? South African? Jamaican? No one could say for certain.

The children cowered behind Seldom. In truth, she was a little afraid of the woman, too. She was large and in charge. "We made cookies," Seldom announced brightly, holding out the plate like a peace offering. Mrs. Walsh reached for one and took a bite, waiting to chew and swallow before she made a reply.

"Now thoose be fair tasty," she said, wiping a crumb off her mouth with the back of her hand. "And where did a trifle like yous learn to baker like dat?"

"I worked in a bakery," Seldom said.

"Did ye now?" Mrs. Walsh asked, eyes narrowed suspiciously. Her gaze scoured the kitchen once more, looking for anything out of place. "Weel, if yous keep on cleaning up afters yourselfs, you can baker anytime you please. As long as you share like." She added a wink as she reached for another cookie.

Pressing her luck, she gave Mrs. Walsh a one-armed hug and kiss on the cheek. "Thank you, it's an amazing kitchen. So well stocked." It was probably an odd compliment, unless you routinely worked in a kitchen and realized how difficult it was to get everything just so.

The cookies took so long that as soon as they changed clothes and got themselves cleaned up, it was time for Callum to arrive. The kids shyly presented him with the cookies they'd packed for him, and he spent due time exclaiming over them. By the time the kids were tucked in the back seat, they were glowing with good cheer, squirming with excitement, their noses pressed to the window. They had never been to the Bronx before, and certainly never to anything as pedestrian as a baseball game.

"I don't suppose you could use your prophetic knowledge to tell me if the Yankees win the World Series this year," Callum said, reaching over to squeeze Seldom's knee.

"Sorry, my knowledge of world history does not extend to sports. I've been to games in the new stadium, but I like the old one better. More nostalgia."

"What? They got a new stadium? That's a sacrilege."

"You're not the only person who feels that way. I remember there were a lot of protests when it opened."

"What did they do with the old one?"

"Tore it down. It's a park now."

He made an "oof" sound as if the future destruction of his beloved baseball stadium was physically painful.

Callum insisted on buying their tickets, despite Seldom's protests that she had an expense account for the kids. Finally after a few minutes of back and forth bickering, he pressed his palm over her mouth and said, "1946. The woman doesn't pay."

Resigned, she gave up, also allowing him to buy their hot dogs, soda, peanuts, and ubiquitous Cracker Jack. The children had never eaten any of it before and would likely get sick, but it was worth it to see their shimmering joy and excitement. Seldom and Callum shared a lot of smiles over their heads, especially when they realized Cracker Jack came with a toy at the bottom of the box.

After all the food had been consumed, Daisy crawled into Seldom's lap and promptly fell asleep. But Mathew, like Callum, was raptly focused on the game, barely bothering to blink or breathe. Seldom wasn't a sports fan, but even she had heard of Joe DiMaggio and Yogi Berra.

"Has Joe DiMaggio married Marilyn Monroe yet?" she asked during the seventh inning stretch.

"Who?" Callum asked.

"Never mind, that must happen later." The timeline of certain events was all mixed up in her mind. She had a vague awareness by decade, but not a year-by-year certainty of events. She'd always liked history, had read books on world events for fun. Now she wished she'd paid even better attention.

By the time the game finished, Daisy was awake but Mathew was lagging, so much that he didn't protest when Callum picked him up and carried him to the car. They tucked the kids into the back seat and began the drive home. It was less than twenty miles, but it took forever with traffic, even in 1946.

"Thank you so much, Callum. This was fun."

"You're welcome. And this was fun," he agreed. "Feels good to get away from everything for a while."

"How's work?" she asked.

"I've been reaching out to the other precincts, asking around to see if anybody has any cases like ours. So far nothing. I suggested to the captain that it might be in our best interest to go public, but he looked at me like I lost my marbles. It's only a matter of time until that happens anyway. Beyond that I've been trying to make a list, see if I can find any connection between the two cases." He tipped his head thoughtfully at her while they waited at a red light. "And your case, I guess. It's so similar to the others, I might ought to include it."

"That would give you a definitive starting point because if the other women started their evening with a date, it means they also knew their attacker and that it wasn't random."

He whistled softly. "That's a kick in the teeth. Somehow it seems better if it's random."

"Not for the dead women, but I see what you mean. It's an altogether different kind of monster to prey on someone you've met, talked to, maybe even kissed." She shuddered, thinking of Christian's lips on her fingers. Had the women who'd died sensed something off? Had they tried to get away, too?

"You're safe, sweetheart," Callum assured her, reaching over to pat her knee. "How come you always sit over there by the door?"

"I don't know. Habit, I guess. We don't have these long seats anymore; we have captain's chairs." She slid closer to him, aligning the left side of her body with the right side of his. He was warm and solid and secure. Seldom let out a breath she didn't know she'd been holding. *Safe.* That was the word that came to mind when she thought of Callum, but in a good way. Not "safe" like there was no attraction between them, but "safe" like home, like the home she'd never known or had. With Callum, she felt she could let go and unburden herself, could stop holding everything in and fighting to survive. It was a new feeling, something she'd never experienced with anyone else. For that reason it terrified her as much as it soothed her. How could a person be trustworthy and scary at the same time? Somehow Callum accomplished both.

He eased his arm around her, driving with one hand. She rested her head on his shoulder. They finished the drive home in cozy, pleasant silence. Both Mathew and Daisy were awake by the time they reached the mansion. Callum walked them to the door. Seldom sent the children inside and told them to go upstairs and begin getting ready for bed. When they were safely away, she turned and faced Callum. He eased his arms around her and rested his head on hers.

"What's this thing between us?" he asked.

"I don't know, but I like it."

"Me, too," he agreed. He pulled back, tipped her face to his, and kissed her. Then he opened the door and waited to leave until she was safely inside.

15

"Miss Murphy, may I have a word with you, please?"

Andrew Pierce stood in the foyer, arms crossed over his chest. Seldom froze, feeling caught for no reason in particular. "I need to get the children ready for bed," she said.

"I sent Janet to do that. My study, if you will." He turned and began heading there without waiting for an answer.

Seldom trailed after him, trying not to feel nervous. She had an idea what this was about, and it had the potential to be very unpleasant. He sat behind his massive walnut desk and indicated the leather club chair in front of it. Seldom sat. He stared at her, regarding her with a serious expression. She stared back, maintaining eye contact. She had the sense he was used to making people cower with that look and she had no intention of allowing it to work on her, especially when she'd done nothing wrong.

"So." He was the first to speak, and she felt a small thrill of victory. "I've had quite an earful about you lately. Would you like to know what I've been hearing?"

"I could probably venture a guess, but go ahead," she said.

"According to my staff, your behavior is unorthodox, overly familiar, and inappropriate."

She remained mute.

He raised an eyebrow. "Nothing to say in your defense?"

"So far nothing sounds like it requires a defense," she said.

"You insisted the children call you Seldom."

"That's my name." *Don't wear it out.* She refrained from saying the last part, with maximum effort.

"You took them to a public library."

"Books are the best way to expand the mind," she said.

"You baked these cookies," he pointed to the plate they'd left on his desk as a surprise.

"Yes."

"You took them to a baseball game."

"Turns out Joe DiMaggio is as good as everyone says he is," she replied.

They stared at each other again. He leaned forward and clasped his hands on his desk. Previously he had been in shadow, but now that he was in the light she could see the faint outline of a bruise around his eye. Was his nose swollen? Had it always been that large? Her eyes fell on his hands, noting the bloody scrapes on his knuckles. What on earth had he been up to?

"As you can guess, the children are not used to this sort of informality, hobnobbing with riffraff, riding the subway, eating who knows what immigrant street food. Arthur has been especially mortified, has warned me multiple times about what he terms your looseness, your slovenliness. Whatever you've done has certainly stirred his passions." His tone was stern, foreboding. Seldom remembered Callum's warning about his ruthlessness and had to make a conscious effort not to squirm. What was the worst he could do, fire her? She'd have no trouble getting another job. But she'd have to leave Daisy and Mathew, and already she'd grown unbearably attached.

His face broke into a wide smile. "On the other hand, my children very obviously adore you. I can't remember the last time I saw them having so much fun."

"Oh." Was she in trouble or not? It was hard to tell. He left the desk and perched on the edge of it, bringing his body in close proximity with hers. He reached for a cookie from the plate and bit into it.

"I can't seem to stop eating these blasted things. They're delightful. Did you really make them?"

"Yes."

"Hmm. Who won the game?"

"We did."

"And you went with your police officer friend?"

"Callum, yes."

"Is he your beau?"

Seldom thought about that. In 2020, she would never say such a thing about a man, especially after such a short acquaintance. At the very least she would wait for him to say it first, to define the relationship so she didn't come off looking needy or desperate. But this was 1946 and casual dating wasn't much of a thing here. "Yes."

"Are you betrothed yet?"

"No."

"Hmm." He was eyeing her, arms still crossed. "You'll have to pardon my fascination. My wife and I never went through that sort of thing."

"You didn't date? Er, court?"

He shook his head. "I suppose you could call us an arranged marriage of sorts."

"I didn't know people still did that back then."

He laughed. "It wasn't so long ago, only seven years. I'm not *that* old."

"No, I meant..." there was no way she could explain that she'd meant eighty years ago. It had been a slip of the tongue. His frank gaze and conversational fast pitches were putting her off kilter, making her careless. "I didn't know arranged marriages still existed."

"It wasn't called that, as such. But it was the same nonetheless, a combination of dynasties, a consolidation of power. Both our parents got what they wanted out of it."

"And you and your wife?" she chanced.

"I got Daisy and Mathew out of the bargain. Hillary...well, Hillary drew the short straw, didn't she?" His smile was...odd. Or maybe it was odd that he was smiling while talking about his dead wife.

"Maybe it will be a love match next time," she suggested.

"I highly doubt it," he said. "That's not really how it works in my world. One of the advantages of being poor is that no one cares who you marry. Enjoy it."

She snorted a laugh. "There are so many advantages to being poor; that one has to be the biggest."

He gave her a wry smile. "Do you want me to apologize? Because I thought you were unconventional enough to enjoy frankness."

"No, I don't want you to apologize. It would be nice if you were a bit less pretentious, but," she shrugged, "at least you're an honest snob."

"And why shouldn't I be? I've worked hard to maintain my family's wealth and position, married a woman I don't love, given up friends and hobbies in the interest of propriety. Might as well enjoy it."

"I guess where I'm from it seems that hard work usually leads to a bit of humility," she said.

"Canada, you mean?" He gave her the wry smile again.

"Canada, right. With a heavy Austrian influence."

"Where are you really from? You can tell me, I won't be angry."

"I can't tell you because you wouldn't believe me," she said.

"Try me," he commanded.

"No."

"Why not."

"Because I don't trust you," she said.

He blinked at her, shocked, and his answering smile was slow. "Smart girl."

"I'm twenty eight. Smart *woman*."

"Twenty eight? That's only four years younger than me. No wonder you're going for the copper; you're an old maid."

"You enjoy trying to shock me, huh?"

He nodded. "Is it working?"

"Not even a little," she said.

"I suppose I'll have to try harder then," he said. He stood and resumed the seat behind his desk. "What are you doing next weekend?"

"Working." She worked every weekend. Sunday was her day off, but she usually spent it with the children, mostly because they had no one else.

"Good. We're going to Montauk. Pack appropriately for the children." He tipped his head at her. "Do you know what Montauk is, and do you understand what I mean by appropriate?"

"I know Montauk is a playground for spoiled rich people, and I know that by appropriate you mean swimsuits and party clothes." She paused, thinking. "I'm going to have to procure a swimsuit for myself, I guess."

"I'll have Arthur give you some money. Buy more dresses. The ones you've been wearing are cheap and hideously out of fashion. There will be parties, and they're not the sort I want my governess to attend in rags."

"Such a charmer, Mr. Pierce. Am I dismissed?" She stood.

"One more thing. How did you know about the stocks?"

"What about them?" she asked.

"They've skyrocketed already, all of them you recommended."

"Maybe I'm a witch," she suggested.

"I don't believe in witches," he said.

"Neither do I." She turned to go. His hand shot out to hold her back, gripping her wrist hard.

"Whatever you are, here's a word to the wise. Witches get burned."

They stared at each other, the six inches between them radiating with an odd sort of tension. "I'll keep that in mind," Seldom said at last. She yanked her arm free and walked from the office, waiting to rub her aching wrist until she was out of Andrew Pierce's sight.

16

"There she is," Callum said when he let himself into his house after work and saw Seldom sitting at the table, waiting for him as she had done for that brief time when she was solely theirs.

"Hiya, Copper," she said, giving him a smile that made his heart turn over.

Because she was going away for the weekend, she had taken a different day off. And she had chosen to spend the night, to get a full break from the mansion. The longer she spent in that world, the more she understood Callum's warnings. They weren't like her; they weren't like anyone. The super rich lived by a different set of rules, rules Seldom didn't know or understand. As much as she didn't care to learn them, she grew weary of the disapproving looks from the staff when she unknowingly broke them. Getting away now felt like a luxury. Visiting Callum and his mother felt like coming home. *Home.* Funny how often that word came up when she was with him.

He rushed through his supper, barely tasting the food. The pastry beside his plate gave him pause. He picked it up and turned it over, studying it. "You made this," he guessed.

"It's an apple Danish," she said, nodding.

He took a bite and closed his eyes; this couldn't be rushed. "That's a killer Diller," he said, resisting the urge to lick the napkin when he was finished.

"I'm glad you liked it," she said.

"Did the kids help you with that one?"

"No, I made it last night after they went to bed. Everyone thinks I'm insane because I bake at odd hours," she confessed. Though, to be fair, they thought she was insane no matter what she did.

"Nervous?" he guessed. He stood and took her hand, leading her to the couch. This time he didn't wait for her to sit in his lap. He sat and pulled her into his embrace. She snuggled closer and he wrapped the afghan around her, using it as an excuse to give her a squeeze.

"A little," she admitted. "I've never been to Montauk before."

"It's a pretty grand affair."

"It's not that. It's all the scrutiny I'm going to be under. Here the kids and I do our own thing. We leave in the morning and often don't come home again until night, and that's how I prefer it."

"Because you like to be the one in charge," he interjected.

"Unnecessary," she said, poking him. "But true. There I'm going to be under close watch. Andrew may only find my 'unorthodoxy' amusing when he doesn't have to see it up close."

"It's Andrew now, is it?"

"Only in my mind. I'm not from a time that does well with formality. Everyone goes by their first names, mostly."

"You call my mother Mrs. O'Rourke."

"Yes, well, your mother is the type of woman who garners automatic respect," she said fondly. His hand rested on the back of her neck, his thumb smoothing from the nape to her shoulder. She closed her eyes and focused on the sensation.

"Found another girl," he said softly, and she jolted.

"Like the others?"

"Yes. You know what's really been bothering me about these girls? No one has reported them missing. Where did they come from?"

"What if..." she began, but he cut her off.

"No."

"But what if they are?" she countered.

"They're not from the future," he said, his tone dismissive.

"You could at least check their teeth. Their fillings would be white instead of silver."

"Do you have white fillings?" he asked.

"A couple."

"Show me so I know what to look for," he said.

She tipped her head back and he kissed her. "You tricked me," she said when the kiss was over.

"Yes, and I have no regrets," he said. They rested their foreheads together.

"I'm going to miss you," she said.

"It's only three days," he said.

She pulled back to look at him, frowning. "You don't have to do that."

"Do what?"

"Downplay any emotion. You could say you'll miss me, too," she said.

"If you know it, why do I have to say it?" His hand reached up to brush her cheek. She batted his hand away and stood.

"I'm getting a sip of water. Do you want anything?"

"No."

He stayed in the living room while she went to the kitchen and reached for a glass. She turned on the tap and glanced to her right and the glass slipped through her fingers, landing in the sink with a thud. On the other side of the window to her right was her bakery, as clear as if she were passing it on the street. She walked toward it, hand outstretched. Unlike the actual night outside, the bakery was well lit and sparkling. Her hand touched the wall and felt a blast of cool air that numbed her fingers.

"Seldom." Callum stood behind her in the entryway of the room. Seldom snatched her fingers back and turned to face him, mouth ajar. He wasn't looking at the bakery, though; he was looking at her, his eyes narrowed in concern. "What's wrong, sweetheart? You look like you swallowed glass."

"It's...it's..." she looked at the window again. Her bakery was *right there.*

Callum blew out a breath. "I'll miss you, okay? I always miss you when we're not together. I don't know why things are hard for me to say sometimes."

She looked at him, her heart wrenching painfully at the thought of leaving him, probably forever. She looked at the bakery, so bright and inviting. She took a step back, away from the window, toward Callum. Like a vision going dark, the bakery faded slowly from view. Her fingers reached out and skimmed the wall, finding it solid once more.

"Are you coming?" Callum asked softly. When Seldom turned to face him, he was holding out his hand. She stepped forward and took it, sliding her fingers into his big, warm hand.

"Why were you staring out the window?" he asked, easing his free arm around her.

"I was thinking."

"About what?"

"Home."

"You miss it pretty bad, huh," he said, giving her shoulders a squeeze.

"Not as much as in the beginning." She stopped short and faced him, clutching his shirt in her hands. She stared at his buttons. "If our situations were reversed and you had the choice of coming back here or staying with me in my time, what would you do?" He was quiet so long she chanced a glance at his face. He regarded her with a serious expression, brow furrowed.

"I'm not certain that's a question I could answer in the hypothetical," he said at last.

Seldom forced a smile and gave him a little nod, trying hard to cover her hurt. Obviously she wanted him to say that he would choose her. After all, hadn't she just chosen him? She swallowed past a sudden lump and turned to stare at the window again. If the choice ever came back around, at least she'd be prepared. This thing between her and Callum, it must not mean as much as she thought it did. It couldn't mean enough to keep her here forever, a place she so obviously didn't belong.

Callum wrapped his arms around her and gave her a tight hug, crushing her to his chest. "You should get some sleep, sweetness. You've got a big weekend coming up."

She nodded against his chest, fighting the sudden surge of tears. In that moment she'd walked away from the bakery, toward him, she'd been so certain. And now she felt so monumentally stupid. It's not like he rejected her; he was right there, after all, his arms swallowing her in a crushing embrace. But in her mind, feeling like a fool was worse than feeling hurt. She took a step away from him.

"Good night, Callum." She bypassed him without a kiss goodnight, closed her door, and leaned against it. She took a deep breath, held it, let it out slowly, and scrubbed her eyes. If she didn't fit in her world, and she didn't fit with Callum in his, where did she fit?

Nowhere, a little voice inside her echoed. Worse, the little voice had always been there, and it had been right the whole time. She had allowed herself to hope that maybe she *had* been born out of time, that at last she'd finally found her place and her people. But, no. She was on her own as much as she ever had been, maybe more. And she was once again stuck here, maybe forever this time. She might have blown her only chance to get home, and for what? The chance at happily ever after with a man who had to have his arm twisted into admitting he'd miss her when she went away.

Seldom wouldn't twist his arm anymore. She had gotten herself through twenty-eight years just fine. She would make it through however many she had left the same way—alone.

With that decided, she hung up her dress, slipped into her gown, crawled between the sheets, and fell into a deep and dreamless sleep.

17

"What's wrong, Miss Murphy?" Andrew Pierce asked. She thought Pierce an apt name. His eyes watched her hawkishly, tearing through her defenses. Somehow she and the children had ended up riding in the limo with him on the trip to Montauk. He and Mathew shared one seat while she and Daisy shared the other, facing them.

"None of your beeswax," Seldom said, peeved. She was weary of him ogling her, weary of all people, really, except for Daisy and Mathew who were currently asleep. "I think your children may be narcoleptic."

He smiled as he gazed at the children fondly. "They've always slept well in the car. But back to you. Did you have a rhubarb with your beau, Miss Murphy?"

"Slang doesn't suit you, Mr. Pierce. And can you please call me Seldom? Being called Miss Murphy makes me feel like the spinster everyone keeps accusing me of being."

"I suppose I could manage to call you Seldom, as long as no one else is around."

"It will be our dirty little secret," she said, pressing her finger to her lips.

"You make me laugh," he said, deadpan.

"Tone it down, would you? You're going to bust something," she said, turning her gaze out the window.

"What did you and the officer fight about?" he tried again.

"Nothing," she said and meant it. They hadn't fought. Callum had been confused and wary the morning Seldom left his house, quiet and withdrawn. *Are you mad at me?* he had asked. *Of course not,* she had replied. Then she had refused his offer of a ride home, kissed his cheek goodbye, and ridden the subway, fighting tears the whole way. If she hadn't been able to explain to him why she'd been upset, there was no way she could explain it to her uppity boss.

"Did he try to take advantage of you?" he asked.

"No."

"Did you try to take advantage of him?"

She laughed, and he smiled. "No. Believe it or not, not everything in a woman's life revolves around a man." Though in this case it did. Come to think of it, most of the time when she was upset, it was because of a man. Drat them and their infuriating charm and kissable lips.

"It would appear I've lost you again," Andrew said, snagging her attention from the window where she'd unconsciously been gazing, unseeing. "You'll have to forgive me, but I did warn you I find such things fascinating."

"Which things?"

"The love lives of the servant class," he said with zero irony.

"Are you auditioning for the role of Jay Gatsby?" she asked.

"Gatsby is new money. I'm Tom Buchanan," Andrew said, completely unbothered by what she'd meant as a putdown.

"If we're being literary, I guess that makes me Jane Eyre," she mused.

"No, Jane Eyre was ugly," he said.

"No, Jane Eyre was plain, hence the term Plain Jane."

"In either case, doesn't fit. You are neither ugly nor plain. You are, well, you are uncomfortably pretty."

"Uncomfortable for whom?" she asked.

"Anyone unfortunate enough to find you off limits," he said.

She rolled her eyes and faced the window again.

"I would love to know where your high opinion of yourself hailed from. I find it fascinating."

"Fascinating must be your word of the day," she said dully. She hadn't slept much the night before and they'd had an early morning. Her body was trying to work itself into a headache. She ground the heels of her hands against her temples and squeezed her eyes closed.

"That, for instance, that you should choose to talk to an employer so is," he shrugged helplessly, "fascinating."

She sighed. "I am sorry. I'm honestly not trying to be rude or impertinent. Believe it or not, that's not my go-to mode. But if we're being honest here, you kind of bug me."

"Excellent. Do tell."

"You think you're better than me," she said.

"I am better than you."

She laughed and pressed her hand over her eyes. "You're not supposed to say things like that to people."

"Why not? You're a governess. I'm a multimillionaire. There you go."

"Do you honestly believe your bank account determines your worth?" she countered.

"Fine. I have a high position in an established Wall Street firm, two beautiful children, multiple employees, a world-class education, a large network of friends, and I'm from one of the oldest and most well-established families in New York. Your turn."

"My turn to what?" she asked.

"List your amenities. What makes you believe you're better than me? Because from what I see, you're an uneducated pauper with no connection to anyone, save one Irish copper."

"I don't believe I'm better than you. I believe we're equal."

"Very well. What makes us equal?"

"'We hold these truths to be self-evident, that all men are created equal, that they are endowed by their creator with certain unalienable rights, that among these are life, liberty, and the pursuit of happiness,'" she said.

"That's it? That's all you've got? The Declaration of Independence?"

"What else do I need?" she said.

He shook his head. "You naïve child. I'm quite disappointed."

"Does 'disappointed' mean smug and pompous in Montauk?" she queried.

He laughed. "What you lack in debate skills, you make up for in amusement."

"Seriously, though, do you really think you're better than other people? Better than your household staff, better than anyone who doesn't have a summer home and a lineage that dates back to the Pilgrims?"

"Yes," he said, holding her gaze unblinking.

"You're in for a rude awakening," she said.

He laughed again. "How so, delightful girl?"

"The coming post-war rise of the middle class. Soon it's not going to be the haves and the have nots. It's going to be the haves and the haves a little less. Your precious Montauk? It's about to be transformed into a tourist trap because everyone is going to have money for travel, for vacations, for leisure time." She thought of her lack of travel, of her early struggle for survival. "Well, almost everyone. A lot of people. And the large household staff? It's about to go the way of the dinosaur. I bet in ten years you'll be down to a cook, a chauffer, and a maid from a service."

"Perish the thought," he said, full sarcasm. "I suppose it's true that there might be a wealth boom in the coming years, but I think you underestimate my wealth and status if you think it will affect me. Our rules aren't your rules."

"You sound like Callum," she said, pain slicing through her midsection at the thought of him.

"It stands to reason that your proletarian beau does not like the wealthy," he said.

"He's not a character in a Victor Hugo novel," she said.

"What is he, then?"

"He's a man who works hard to do the right thing every day."

"How quaint," Andrew said.

"I like quaint," she said.

"I can't get a read on you. At times you seem refreshingly naïve, at others sharp and cynical."

"I'm all of those things, a melting pot of unflattering adjectives," she said.

"You're certainly not like anyone I've ever encountered, man or woman," he said. "Then again, my circle is admittedly small, consisting of my contemporaries and a few servants."

"Didn't you meet a lot of other people in the war?" she asked.

He shook his head slowly. "I didn't go to war. I had a deferment because Hillary was critically ill, lucky me."

His tone was bitter. It might have been for the loss of his wife, but he'd already established that it wasn't a love match. Instead Seldom thought perhaps it was bitterness over not being included in the war. As horrific as it had been for men like Callum to go, how hard must it have been for men like Andrew to stay? To see their fellow countrymen going off to prove their manhood? Had he felt left out? Emasculated?

They stared at each other. "That must have been difficult," she said at last. His other eye looked puffy and bruised today, the knuckles on his other hand skimmed. Last night he had disappeared for hours, in the midst of getting ready for the trip. Where had he gone? "Was it difficult for you?"

He held her gaze for a few more beats before turning away to look out the window. "You see too much, Seldom."

"Should I apologize, Mr. Pierce?"

When he returned his attention to her, he was smiling, his eyes clear and guarded. "Come now, call me Andrew. But only when no one is listening."

Now it was Seldom's turn to tear her eyes away and stare out the window, feeling suddenly nervous and half-sick for reasons she couldn't articulate.

18

Compared to the mansion in Manhattan, the house in Montauk was a cottage. Compared to the O'Rourke's brownstone, the cottage in Montauk was a mansion. It was huge, but not as grand and glamorous as the mansion in the city. Once again Seldom had her own room, but this time Daisy and Mathew would have to share, an option that suited them both very well, if their enthusiasm was any indication.

Ironically the only staff would be the chauffer, one maid, a cook, and Seldom, exactly as she had predicted to Andrew in the car. He'd seemed more relaxed since their arrival. And he was going to accompany them to the beach, furthering the children's excitement to a fever pitch.

Seldom set out their bathing suits and helped them change, warning them with dire threats to stay put while she changed. Losing them at the ocean would be her worst nightmare. For that reason she changed with haste, tossing on her bathing suit and cover up without checking her reflection.

Andrew was waiting for them in the foyer. The four of them walked to the beach together. Seldom's bag was weighted down by anything she thought they might need, including an ugly glass bottle of Coppertone. The pharmacist at Woolworth had stared at her like she was insane when she asked for Sunscreen, a thing which was apparently not common yet. She had thrown out a few brands, just in case. Coppertone stuck, though it neither looked nor smelled like the suntan lotion from her memory. Andrew was as mystified by it as the pharmacist had been.

"What are you doing?" he asked as she began smearing it on the chil-dren. She had no idea what the SPF was on it, but it had to be better than nothing, right? Daisy and Mathew were so pasty from the long months in the city that they would be crispy red in less than an hour.

"I'm putting sunscreen on the children," she said, smearing it on their arms, legs, and faces while they squirmed impatiently to get away.

"Why?" he asked with the pervading mix of mocking amusement he always used with her.

"If I don't, they'll get burned," she said

"They burn the first day and then it gets better. They need to build up a resistance," he said.

"There is no resistance, and they're doing irreparable damage to their skin," she said.

"If you say so," he said, shaking his head, still clearly disbelieving. "Nice hat, by the way. Did they not sell anything larger?" His eyes landed on her overly large straw sunhat.

"Not that I could find," she said, unbothered by his teasing. "You'll be sorry when you bu...rn." She happened to look up at him just as he took off his shirt, revealing a shockingly well-developed torso. How did a stockbroker get a body like that, she wondered, and how long could she get away with staring at it in 1946 before it became inappropriate?

She'd already passed that point, if the way he quirked an eyebrow at her was any indication. She cleared her throat, closed the bottle of sunscreen, and tucked it back into her bag. She'd been in such a haste to leave that she hadn't had time to cover her tattoos. Ever mindful of Callum's warning to do so, she removed Band-Aids from her bag and applied them to the tiny cupcake on her ankle and the little heart on her shoulder. The tiny butterfly on her thigh was well hidden by the bathing suit's little skirt.

When she looked up again, Andrew's piercing gaze was on her. De-spite her efforts to be surreptitious, he'd apparently spied her tattoos. They made eye contact and maintained it unblinking. *I see you, and I know something's not right about you,* his eyes seemed to say. *What are you going to do about it,* her eyes asked in return.

He was the first to look away, pulling his eyes off her with effort as he turned to stare at the ocean. Seldom removed her cover up and laid it carefully aside. The swimsuit was adorable, cherry red with white lace trim. It had a halter design up top with the cute little skirt at the bottom. It was definitely something she would have selected for herself in her own time, not only because it was cute but because it showed her hourglass figure to its best advantage. She had always been a pin-up girl lacking a calendar. Her body, at least, was very happy in 1946. For once her shape was considered the ideal, and she was relieved not to have to try to stuff herself into straight leg skinny jeans. Despite everything she'd read to the contrary, those didn't seem to be flattering on anyone over a size zero. The last time she tried to wear them, she'd suffered a muffin top so epic she felt like a walking mushroom.

She smiled, thinking of the ads she'd seen since she'd been in this time, targeted to skinny girls who wanted to gain weight in their hips and bust. *How the tables have turned,* she thought with no small amount of satisfaction. She had the sudden desire to call up Deidra Hall, the skinny girl in high school who'd called her fat, and brag that it was now her time to shine. But of course she wouldn't, even if she could. Not all skinny girls were mean, and a lot of people in this time were thin because they'd been malnourished. When she thought of it like that, she stopped smiling, grabbed a shovel and pail, and went to make a sand castle with her charges.

They were in hour two of the beach when the newcomers arrived. Andrew had been playing with them the entire time. If the children found this unusual, they didn't show it. It seemed he was a different person in Montauk—relaxed and able to enjoy his children.

"Hello, Pierce," a man called from the mansion next door, waving his hand in a high hello. Andrew stood and brushed the sand from his body, shading his eyes before offering his own wave hello. He stood sentry until the man arrived, his wife, children, and governess in tow.

"What's new, Old Man?" Andrew asked, reaching out to shake hands with the man before leaning forward to kiss his wife on the cheek. Seldom didn't realize she was waiting for an introduction until one didn't occur. Of course it wouldn't, though. No one cared to introduce their servants.

The three manor-bred individuals retreated to their lawn chairs, leaving Seldom, Mathew, Daisy, the new children and their governess to themselves. Mathew and Daisy knew the other kids, if their enthusiastic greeting was any indication. The kids picked up their toys and resumed building their castle, chatting happily. Their governess sat down in the sand beside Seldom.

"I'm Seldom," she said, turning to the newcomer with a smile.

"I'm Mable," she replied, pearly teeth glinting bright white in her pretty ebony face. "That's Betsy and Daniel. And those are my employers, Giles and Jillian Montgomery. How long have you been with Mr. Pierce?"

"A few weeks," Seldom said. "How long have you been with the Montgomerys?"

"Since Betsy was born, seven years ago. Daniel is five."

"Do you come to Montauk every weekend?" Seldom asked.

"Yes," Mable said, rolling her eyes to indicate her displeasure.

"You don't like the beach?" Seldom queried.

"I like the beach just fine. It's everything else I hate," Mable said.

"Like what?"

Mable glanced over her shoulder to make sure they were far enough away that sound wouldn't carry. She leaned in to whisper but, "It's Montauk," was all she said.

"What's wrong with Montauk?"

"All those rumors you've heard? They're true."

"I'm afraid I don't know what you're talking about. I'm from Canada."

"Camp Hero," Mable said, her tone ominous.

"The park?" Seldom guessed.

Mable tilted her head at her, confused. "No, the new Air Force Station."

"Oh, right," Seldom drawled. There was no Air Force Station on Montauk in her day, of that she was certain. They must have converted it into a park at some point. "I was thinking of something else. What about it?"

Mable looked around again and chafed her arms. "It's creepy, that's all. My guy, Boots, has a buddy who works there. He's told me some things, secret things."

Seldom thought Mable had a propensity toward drama. "What kinds of things?" Belatedly she realized her tone sounded a lot like Andrew's, amused and mocking.

Mable frowned slightly. "Like that they do all kind of experiments on people and animals. Like that they brought in some Nazis to work on their secret projects."

What she was describing sounded suspiciously like The Manhattan Project, but that had for certain already taken place. And nowhere near Montauk. Could there have been something else like it going on now? Another bomb or weapon that never made it off the ground? "What kind of secret projects?" Seldom asked, being careful to keep the amusement out of her tone this time.

Mable scanned the horizon again. Her paranoia was contagious because Seldom found herself doing the same thing. "Time travel," she whispered.

Seldom froze, not daring to blink or breathe. "What?"

Mable nodded, satisfied that she had finally captured Seldom's interest. She forced her lungs to take a breath and made herself relax. If the Air Force had been working on time travel since the forties, surely she would have heard of it by her time, wouldn't she? It was probably so much fear mongering, rumor, and conjecture. Conspiracy theories were nothing new. On the other hand, was it merely coincidence that someone mentioned time travel when she had, in fact, traveled through time?

"That sounds a little far-fetched," Seldom said mildly.

Mable drew herself up haughtily again. "If they're not up to something bad, how do you explain those dead girls?"

Seldom froze again. "What dead girls?"

There was no mistaking Mable's smugness this time. She had a captive audience, and she knew it. She leaned in, whispering so the children wouldn't overhear. "Last summer they found two dead girls, drained of all their blood."

"Was it in the news?" Seldom asked.

Mable shook her head. "Things don't make the paper here." She waved to their combined employers, indicating, what? That they had a way of making news disappear?

"What makes you think the Air Force had anything to do with it?" Seldom asked.

"Who else?" Mable replied.

Who else, indeed?

<h1 style="text-align:center">19</h1>

"You're quiet," Andrew observed over supper. In Montauk, they ate together, the four of them huddled at the table, continuing the illusion that they were a family.

"Days at the beach are exhausting," Seldom said, pointing to Mathew and Daisy, their faces bowed sleepily over their plates.

"For children, maybe. But this is something else. I've watched you enough to read your moods. Why so contemplative?"

Seldom's eyes flicked to the children again. "It's not talk for little ears," she said. It was better to change the subject. "Have you known the Montgomerys long?"

"Yes. They've been my summer neighbors for years. Hillary and Jillian were friends."

The way he said it was odd. "You and Giles aren't?"

He gave her the wry smile again. "So painfully observant, Seldom. We're not *not* friends, if that makes sense. We ran in different groups."

"How so? In my mind, all rich people are lumped together, lounging in groups and drinking bathtub gin."

He smiled fondly. "I was nineteen when prohibition ended. Those were some grand times. It was more fun to drink when I wasn't allowed to. I wonder why that is." He shrugged one shoulder. "In any case, my set was more fun loving. Giles was always stuffy, always serious and bent on following the rules."

"He didn't seem stuffy to me," Seldom said.

"Perhaps age has mellowed him," Andrew mused.

"Or perhaps he's grown better at hiding it."

"Why would he do that?"

"To be liked. No one wants to be friends with a scold."

"You sound as if you speak from experience," Andrew said.

"I was neither scold nor rebel," she said.

"What were you?" he asked.

"Alone," she replied. It wasn't that she'd been an outcast. She'd had friends. It was merely that those friends never reached her core. She'd kept them outside of herself, never letting them touch her heart. Only Josh, seven years her junior, had felt safe enough to let inside. And now Callum. How he wormed his way in there was still a mystery. Had it been her capture by Christian that lowered her defenses? Or was it something about Callum himself? She'd likely spend the rest of her life pondering that question and never get an answer. And she'd likely do it alone.

When she pulled herself free of her trance, Andrew was staring at her, mocking smile firmly in place. "You're not like other women."

"It will likely not surprise you that I've heard that one before," she said.

"I've never encountered a female so heartily uninterested in procuring a husband," he said. "Even among the servants. I listen to Katherine and Janet whisper, when they think I'm not paying attention. Their chatter is perhaps more ribald and coarse than the women of my ilk, but it's basically the same, a near obsession with scoring a mate. It defines their entire being. But you, Seldom Murphy, seem undefined by men."

"That may be the nicest thing anyone has ever said to me."

"But here's where it gets interesting because I encountered suffragettes in college, women so absorbed with their cause that *that* became their identity, the rights and benefits of womanhood. And yet you're not one of those, either. I've yet to find a name for what you are. Perhaps when I do..." He trailed off, picked up his glass, and swirled it absently.

"What?" she prompted.

He pulled his gaze from the window and fastened it on her. "I'll end my fascination and get rid of you."

"I guess for the sake of my job, I'd better keep being a mystery."

"Your job, yes," he said vaguely. He set his drink down and surveyed his children. "Time to put the moppets to bed, I think."

They roused the children and herded them upstairs. Andrew turned down their beds while Seldom washed their faces, helped them brush their teeth, and struggle into their pajamas. They barely made it to the bed before they were asleep, drained by hours in the sun and water. For a moment the two adults hovered together at the periphery of the room, drawn together by their mutual love of the room's inhabitants.

"I love to watch them sleep," Seldom whispered.

"So do I," Andrew confessed as if it were a dirty secret. "I always have."

They eased from the room and closed the door. "Was your wife a good mother?"

He contemplated that before he answered. "I suppose it depends on one's definition. She was a mother much like her mother, like my mother. Remote, detached, busy with social engagements. She didn't know how to be any other way. In the intervening years, I've come to want something different for them, someone more like the nanny I had growing up."

"What was your nanny like?" Seldom asked.

"Warm, affectionate, gregarious, but willing to dole discipline when called for."

Seldom smiled at the mental image. "Is she still alive?"

"I've no idea," he said.

She stopped short and peered up at him. "How could you not know?"

"How could I? She was just a servant. When I had no need of a nanny anymore, she found another placement." He continued walking, undaunted.

Behind him, Seldom sighed and slowly caught up. "You're a hot mess, Andrew."

"Surely that is some Canadian phrase, of which I'm unaware. For both our sakes, I'm going to pretend it's a statement of deferential respect," he said as he reached for the buttons of his shirt. Once undone, he pulled it off and reached for another, conveniently lying on a chair.

"What the what?" Seldom said, her eyes riveted on his impressive physique once again. She didn't know a lot about etiquette in this decade, but she was fairly certain men didn't routinely undress in front of women. And how did a man who worked in an office six days a week maintain such an amazing body? It wasn't like he met with a trainer before work, like men of her generation did. There was no gym equipment in either of his houses. She told herself that was why she continued to stare at him as he buttoned the new shirt: to try and solve a mystery. In reality he was just that attractive. Besides the body he had deep blue eyes and thick, dark hair. She wasn't certain what was fashionable and attractive for men of this generation, but where she was from he would be completely drool-worthy.

"I'm going out," he announced, drawing her attention back to his face.

"Where?" she blurted without thinking. She had no claim on him, zero right to know where he went or why, a fact he promptly reminded her.

"None of your beeswax. Don't wait up. And Seldom," he had taken a step toward the door. He paused and faced her, one hand on the jamb.

"Yes?"

"Lock the door behind me."

It was his tone more than his words that gave Seldom a chill as she watched him go and then dutifully slid the bolt in the lock.

20

Andrew didn't show for breakfast the next morning. Seldom knew he was there because she'd heard him, heard the soft click of the door at three in the morning.

After they ate, she helped the children change into their suits and herded them back to the beach, forcing more sunscreen on them before she let them run free. They had burned the day before, but not as badly as she thought they might have without her hourly reapplication of Coppertone.

The beach was magical because it required zero interaction from her. The children were content to play in the sand and water while Seldom sat and let her mind roam free. It was the first time since she took the job as governess that she had a break long enough to do so. Left to its own devices for the first time in weeks, her mind turned to murder.

Had there really been dead girls in Montauk? If so, were they related to Callum's cases? Thinking of him made her heart twist painfully. Was he thinking of her? If so, he was likely wondering what happened to set her off that night. She had been unfair, she realized it now. He hadn't seen her bakery shimmering on the other side of the wall, hadn't been privy to the momentous decision she'd made. She had sprung an important question on him in the middle of the night, after a long day at work, when he'd dealt with yet another murder. And then she'd become easily hurt and upset when he hadn't readily given her the answer she wanted. Andrew said she wasn't obsessed with procuring a mate, and that was true, but her thoughts had been focused on Callum more than any other man she'd ever met. Perhaps it was merely the fact that she'd fallen through time and into his grasp. He was the only person here who knew the truth of where she came from, besides his mother. Of course she felt an affinity for them; they were the only people with whom she didn't have to pretend. It was highly possible there was nothing special about Callum, save the fact that he'd rescued her from a madman. Was that it? Was it merely a case of hero worship on her part? How embarrassing, if so.

"Well, good morning, Miss Seldom," Mable said, sitting down beside her in the sand.

Seldom smiled, glad for the interruption in her dreary thoughts. "Good morning, Mabel. How are you this morning?"

"Right as rain. Are you going to the party tonight?"

"There's a party tonight?"

"Mr. Pierce didn't tell you? Maybe he's not going to go. Doubtful, though. From what I've heard, he never misses."

"I really couldn't say," Seldom said honestly. She knew very little about Andrew, minus the few things he'd told her. *We're not friends*, she reminded herself. Unconventional though he was, he was her employer, nothing more.

"I'm going to be there," Mable said excitedly. "And Boots."

"Your boyfriend is invited to the party?" Seldom said.

Mable laughed. "Of course not. Invited. Pshaw," she gave Seldom's arm a shove. "He's the Montgomery's chauffer. All the working folk will gather in the stable, like we always do. Boots is going to get some hooch, the good stuff. He has connections."

"Where will the children be while everyone is partying?" Seldom asked, casting a worried glance at the four kids who were playing happily together, oblivious that they were the topic of conversation.

"They'll be in the playroom, where they usually are. We take turns checking on them. This is Montauk, Seldom. It's a bit more relaxed." She stretched out, tipping her face to the sun with a smile.

Seldom spent a moment envying her built-in sunscreen. If Seldom tried that same pose, she'd crisp like a lobster in minutes. Instead she sat huddled under her giant sombrero, applying Coppertone to her extremities as often as she applied it to the children.

"What do you know about the dead girls?" she asked Mable, seemingly apropos of nothing. It had weighed heavily on her mind, however, since learning of it. She needed to tell Callum. And yet fear kept her from making the call, the old fear that she would come off looking needy or desperate. Hadn't she already done that with her breakdown last time she saw him? It was obvious she'd been upset. What wouldn't have been obvious was that it was a rare event for Seldom to overreact that way. He didn't know her well enough to understand she usually kept an emotional barrier between herself and everyone else. Still, it affected his job and his cases. Also, she missed him.

"Only what I heard from the pipeline."

"What's the pipeline?"

"Man, you are green. The pipeline is the what we call the help's network. We know more about what's going on in our employers' lives than they do, I expect."

What did she know about Andrew? She opened her mouth to ask as much when Andrew folded himself into the sand on Seldom's other side.

Mable sat up, back suddenly ramrod straight. "Mr. Pierce, sir."

He gave her a dismissive nod. Quickly, she gathered her children and moved farther down to the spot in front of her mansion. Seldom turned to survey her employer. Today he wore sunglasses, blocking her view of his eyes. There was no hiding his fat lip, however, or the deep scratches on his arm.

"What happened to you?" she asked.

"I hit the broadside of a barn," he said. He tried to smile, remembered his sore lip, and quickly gave up.

"And these," she said, laying her finger alongside the scratches.

"I don't know, tree or something. What were you and Mabel discussing?"

At that moment the children realized his presence and pelted themselves at him, begging him to play with them. He complied, saving Seldom the trouble of an answer.

Later, as they walked back toward the house for lunch, Andrew told her about the party. "It's next door, at the Montgomerys," he said, pointing, as if there was some doubt about which mansion was theirs.

"Mable said the servants have their own party in the barn."

He barked a laugh. "You're not supposed to tell me that. The servants do their thing and we do ours and everyone pretends they don't know what the other is doing."

"And the children?" she asked.

"Will be fine for a night unsupervised. My goodness, Seldom, you're not a prisoner. Let your hair down once in a while and cut loose, why don't you?" He slicked his hand through his freakishly thick hair.

"I suppose I'm not very good at balancing my work with my personal life." She always felt as if she were on the clock, no matter the job. It was what made her both a wonderful and terrible entrepreneur. No one was as hard on her as she was.

"Let me help. After lunch, the children should nap. Tonight will be a late one. While they're resting, I insist you do something for yourself," he said.

"Thank you," Seldom said.

The cook had their lunch prepared by the time they reached the house. The children were lagging, practically asleep at the table by the time lunch was finished. Seldom led them upstairs and read them a story. They were out by the time they reached the third page. Seldom tiptoed from the room and closed the door behind her. She leaned on it and scanned the hallway. What to do with her unexpected free time? She breezed down to the library and scanned the shelves, feeling restless. Hands clasped behind her back, she continued her inspection of the house until she reached the telephone in the hallway. She paused, staring at it. It stared back. Tentatively, she picked it up and dialed Callum. He would be prepping to go to work now. Seldom expected Mrs. O'Rourke to answer, as she usually did. But on the third ring, Callum's smooth, warm voice said hello.

"Hi. It's me. Seldom." She rolled her eyes. Of course he knew it was her.

"Sweetheart, hi. How's Montauk." His voice smiled. She pictured him settling onto the couch seat beside the phone stand and smiled in response.

"So far, so good. The kids are loving the ocean."

"I'm a bit jealous of them," he admitted.

"I didn't know you were such a fan of the ocean."

"I'm not. But they get to see you in your bathing suit all day. Not fair."

"I made friends with the nanny next door. She invited me to a party tonight."

"Are you going to go?" he asked.

She rolled her eyes. It was uncanny how well he knew her. If not for Andrew's comment, she likely would have stayed home. "I think so. But I wanted to tell you something she told me."

"What's that?"

"She said they found two dead girls on Montauk last year. They'd been drained of blood, like the others."

He was quiet so long she wondered if she lost him.

"Are you still there?" she asked.

"Yes, sorry, kid. My mind went into high gear at that. I'll give the police department there a call, see what they can tell me."

"She told me something else," Seldom said.

"What?" He was tense now, clearly expecting more information about his case.

Seldom looked around to make sure no one was nearby. This was not something she wanted to say in front of Andrew or the servants. "She told me the Air Force has been working on a secret project involving time travel."

He was quiet again. This time she knew he was merely thinking. "And you think this has something to do with you," he said slowly. "With why you're here."

"Honestly? I have no idea. I'd dismiss it as a whole bunch of bunk except, well, I'm here, and how do you explain that? It seemed awfully coincidental to hear someone mention it, in light of my circumstance."

"I don't know, honey. Does it matter? Either way, you're here," he said.

"Yes, but it would be nice to have an explanation, don't you think? I mean, is there some logical reason behind it, something scientific that could be explained by a government experiment? Or is it something else?"

"What kind of something else?" he said. By his tone she could tell he was growing weary of the conversation. His mind was probably still on his case, and he didn't like to dwell on things, to delve into the why behind unfathomable mysteries or suppositions. *It is what it is,* she could almost hear him thinking it.

"A different reason, a bigger purpose," she hedged.

"What kind of purpose?" he asked.

You, you big dummy. Am I here for you? Was I brought here because we're in some way connected? Seldom wanted that to be the case. She was desperate enough to need a sign where he was concerned. Then again, if she stayed here, she'd be giving up everything. Didn't that give her the right to ask for some cosmic reassurance? "Nothing," she said, putting her barriers back in place. It wasn't so much that he wasn't giving her what she wanted, but rather that she sensed that he *knew* what she wanted and still wouldn't give it, wouldn't tell her the things she so desperately wanted to hear.

"Seldom," he said but nothing else. It was as if he wanted her to read and believe what he wasn't saying, but Seldom didn't work that way. She needed words.

"I should go. Best of luck with your case, Copper." She hung up before she could hear what he might say. Or, worse, what he might not say.

21

Seldom felt unaccountably nervous as she headed to the Montgomery's stable. She had bathed the children and gotten them ready before walking them to the nursery in the mansion. It felt ten shades of wrong to dump them off in the room with a handful of other children and disappear. She reminded herself that their parents were only downstairs, that the children's father had all but commanded her to go to the party.

Downstairs the A party was already in full swing. Seldom could hear soft laughter, the clinking of crystal stemware, and gentle music. Servants scurried from the kitchen and back again, trays either empty or full of food and drink.

The stable was another scene entirely. Loud music and raucous laughter trundled out. Approximately twenty people were inside, some employees of the grand houses that lined the beach, as well as a few people from town. A tall, thin black man was the first to greet her.

"Mable told me you'd be coming," was his opening line.

"You must be Boots," Seldom guessed.

He laughed and shook his head. "I'm her cousin. They call me Johnny Light Feet."

She glanced down at his feet, overly large compared to his too-tall body. "Do they now?"

"Don't claim all the pretty girls from the get-go, Johnny," another man said. This one was white, his cheeks ruddy from too much time in either sun or wind. He held his hand out for Seldom to shake. "I'm Boots. Heard you met my girl, Mable."

Seldom extended her hand and tried not to let her shock show. She had never given a thought to interracial dating before. It had always been part of her world, and race had never been a determining factor in whether or not she was attracted to someone. But this was 1946. Wasn't it forbidden? She felt disoriented by her perception of history compared to the reality as Mable entered and sidled up to Boots who put his arm around her and kissed her cheek.

Whatever, Seldom thought and shook off her surprise. Maybe it was a secret, or maybe it was Montauk. It didn't much matter to her either way.

"I was about to ask your friend if she dances," Johnny said to his cousin.

"So stop yapping to me about it and ask her," Mable directed, taking the drink Boots had procured for her.

"How about it, Miss Seldom?" Johnny asked, bending low in a courtly bow.

"I'd be delighted," Seldom said, extending her hand to his. He took it and led her to the center of the cavernous barn. The record switched. A new song started to play. This music was also different than what she'd been expecting. She knew most of the songs from the era, but she didn't know this one.

"What is this music?" she asked.

"This is our music," Johnny said before clasping her hand and spinning her away from him.

She got it now, why people called him Johnny Light Feet. Despite the fact that his feet looked much too big for his body, it was as if they never touched the ground as he led her through a fast-paced dance that left her breathless.

The dancing, too, was much different than she was used to, a world away from the dances she'd shared with Callum. This was almost but not quite like the way she'd danced at clubs when she was still young enough to go to them. It wasn't risqué, exactly, but it wasn't something any of these people would have performed in front of a priest. For one thing he moved her so fast and so often that his hands were almost constantly on her, and there wasn't much room for the Holy Ghost. On the other hand, they were moving so quickly that it didn't much matter. She was away from him, then back again, then being swung in a wide arc before being pushed out and pulled away again. Not the sort of iconic USO dancing she had come to associate with the time period.

Seldom was breathless and drenched, but laughing so hard her sides ached. It was a dizzying whirlwind of movement, and then it was over. Seemingly everyone in the stable came to a standstill and faced the door. Slowly, Seldom turned to see what they were looking at and saw Andrew leaning against the jamb in what was becoming a familiar way, studying her. What was unfamiliar was the palpable sense of fear pervading the room. Johnny had taken an actual step away from her. Mable and Boots were rigid and silent, staring straight ahead as if they might go unnoticed if only they could avoid eye contact.

Certain that he had her attention now, Andrew spoke. "Daisy is crying for you. I promised her I'd fetch you." Having delivered his missive, he turned and began walking away. Seldom hurried to catch up with him. As soon as she was clear of the barn, she heard the record player begin again.

Having caught up to Andrew, they walked in silence a few steps while she tried and failed to figure out what had just happened. Why had the room turned so suddenly tense? Was it because an employer had found their "secret" party? That seemed unlikely. According to Andrew, both sides knew the score.

Was it because she'd been dancing with a black man? She glanced at Andrew and found his features impassive. From everything she knew of him, it didn't seem that race was a particularly bothersome issue for him. What then had caused everyone but her to be so afraid?

"What were you talking about?" Andrew said, seemingly out of thin air.

"We weren't talking; we were dancing."

He chuckled. "It hasn't been so long that I don't recognize the Lindy

Hop. I meant last night. You told me you couldn't tell me what had upset you because the children were present, and then we never came back to it." They had reached the front porch. They turned and faced each other, his hand on the door.

"Mable told me they found a couple of dead girls here last year."

He regarded her in silence a few beats. "Did that frighten you?"

What an odd question, she thought. "No. Does it frighten you?"

"No." He held the door for her but remained in place so she was forced to duck under his arm. "But I'm not a girl," he added as the screen door banged closed behind them, making such a loud boom that she jumped and clutched her hand over her heart.

"Why did everyone seem so afraid of you when you were in the barn?" she asked.

"Did they?" he countered, a hint of a smile playing on his lips. "Did they say something about me to you?"

"No, why would they?" she said.

"I can't imagine a reason," he said and disappeared back to his party, leaving her to fly up the stairs and console a weeping Daisy who, it turned out, was heartbroken over some mishap with her doll. Seldom sensed perhaps that she was feeling a little insecure among so many strangers, so she spent a long while rocking her, petting her head, and singing little songs until the girl stopped clinging to her neck and showed signs of being ready to play again. In truth, Seldom would have stayed longer. She had no real desire to go back to the party in the barn, and even less desire to go home by herself. But with the children all playing nicely together, it would have been odd to linger. She could think of few things worse than being an unwanted interloper at a child's party, so she took her leave and eased out the door, closing it in her wake.

She turned to head toward the back stairs and ran, almost literally, into Giles Montgomery.

"Everything all right with the kiddies?" he asked her, concern etched on his features. Like Andrew, he was a decidedly handsome man. Unlike Andrew, his features were pulled slightly taut, giving him a perpetually worried look. She supposed it was possible he smiled often and she merely hadn't seen it in the three glimpses she'd had of him. Maybe it was Andrew's words that made her think of him as being severe. *Stuffy*, he'd called him.

"Everything is fine. They're playing nicely together," Seldom said with a smile.

"Excellent," Giles said, but his face didn't tip into a smile. Maybe it couldn't. Maybe he'd had some sort of nerve damage that kept it in a permanent near-grimace. "Please, let me escort you back down stairs." He motioned for her to precede him toward the back staircase. It was on the tip of her tongue to protest, to assure him he didn't have to, when she wondered if maybe he thought she couldn't be trusted upstairs alone. Did he have visions of her looting their valuables? She, a poor, Irish serving wench?

You're being paranoid, she told herself. Forcing another smile, she turned and headed toward the stairs, this time with Giles bringing up the rear. They turned the corner, taking them into the dim alcove at the top of the stairs. Seldom reached out a foot to take a step down when Giles grabbed her wrist pinned her between the wall and his body, and kissed her hard on the lips.

She gave him an ineffectual shove and wrenched her head away, fighting the numbness of shock with effort. Her brain had become paralyzed when kissed by the psychotic Christian. She wouldn't allow the same thing to happen with the mild-mannered Giles. She tasted some kind of alcohol heavy on his breath, whiskey or bourbon, she had no idea and didn't care. "Stop it," she hissed. "Stop it right now. I don't want to kiss you." She had to say the words, in case there was any doubt, in case he somehow thought she wanted this. She attempted to wrest free of his embrace but, laughing, he put up a hand, grabbed her right breast, and twisted hard, hard enough to take her breath away. But only for an instant. Panicked and enraged now, she brought her knee up as hard as she could between his legs. He doubled over, gagging, and she boxed his ears, preparing to turn and flee down the steps. But when she turned, she came face to face with Andrew who regarded her, his eyes hard and furious.

For one blissful second, she believed he was furious on her behalf, that he was there to rescue her. But when he roughly grabbed her bicep in an iron grip and began to drag her away, she realized the truth: he was furious with her.

22

Neither of them spoke as he frog marched her down the steps and out into the humid night. They were on the vast lawn now, the sounds of both parties echoing dimly around them, creating a nauseating cacophony of music and rhythm and laughter. To Seldom's overheated brain it sounded like war drums, ominous and final.

Andrew released her, flinging her away from him so she stumbled a few steps before tumbling to her hands and knees. She sprang up again, somehow understanding that the coming confrontation would go better for her if she was looking him in the eye.

"What were you thinking? What were you doing?" he roared.

"Me? Why are you yelling at me? He attacked me," she said, hands at her sides, balled into tight fists. She was in imminent danger of dissolving into tears, and she wasn't sure which was in more danger of making her cry—the original attack or the fact that this man was blaming it on her.

"And that's how you handle it? By beating a man like Giles Montgomery?"

"What should I do next time, lie down and let myself be raped?" she hissed. She wanted to yell the words, but she wasn't so far gone that she would risk drawing a crowd to witness this little scene.

"He wasn't going to rape you," Andrew said, waving his hand in dismissal. "He'd had too much to drink. He does this with the help sometimes and then feels immediate remorse. If you'd waited another ten seconds, he probably would have started bawling and tried to press a fiver into your fingers."

Seldom stared at him, dismayed. Callum had warned her that the rich had different rules, but this...this was something altogether different. It was sickening; it was inhumane. "Are you...are you actually saying I should have stood there and let him have his way with me, and then consoled him and accepted money for the privilege of being attacked?"

Andrew swiped a hand over his face. "Of course not. I'm merely stating that unmanning him in his own home..."

"Unmanning him? He wasn't a man to begin with, if he treats a woman that way. This is...this is..." she plunged her fingers into her hair, unraveling it. "I hate what he just did to me, but I equally hate that you're saying these things to me right now. Do you understand that?"

His mouth opened and he blinked at her, as if her words shocked him, as if they possibly got to him. And then it was over and the mask was back in place. He shook his head. "You've no idea what you've done, you stupid, stupid girl."

"What if it was Daisy?" she continued undaunted. "Is that how you want your daughter to be treated by a man some day?"

"That will never happen to Daisy," he said calmly.

"Why not? Do you think she's impervious to the whims of drunk men?"

"No, because Daisy will never be..." He broke off.

"Never be what?" she prompted.

"Never be a servant," he said.

The silence hung between them, an ugly thing. At last Seldom broke it.

"I keep searching for some spark of humanity in you, and you keep snuffing it out," she said sadly, crossing her arms over her chest. Her body was starting to shake, a delayed reaction to shock.

"Grow up, Seldom," he said softly, almost gently.

She swallowed hard and looked away from him, toward the ocean. "I already did, in another time, another place. And it's really no different, is it?" She thought of the times men had put their hands on her body uninvited—Christian, her prom date, a man on the subway, a customer at the restaurant where she waited tables. Then, as now, she'd had no one to defend her, no one but herself. She was suddenly so tired, too tired to argue, too tired to try and make him see reason, to pick apart his argument and defend herself, to defend all women, rich or poor.

All she wanted was a reprieve from fighting her own battles. Short of that, she wanted peace. She turned and began walking away, toward the ocean. Andrew might have called to her. She doubted it, but in any case she didn't hear anything as she stumbled blindly toward the crash of waves, hoping against hope that nature would heal everything that had gone wrong tonight, might erase everything that had gone wrong in her life. She had the irrational sense that if she could just dip her toes in the water, could sink into the sand and let the saltwater wash over her feet, that it would leach away the pain and fear and humiliation that Giles and Andrew had inflicted on her.

She had no idea she was crying until she tripped and fell over something she couldn't see through the glaze of her tears. Swiping impatiently at her eyes, she squinted in the dim moonlight, expecting to see a piece of driftwood.

But when she finally blinked enough times to clear her vision, it wasn't driftwood; it was the lifeless body of a woman, her skin so loose, her skeleton so visible that Seldom knew there was no blood left in her. She stood and began sprinting away with no destination in mind, merely a blind panic that bade her gain distance between her and that inhuman *thing* lying in the sand.

Once again she was either crying or running with her eyes closed because she hit something else, this time it was upright, and it wasn't a thing, it was a person. She took a breath to scream when the person spoke.

"Hey there, kid, what's the fuss?"

She blinked at him, disoriented. "Callum?"

"Sweetheart, what's the matter?" he asked, peering intently at her face.

Giving up the pretense of keeping it together, she burst into violent weeping and threw herself into his arms. He caught her, wrapping his arms around her and running a soothing hand up and down her back. When that failed to garner a response, he bent, swept her into his arms, and sat down in the sand, positioning her in his lap much like she had positioned Daisy a little while ago. And as with Daisy, it began to work its magic so that the hysterical sobs died down to gentle crying and then silent little shudders.

Callum removed his trusty handkerchief and wiped her tears. She remained silent, watching his tender ministrations, noting the intent look on his face as he attempted to put her back together. That, more than anything, finally made the panic begin to ebb because Callum would keep trying until he got it right, until she was comforted and calm. Somehow that knowledge and security made her feel comforted and calm. She took a breath, and then another.

"What's the matter, babydoll?" he asked, his tone filled with all the soft tenderness she'd longed for after Giles attacked her. To delay the inevitable moment she'd have to tell him about the dead woman and break the sweet spell, she asked him a question of her own.

"Where did you come from? How did you get here?" Did he teleport whenever she needed him?

Reading her mind as usual, he smiled. "I drove in my car. You sounded...you didn't sound yourself on the phone. I thought it best to come and check on you, figured I'll sleep in my car and get first crack at finding out about those dead girls you mentioned."

"Callum," she whispered, and then she was kissing him with all the furor of the past hour, and he was kissing her in return the same way with no reasonable explanation for his passion, except that maybe he wanted her as much as she wanted him. Eventually she broke away, feeling guilty that she'd put it off this long. She took a breath and clutched his lapels. "There's another dead girl."

He tensed, pulling himself immediately out of his passion-induced fog and into work mode. "Where?"

She pointed to the spot she'd just come from. "I tripped on her."

"I came to the house, intent on talking to you. I saw you running and followed you here. Why were you running?" he asked.

She shook her head.

He digested her lack of answer in silence a few beats and then said, "Show me, sweetheart." He stood, pulling her up alongside him. She led him back to the spot she'd found the girl. Given her interest in thrillers and mysteries and the serial killer genre, Seldom thought she'd be insatiably curious if she ever came across a murder victim. But now that she'd quite literally stumbled across a dead girl, she had zero desire for a closer inspection. Callum was right; real death was nothing like the movies. She hung back, pointing, and when she was certain he'd found the right spot, she turned her back on him, staring at Andrew's house instead. There was a light inside now. Was Andrew there? She should go get the children and put them in bed. She didn't, though. She remained rooted to the spot until Callum came to reclaim her with a gentle touch to her arm that nonetheless made her start.

"Sorry, sweetness," he whispered, his hand smoothing over the spot he'd touched. "I'm going to walk you back to the house. If you'd call it in for me, I'd appreciate it."

"I can go myself," she said.

"No, I'll take you." He took her hand, weaving his fingers through hers so that they might have been any other couple out for a midnight beach stroll. They reached the porch and he settled his hands on her shoulders. "Do you know how to call the police?"

She started to tell him yes, that she was familiar with 911. Then she realized 911 likely didn't exist yet and shook her head instead.

"Dial zero and ask for the police department. When you talk to them, tell them about the girl and tell them I'm on the beach waiting for them so they won't be surprised." He glanced up at the massive house. "Which room is yours?"

"There." She pointed to her window.

"All right. Get some sleep, angel. I'll be back when I can." He tipped her face, kissed her lightly, and disappeared into the inky blackness.

23

⊚≋⊚

When Seldom entered the house, there was no sign of Andrew. She dialed the operator and waited for what felt like a long time before she was connected to the police. She expected it to be like New York, with a police station that never stopped running. But this was Montauk and everyone in their police department was asleep. The operator connected Seldom with their chief who roused from his slumber with an impatient, "Yeah, what is it?"

After she told him about the dead girl and the Manhattan detective who was waiting for him on the beach, his tone became much more conciliatory. "Thank you, ma'am," he ended the call with a click.

Wearily, Seldom trudged upstairs and poked her head into the children's room. They were in their beds, asleep. Relieved, she eased back out again, readied herself for bed, and slipped between the sheets. Seemingly only a moment later she was awakened by the soft sound of rocks being pelted at her window.

Huh, people actually do that here, was her first groggy thought. She slipped out of bed, wincing as she pulled up the creaky sash, and leaned her head out. Callum stood on the ground below. He smiled and motioned for her to come down. She glanced back and forth and found a ubiquitous trellis conveniently nailed to the wall beside her window. She lunged for it, swayed, and heard Callum hiss below. *This might not support me,* she belatedly thought. But she had reached the point of no return, so she grabbed on and began the long descent to the ground.

When she was within reaching distance, Callum grabbed her and pulled her to him. "What are you doing, crazy woman?"

"You told me to come down," she said.

"I meant through the door. Who uses the trellis? You might have broken your neck," he said, but he was smiling.

"This is how it's always done," she explained. His arms were around her waist, holding her so tightly that her toes skimmed the ground. She circled his neck and pressed her face to it, inhaling the mix of saltwater and sweat she in no way found off-putting. They stood that way for an unknown time, letting the shared serenity wash over him. Seldom knew exactly why the hug was therapeutic for her, and she could only imagine why it was working for him. His hand rubbed a soothing little circle on her lower back, and Seldom melted against him, the evening's trauma long forgotten. In her current state, she believed maybe nothing could ever hurt her again, so long as she had Callum to pick up the pieces.

"How did it go?" she asked at last. She took a step back so she could see his face. He indicated the porch. They walked there side by side and sat on the step, close but otherwise not touching.

"It's like the others. It's connected, I'm certain," he said.

"Oh," Seldom said. They stared toward the ocean. It was impossible to see from where they were sitting, but they could hear waves pounding on the shore. A moment ago it had felt soothing; now it seemed relentless.

"At least this gives me a place to start," he said.

"How so?" she faced him, her expression alight with curiosity.

"What is the connection between Montauk and Manhattan?"

"Me?" she said, pointing to her chest.

He laughed and shook his head. "I was looking at the bigger picture, doll."

Of course he was. It was her Millennial nature to make herself the center of everything. She winced with embarrassment, having been caught doing it by someone who gave no thought to self.

"I meant them," he motioned to the house behind her, and she froze, her mind going immediately to the scratches on Andrew's arm. Before she could tell him about them, he continued.

"All these people, they're summer residents, spending their winters in Manhattan and warmer weekends here, along with their staff. It's a massive list of suspects, but not as much as the entire city of New York." He rubbed his eyes wearily, but his voice was perky with newfound determination. "The timeline should be easy to narrow down—who's here now, who was here last year when the others were found. Someone made a grave mistake by creating two crime scenes, and that's how we're going to nab him."

"If the girl tried to defend herself, say if she scratched her attacker, would you be able to match that evidence to her murderer, if you found him?" She knew DNA didn't exist yet, but how advanced or primitive were their techniques at this point?

"Yes, we could do that, if we found the attacker and if we found evidence on the girl, but here's the thing." He took a breath and eyed her as if not certain he wanted to impart the next sentence. Eventually he must have decided to do so because he continued. "You said we should hold something back from the papers when the stories come out, some memento or something he took from the scene. There's one thing."

"What?" she asked, her stomach fluttering with preemptive dread. Whatever it was, she knew it would be bad.

"Their hands. He's taking all of their hands."

She had told him she was shock proof, but apparently she hadn't meant it because the information had such a visceral impact on her that she closed her eyes, fighting a wave of nausea and dizziness. And as before, she made it about her, picturing the loss of her hands if Christian had had his way. Did that happen after the girls were dead, or did he make them watch? She realized then that she always pictured Christian as the killer, herself as the victim "Oh," she said softly, and she must have done a good job of hiding her dismay because Callum's thoughtful expression didn't shift. He was mentally at work, already plotting how to narrow his field of suspects. She should tell him about Andrew, about his odd disappearances, about the scratches. But she didn't. Why, she had no idea. Maybe she feared she would sound dramatic. After all, what were the chances that her boss was a serial killer? Extremely dim. It would likely turn out to be someone she had never laid eyes on, some butler or delivery driver with a twisted fetish for fingers. She shuddered. Callum eased his arm around her. She rested her head on his shoulder, his fingers gliding gently along her bare arm.

"My friend Mable's boyfriend is white," she said, apropos of nothing. Why her mind returned to that earlier conundrum was a mystery even to her.

"Hmm," Callum murmured, clearly not surprised or shocked.

"I was under the impression that wasn't allowed in this time."

"Not celebrated, maybe, but it happens. Marriages between the blacks and the Irish have been common for decades. Mutual oppression, and all that."

"Really?" Seldom asked.

"Where do you think all the mulattos come from?" he asked, and she flinched. "I've stumbled upon another forbidden word, huh?"

She nodded. "The forbiddenest. I've never even heard anyone use that one before. What would happen if someone in authority came across a black man dancing with a white woman?"

"Depends on the context, upon the man in question, whether he had a reputation for viewing race as an issue," Callum said. She liked how he could give a thoughtful answer without getting emotionally invested. It helped her to talk about things when they kept it in the realm of the hypothetical.

"It was a casual, mixed race party. The authority in question seemed progressive in his views."

"Then I can't imagine it would be a problem, not this far north. I've heard rumors things are different in the south, but as I've never been there, I couldn't say for certain."

That was helpful, but also not. If the party's fear reaction to Andrew hadn't been about race, what had it been about?

"Callum."

"Hmm."

"What would you do if you saw someone touch me in a way they shouldn't, forcefully and without my permission?"

He froze, suddenly tense. "There's a very fine line between teaching someone a lesson because they have it coming and murdering them for retribution. I suppose I'd pray that in that moment I'd be able to tell the difference." He forced himself to take a deep breath and then his fingers continued their gentle path along her arm. "Seldom."

"Hmm."

"Did Pierce do something to you?"

She pulled away and looked him in the eye. "No. Andrew didn't lay a finger on me."

He stared at her, trying to read the depths behind her eyes. "I should probably go. They're going to open the station, let me see the evidence from last summer." His fingers trailed along her cheek. "I don't like leaving you here."

She smiled and cupped his face in her hands. "Maybe someday you'll realize I can take care of myself."

He mimicked her pose, cupping her face in his hands. "Maybe someday you'll realize you don't have to." He kissed her, gently, tenderly, and let her go. He stood to open the door for her. "Goodbye, darling girl. I'll see you when you get home."

Home, that word again. She stood on her toes and brushed her lips to his. "Thank you for being here."

"Always," he said, his voice a bit husky. He waited until she was safely inside before closing the door behind her.

"And how is Officer O'Rourke?" Andrew's voice spoke from the darkness to her left. Seldom's head whipped in that direction, but all she could see was the tip of his cigarette, glowing red in the darkness.

"As ever, dependable and compassionate. I didn't know you smoked."

"It's been a harrowing day," he said, his voice loaded with its usual wry amusement.

"I think it's fairly obvious I can't work for you anymore," Seldom said.

Andrew made no reply at first, but the cigarette glowed brightly as he took a long draw. "You're ready to run off and abandon the children that easily?" he said eventually, his tone casual.

Seldom's heart twisted at the thought of Daisy and Mathew. "I'll stay until you find a replacement. They'll be fine. I've only been a part of their life a few weeks."

"They won't," Andrew disagreed. He stood and made his way toward her, easing gradually into view as the moonlight began to illuminate his body. His hair was standing on end, his tie disheveled. "Mathew especially will take it hard. He keeps pieces of himself tucked from view, doesn't let anyone know how much he's bothered."

She turned away, trying to block herself from his words. She didn't want to hurt Mathew and Daisy; she loved them. But how could she stay, after what happened tonight? Andrew reached out and stubbed his cigarette in an ashtray to her right, bringing him in close contact with her body. Seldom remained frozen, unwilling to back away, in case it had been his intent to intimidate her.

"The thing with Giles was for your benefit, though you can't see it now," he said conversationally.

"My benefit?" she snapped.

"Yes," he said, some anger leaking into his tone. "You have no idea what it means to make an enemy like Giles. You can't play a game whose rules you don't understand." He reached out and pressed a finger on her shoulder tattoo. Despite the darkness, despite the gown that covered it, he touched the exact spot where it was and pressed down hard, as if trying to make a point.

She wrenched away from him. "Some rules are universal. I don't have to let a man lay hands on me if I don't want them, no matter the time or place."

"In what time and place might a man lay his hands on you?" he asked. Was his tone full of mocking or flirtation? In his world, she wasn't certain there was a difference.

"You weary me, Andrew," she said, taking a step to move past him. When he spoke, it was so soft she almost missed it. In the morning, she would wonder if she'd imagined hearing him respond, "I weary myself."

24

"Where's Father?"

It was the fifth time Daisy had asked the question, and the fifth time Seldom gave the same answer. "Father had to leave early, to go back to work." She hadn't known that when she woke in the morning. She'd thought Andrew was still sleeping when she quietly readied the children for the beach. But when they returned to the house for lunch, the cook informed him he had left at dawn that morning and the chauffer, Stephen, would return soon to drive them back to the city.

Daisy had cried, both because she didn't want to leave the beach and she wanted her dad. "I like him better in Montauk," was all Mathew had said, staring off into the distance with quiet resolution.

So did I, Seldom thought. Until the moment at Giles's party, Andrew had felt like a friend, a real one. And now he was back to being a cold stranger. Or worse, a soon to be former employer. *Now what?* She asked herself the question the whole way back to Manhattan and still failed to find an answer.

The children, happy to be back among their toys, played contentedly the remainder of the afternoon, and then it was time for supper.

"Mr. Pierce requests your presence with him in the dining room this evening," Arthur told her. His eyes flicked up and down her body. "Dress accordingly."

Seldom was too shocked for a reply. She and the children always ate in the kitchen, but since the children didn't seem surprised by the request, she deduced it was a thing that happened occasionally, likely whenever Andrew had a whim.

She changed the children out of their play clothes, put Daisy's hair in ribbons, slicked Mathew's hair with water, and made herself ready. Since she had the first stirrings of a headache, she pulled her hair out of its twist and left it down, closing her eyes as she fluffed her fingers through the mass.

Makeup was a tricky thing, much less forgiving than its modern counterparts. The pigmentation played for keeps, with fewer emulsifiers to make it smooth. She had to be especially careful with the bright red lipstick, lest she wanted to be left with unnatural red smudges that would take hours to go away. Satisfied, she took the children by the hand and led them downstairs.

Andrew was waiting for them in the den, reading the *Wall Street Journal*, as was his standard. At the sight of them, he stood and set the paper aside, opening his arms to receive and bestow hugs from his children. They chattered about their morning at the beach. Seldom stood at the periphery, her eyes skimming Andrew's discarded paper. She had started fishing them out of the bin to read at the end of the day. The stock market was becoming a tempting fascination for her. Maybe it was because she knew what it was about to do in the coming decades, that it would have unprecedented gains until the eighties, then rebound and explode again. Or perhaps it was because she now knew a stockbroker. Whatever the reasons, it intrigued her, calling to her the same way the competitive world of pastry had once done, as if issuing a challenge.

"Do you see anything interesting, Seldom?" Andrew asked, calling attention to the way she was lurking over his paper.

"Yes," she said simply. She hadn't been certain how things would be between them, but Andrew was acting as if nothing had happened. Relieved, she decided to follow suit.

The butler opened the door to the dining room then, their signal to go inside and be seated. Seldom made sure the children were properly situated before allowing the butler to hold her chair. The table was set formally, five forks lined neatly in front of her. She had no idea what they were for but wouldn't give Andrew the satisfaction of admitting as much. He was staring at her as if he sensed her dismay, as if he was waiting for her to either give up or mess up. Instead she met his smile with one of her own.

"How does someone become a stockbroker?"

He blinked, surprised, and she put a point in her column for throwing him off kilter. "Why do you ask?"

"Because I'm looking for a new career," she said, and he laughed, hard.

"That's delightful. You make me laugh." He used the butt off his hand to dab at his eyes.

"Why is that funny?"

"Not funny so much as ludicrous," he said.

"But why? Why can't I be a stockbroker? Because I'm a woman?"

He sighed expansively and rested his arms on the table as if gearing up for something arduous. "Have you ever heard of the Buttonwood Agreement?"

"No."

"On May 17th, 1792, twenty four men stood under a buttonwood tree and signed a piece of paper, agreeing to trade stocks. That signing took place in front of 68 Wall Street, and it was the beginning of the New York Stock Exchange."

"Fascinating," she said sincerely. She'd never heard of such a thing, but she was an avid fan of history.

"My grandfather, several times removed, was one of those original signers. Since that day, every generation of my family has been involved in the stock market. My father bought me a seat on the New York Stock Exchange, as did his father and his father before him."

"I didn't know you had to buy a seat," she said.

"Of course you didn't," he said dismissively.

"Maybe I could do that. How much does it cost?"

"Last I heard, it was running somewhere around four thousand dollars. The price went down after the crash, obviously, and hasn't rallied much in the intervening years."

"That's not so much," she said.

He blinked at her. "Your salary is four hundred dollars a year. Tell me, do you have ten years of pay sitting idle in some unknown bank?"

"Oh, right. I forgot to account for inflation. I guess four thousand dollars is a lot of money these days."

"It's not pocket change," he agreed. The first course arrived, soup. He picked up his spoon, convinced the conversation was finished.

"Pretend we're talking about someone else for a minute," she said.

"I'd love to," he agreed.

"Hypothetically speaking, how does someone without family connection become a stockbroker?"

"Typically you go to one of the big schools, Harvard, Yale, Princeton, major in business, and apply to one of the big firms," he said.

"That's it? You need a degree from an Ivy League?"

"Why, do you secretly have one of those as well?" he asked, full sarcasm.

"No, but it seems like there should have been *someone* who has made it without a degree," she said.

He sighed again. "Of course there are people who have done so, but the best way, the most traditional way, is to go through the proper channels."

"The best way for whom? The only people those traditions serve are the people who benefit from them, the already rich and privileged."

"Exactly," he said, nodding, glad she finally understood.

She rolled her eyes. "But that's wrong on so many levels."

"Why?"

"Because it discounts all the people who could make it on their own merit or talent," she said.

"People like you, you mean? I would love to glimpse inside your head, Miss Murphy, and try to discern what has given you such an overflowing belief in yourself and your nonexistent abilities. How you can admit to me in one breath that you have no idea how to become a broker and in the next breath declare your worth and capability to do so is astounding," he said.

His words gave her pause because they echoed every accusation she'd ever heard about Millennials. How many times had older generations complained about their entitlement? *The product of too many participation trophies, they want to be the CEO without any of the grunt work it takes to get there.* She forced herself to take a breath and answer rationally. "I suppose you have a point. But it's not so much my belief that I have the capacity to be an amazing stockbroker, so much as my belief that I have the capacity to do anything I set my mind to." Hadn't she already proved herself by opening a business all on her own? Everyone had warned her away from such a risky venture, had quoted her the statistics of how many businesses in New York fail within the first year, had laid out for her all the hurdles she would have to overcome to get there, her young age and lack of assets chief among them. But she had persevered and prevailed. If she could do it there, she could do it here. Andrew might not believe that, but Seldom did because she knew herself. Once she set her mind on something, she wouldn't stop until she had it.

"How quaintly adorable you are, Mr. Smith, but your ardor would be better spent in Washington," he said. His smile was so pedantic it set her teeth on edge. "Despite how utterly rousing that little speech was, I believe I'll set my stores in institutions that have been in place for the last hundred and fifty years, institutions begun by my own forebears."

"Those institutions are about to topple, if not by me, then by someone else, so I wouldn't get too cozy, Mr. Pierce. Someday a woman will own a seat on the New York Stock Exchange. Someday there will be brokers of every nationality, not just white."

"Yes, the coming revolution. Do go on, Patrick Henry, but don't be offended if I eat my soup while you soliloquize. Wouldn't want it to become chilled."

"It's gazpacho," she snapped.

"Then I wouldn't want it to become warm," he said, giving her a roguish smile that made her want to punch him more than a little.

"You vex me," she said, reaching for her spoon.

"Perhaps I do it on purpose, did you ever consider that?" he said.

"Is your life so void of amusement?" she asked. Despite her irritation, it didn't pass her notice that the soup was delicious. She'd never really enjoyed cold soup before, but then she'd never lived in a time or place without air conditioning. The summer heat was high and sticky outside, barely kept at bay by the cool brick of the immense mansion.

"No, but your cheeks flush prettily when you're angry. Has anyone ever told you you look like Vivien Leigh?"

"No. Someone said Elizabeth Taylor once," she said. It was one of her regulars, a little old lady who showed up every Friday and bought exactly one cupcake. She smiled fondly, though her heart stabbed with remembrance. She missed her customers, and she desperately missed Josh. How long would it take before the bakery would go under without her? She had a lease, of course, but did her landlord have to honor it if she wasn't there?

"The little girl from that horse movie?" Andrew said, squinting. "Why would they compare you to a child? Seems risky. She might grow up to be ugly."

"She doesn't," Seldom said. Andrew tipped his head at her. "I mean she probably won't. Hollywood has a way of making everyone look good. Have you ever met any actors?"

He grimaced. "No, why would I? That's not my world."

"Ah, I forgot. Old money lives by a different set of rules."

"Now you're getting it," he said, and smiled when she laughed.

"What about other famous people?" she said.

"Define famous," he said, his tone wary.

"The Kennedys," she said.

He squinted, in confusion this time. "Of Massachusetts?"

"Yes."

"Certainly I know them. I wouldn't say they're famous. Famously ambitious, maybe."

"What about Jackie O, I mean Bouvier? She was from New York."

"Are you referring to John Bouvier's daughter?"

"Probably," she said.

"I know John quite well. He's a senior broker at my firm, a fellow

Yale alum, and he has a house in the Hamptons, not too far from mine. He has two daughters, both teenagers, and I think one of them is named Jacqueline. You have some odd definitions of fame, Miss Murphy."

"I suppose I see the potential in people," she said.

"You may be right on that one. Last I saw little Jacqueline, she was a beauty in the making," he agreed. He finished his soup and dabbed at his lips. "Here's the thing, Miss Murphy. Part of knowing prominent people is not talking about all the prominent people one knows."

Like fight club, she thought. "If you don't talk about the people you know, how do people know that you know them?" she asked sincerely. It was as if he was giving her a glimpse into a world she didn't understand, a world that made her insatiably curious. In her real life, she never brushed elbows with the upper crust. She'd always been firmly established in the hoi polloi.

"I suppose it's presumed in one's deportment, connections, status." He motioned to the massive dining room around them, a bevy of servants on standby.

"So by your unwillingness to name names, I'm to assume you have an in with all of them," she said.

"Now you're cooking with gas," he said, tossing her a wink.

She laughed. "It disturbs me greatly when you try to be relatable."

"I *am* relatable. I went to college, after all."

"Tell me more about how your years in an exclusive fraternity at an Ivy League school made you relatable," she commanded.

"It was in Connecticut, practically a world away," he said, his tone stuffed with a healthy amount of self-mockery.

She laughed. "Pardon me, I'm sure you had the full cultural experience in Connecticut. No rich white people there."

"What is your obsession with other ethnicities?" he asked.

"I'm not obsessed," she said.

"Aren't you? You looked to be when I saw you dancing with Mable's cousin."

"How did you know he's Mable's cousin?" she asked.

He leaned forward and spoke seriously. "I know everything about everyone."

"That was weirdly ominous," Seldom said. He wagged his brows at her, and Seldom had the shocking realization she was having fun. After their last encounter in Montauk, she wasn't certain she ever wanted to be in the same room with him. Now not only were they eating supper together, but his children were glancing back and forth between them with smiles of delight at the easy camaraderie.

The butler entered the room and approached the table. "Pardon me, Mr. Pierce, but a Mr. O'Rourke is at the door."

"Tell him she's otherwise engaged and he'll have to try back later," Andrew said, his eyes still on Seldom, daring her to protest. Before she could do so, the butler spoke again.

"Beg pardon, Mr. Pierce, but he says he's here for you."

25

Andrew made him wait, a long, long time, until supper was finished and the children had been put to bed. Every time Seldom suggested going to greet Callum, Andrew shot her down.

"Why don't I...," she began toward the end of what had begun to feel like the world's longest supper.

"No," Andrew said.

"But..."

"Seldom, you may not know this, and your officer may not know this, but showing up unannounced in the middle of dinner is rude behavior. As penance, he can wait until we are finished."

"Let me go say hello, and I'll come back and help put the children to bed," Seldom suggested.

Andrew didn't reply; he merely kept eating. Seldom set down what was undoubtedly the wrong fork and stood.

"Walk out that door, and you'll leave with him tonight with no salary and no job recommendation," Andrew said, not bothering to look at her as she spoke.

Pride compelled her to go; common sense bade her stay. It would feel wonderful to walk out of her own accord and leave him sitting there, but she needed the money he owed her, and she needed his recommendation for her next job. Otherwise he could make her life unpleasant, could make her unhireable. It chafed her independent nature to be so dependent on him, or anyone, for that matter.

"You can make me stay. You can't make me eat," she said, placing her fork and napkin on her plate.

"Suit yourself," Andrew said unconcernedly as he meandered through the remainder of his beef roast and potatoes.

"Sometimes I really..." she was going to tell him exactly what she thought of him when she became aware that Mathew and Daisy were staring at her, eyes wide. No matter how angry she might be at Andrew, and make no mistake she was livid, she wouldn't unload on him in front of his children.

Guessing as much, he gave her his usual amused smile. "You're much too nice for your own good sometimes, Miss Murphy."

"And you are..." Once again she caught sight of the children in her peripheral and pressed her lips together. In disgust, she turned away and faced the far end of the room. Unfortunately that wall was anchored by a massive mirror, one that allowed her to see how much Andrew was enjoying the little scene. His eyes practically danced with merriment as he painstakingly ate his meal, one tiny bite at a time.

Finally, it was over. Seldom assumed Andrew would want her to put the children to bed while he met with Callum privately, but she was wrong. "Janet can put the children to bed. I'm sure your officer wants to see you," he said. She didn't understand his conciliatory tone until he put his arm around her and ushered her into the room. She saw it from Callum's point of view, the two of them arriving together, Andrew's arm snugly around her waist. The nefarious plan crumpled, however, when Seldom gave Andrew a light shove and went to take a seat by Callum instead. He turned to survey her, raising his eyebrows in question. *Are you okay?*

No, I want to stab him, she thought as she wrinkled her nose at him to convey her displeasure. He must have caught the gist at least because he smiled and gave her a little wink before turning his attention on Andrew.

"Mr. Pierce, thank you for working me into your busy evening," Callum said.

"I'm happy to oblige, Officer O'Rourke," Andrew said.

Seldom thought it was strange how easily she could tell both of them were lying. The tension in the room was at a light simmer, or maybe it was all coming from her, still so angry with Andrew she wanted to have a tantrum, to physically pound her feet and fists until she felt better. Based on how angry she felt, it might take a while. Could it really bring him so much joy to be such an egotistical puppet master? He was a successful millionaire. Why did he feel the need to rub his status and wealth in Callum's face?

"As I'm sure you're aware, there was a murder this weekend near your home in Montauk," Callum began.

"Yes, I read about it in the paper," Andrew said, his tone somber.

Seldom was so shocked she momentarily forgot her anger. "It was in the paper?" She was looking at Callum. Had he finally been allowed to release the news, or did they run with it on their own? Was he pleased with their coverage or angry at the lapses? What kind of blowback was he getting now that everything was public?

"There was a leak in Montauk, sweet," he said, giving her knee an affectionate squeeze before turning back to Andrew.

"Tender and enjoyable as this scene is, I fail to see how it involves me," Andrew said coolly.

"It involves everyone who was there this past weekend, who might have been there last summer when the other bodies were discovered," Callum said.

"I fail to see how physical proximity gives me any insight into your investigation," Andrew said. "Unless you're hinting you think I'm a suspect. Is that what you're hinting, Officer O'Rourke?" His tone was still conversational, calculated. But then he withdrew a pack of cigarettes, tapped one out, and lit it before taking a deep draw. Seldom watched him, eyes narrowed. It was his tell, she knew, his remedy for nerves. He felt her eyes on him and flicked his glance in her direction, annoyed.

"Is there a reason you ask?" Callum countered.

"Why else would you be here?" Andrew said.

Callum let the uncomfortable silence linger a few minutes before speaking again. "Let me put your mind at ease on that score, Mr. Pierce:

I have no suspects. This is merely a fact finding mission, and any help you can provide would be greatly appreciated."

Was it Seldom's imagination or did Andrew seem to relax perceptibly? In any case, he stubbed out his cigarette and didn't withdraw another. "I'll do what I can, but I can't imagine what help I could be. I go to Montauk to rest and renew. My senses aren't sharp or attuned to possible murder suspects."

"Are they attuned to possible murder suspects when you're here?" Callum asked.

"They're attuned to everything," Andrew answered easily. "Ask your questions, Mr. O'Rourke. I'm reaching the end of my patience with this interview."

"You attended a party on the night the young lady was discovered, is that correct?" Callum said.

"That is correct."

"Did anything unusual occur at the party? Did anyone's behavior seem off to you?"

Andrew's eyes settled on Seldom. He stared at her while he spoke. "Nothing unusual at all."

"We believe the young woman in question was actually killed the day before. Did you see or hear anything suspicious or out of the ordinary on that day?"

"No."

"Were you home all evening?" Callum asked.

Again, Andrew watched Seldom as he answered. "No."

"Where did you go, sir?"

"To a party."

"Where was this party, and can you provide a list of fellow attendees?"

Andrew's answering smile regained its wry amusement. "It's not the sort of party anyone in my position would admit to attending, if you take my meaning, Officer. In any case, it was on the other side of Montauk, far away from your murder."

"You're assuming she was murdered at the beach," Callum said.

"Yes, I am, "Andrew said. "Wasn't she?"

Now it was Callum's turn to pause before answering. "No. She was dumped there sometime after."

"I suppose that explains why we didn't see her when we were there during the day, eh, Seldom?"

Seldom didn't answer, beyond a wrinkling of the nose that amused him further.

"Pardon me, but it's a private beach, isn't it, sir?" Callum said, redirecting Andrew's attention back to him.

"Yes, it is."

"How difficult or easy would it have been for someone who didn't belong to access that stretch of beach and dump a body?"

"I suppose it depends on your definition of belonging. The Montgomerys held a party that night, as you mentioned, with approximately twenty attendees. And then there was the party in the stable. But I'm sure Seldom would have told you all about that by now, seeing as how she obviously had such a good time," Andrew said. "Quite the dancer is your girl, Officer O'Rourke. Very light on her feet."

"Yes, I know," Callum said easily. "Back to the matter at hand, if you please, sir. I have one final question and then I'll let you get on with your evening. Taking into account everything you know about everyone who was at that party, do you have any reason to suspect that any of them may have dumped the body there that evening?"

Andrew laughed, but the sound lacked amusement. "Do you understand who you're asking that question to and who you're asking it about?"

"Yes, sir," Callum replied.

"I don't think you do because, if you did, you wouldn't be here right now, wasting my time. It's obvious who your killer is."

"Is it, sir? How so?" Callum asked.

"I think you'd have better luck asking Seldom," Andrew said.

"How would Seldom have a better answer?" Callum returned, his voice tightening slightly.

"Because Seldom has an in with the servant class. Which is more plausible to you, that someone born and bred with every advantage, educated in the finest schools, surrounded by every possible luxury, would turn out to be a cold-blooded killer? Or that it was someone birthed into violence and debauchery, surrounded by the stink of poverty from an early age?" He held up his hands like Pontius Pilate must have all those years ago, declaring himself clean from filth by association. "I'm not the one in this room who could testify to the violent passions of the lower born. You'll have to look a little closer to home for that. Good evening, officer. I trust you can see yourself out." He held Callum's eye in a death stare until Seldom intervened.

"There's no need. I'll walk him to the door." Shakily, she stood and preceded Callum from the room, the eyes of both men on her back.

26

"He is so..." Seldom waited to speak until she and Callum were on the front porch. But then when she finally felt free to speak, words failed her.

"Yes, he is. But I did try to warn you," Callum said. "Why did you take your hair down?" He eased his fingers into her hair and let them scrape gently along her scalp.

Seldom closed her eyes and swayed toward him slightly. "I had a headache. Why do you ask?"

"Because you only take it down when you're relaxed and at ease. I suppose I don't like to think of you that way with him."

"Is that what this is, a jealousy reaction?" she asked as his fingers continued their gentle assault on her scalp.

"No, a jealousy reaction would be planting my fist in his face. This is for my enjoyment, because you're too lovely not to touch," he said.

"Good line, Copper, I approve," she said and he chuckled.

"Not a line, doll. You're looking especially gorgeous tonight. It was all I could do to keep my mind on my interview," he said.

"Is it true what you told him?" she asked.

"Which part?" He had added his lips to the mix and was now kissing her face as his fingers continued their march through her hair.

Her headache was gone now, but so was her train of thought. "Um, suspects."

"What about them?" He punctuated each word with a kiss, on her temple, on her cheek, on her jawline.

"Do you have one?"

"Nope. I'm still gathering facts, trying to interview people, see what shakes out."

"He was right, you know," she said.

His hands slid under her face, tipping it so he could kiss her neck. "About what?"

"Me."

"What about you, darling girl?"

"That...," she clutched his shirt, fighting to hang on to some semblance of reason, "that I'm your best connection to the other party."

He paused and withdrew slightly. "Other party?"

"The servants' party. I was there. I could talk to people, see what I can find out. Servants talk to each other. They have a pipeline. Mable might..."

"No," he said, shaking his head for emphasis.

"No what?" she asked. She angled herself closer, urging him to return to work on her neck, but he didn't take the hint.

"No, you can't talk to people. No, you can't help with this investigation," he said.

"Why not?"

"Why not? Are you pulling one over on me? How do you think it would look for my girl to do my job for me? Not only that, but it's not safe, like poking a hornet's nest with a stick."

"Why does it seem like the men here keep telling me not to do things?" she mused.

"Maybe because the things you want to do here are bonkers," he said.

"I suppose you also think me becoming a stockbroker is inappropriate," she said, pulling away and taking a step back.

He was momentarily confused by the rapid conversation shift. "What? Why would I care about that?"

"Don't you?" she countered, and now she was the one who sounded confused.

"It's apples and oranges, sweetness. Making paper trades of invisible stocks is hardly the same as trying to track down a mass murderer. As far as I can tell, all it takes is a little bit of brains to become a broker, and you have plenty of those."

"It wouldn't, you know, challenge your masculinity if I did something like that, worked in a man's world, made a lot of money?"

He chuckled. "No. It's nothing to do with me. Have at it." Sensing the argument had been resolved, he took a step closer and eased his arms back around her. "Now, where were we?"

"We were discussing gender norms as they relate to our generational paradigms," she whispered, closing her eyes when he pressed his lips to her neck.

"Now I remember," he whispered.

"And I was winning," she added, balling his shirt in her fist.

"And you were winning," he agreed.

"And I was going to talk to some people for you," she said.

"Nope."

"That was so close to working," she said.

"Not even a little," he remarked, pulling away from her again. "I want to be clear on this. You are not allowed to interfere in this, not allowed to talk to any of the people at that party. Do you understand?"

She nodded.

"Good." He kissed her forehead. "I have to go, sweet. I have a couple more people to talk to while I'm here in Poshville. Sleep tight."

"You, too." She stood on the porch and gave him a little wave as he bounded off the steps and headed to his car. When he was safely away, she went inside and made a call.

"Mable, it's Seldom. How about that play date tomorrow?"

She didn't see Andrew the rest of the evening but much later, when she was asleep, she was certain the front door opened and a car started. Dreamily she wondered who was going out.

The next day Seldom and Daisy and Mathew met Mable and her children for a picnic in the park. The kids were ecstatic and took off, looking for sticks with which to bash against each other like swords.

Seldom and Mable spread out their blanket beneath a tree and sat down.

"I'm surprised you called me, Seldom," Mable said.

"Why?"

"After Mr. Pierce showed up, you left the party and never came back," Mable said. "Then news of the dead girl broke. I've got to tell you, I thought maybe it was you at first. I had to call Boots to check around and find out it wasn't."

"Why would you think it was me?"

"You never came back. And the way Mr. Pierce looked when he stood in that door..." she shrugged helplessly as if embarrassed.

"Andrew wouldn't hurt me, at least not like that, not physically," Seldom said.

Mable's glance darted to her face and lingered. "Wouldn't he?"

"Mable, do you know something about my boss that I should know?"

Mable shook her head. "No, it's just rumors you hear about people, you know? Boots has said some things."

"What kind of things?"

"The odd thing about it is that I can't recall one specific thing he's told me about him, merely the overall impression I get, that Mr. Pierce keeps secrets, that Mr. Pierce isn't safe."

"How would Boots know?" Was there a hint of defensiveness in Seldom's tone? She didn't mean for there to be.

Mable, unoffended, waved her hand dismissively. "Boots knows everything about everyone. He gets around." Her expression turned sly and she nudged Seldom with her elbow. "My cousin, Johnny, hasn't stopped talking about you."

"He's quite the dancer," Seldom said.

"He's a mainstay at the Savoy," Mable said proudly. "He was smitten with you, all right."

"That's sweet, but I'm not exactly available," Seldom said, smiling.

Mable frowned. "Your boss, Mr. Pierce?"

"What? No, of course not. Someone else." She didn't know why she didn't want to reveal Callum's name, nor the fact that he was a police officer. Instinct warned her away.

"Seldom, I have to ask you something, and I need an honest answer."

Seldom braced herself, alerted by Mable's serious tone. "What?"

"Where did you get those shoes?" She reached down and picked up Seldom's foot for a closer inspection. "I've never seen anything like them, and I need them."

Seldom laughed. Apparently what to her had been an approximation of 40's fashion was something else entirely because Mable wasn't the first person to comment on her footwear. Wherever she went, women stared at them in speculation. Maybe she was about to start a trend. "Canada," she lied smoothly. "How long have you and Boots been together?"

"Five years," Mable said.

Seldom blinked at that. "It doesn't seem like most people I've met here date that long."

Mable sighed. "It's complicated, you know? The Montgomerys look the other way on our relationship, but they couldn't if we were married. And the sort of people they entertain, well, a white chauffer and a black governess married to each other, both in their employ," she shook her head sadly, "doesn't work out too well. But the children will be in school soon, and my job will be finished." She shrugged as if to say, *We'll see what happens then.* Seldom wondered if the job thing was an excuse. To her it sounded like Boots was a weasel.

Seldom realized she had become distracted by relationship talk and worked to refocus the conversation. "Who do you think killed that girl?"

"The air force, I told you. I think they do experiments on people. Why else would she be missing all her blood?"

"If the government did it, don't you think they'd be a little more adept at hiding the body? Why dump her on a beach, waiting to be found?"

Mable squinted, thinking. "To make it look like it was random."

"Why let her be found at all? Why not incinerate the body, cremate it, get rid of all the evidence?"

Mable shrugged helplessly.

"Do you have any idea who she was?"

Mable did the thing where she looked around to make sure they weren't about to be overheard, even though there was no one nearby except the children who were currently pelting yew berries at each other. "I don't know for sure, but I can guess."

Seldom leaned in and lowered her voice. "Who?"

"Sometimes when the rich folk don't want to pay a premium for domestic help, they import them from the Eastern European countries, places that were hard hit during the war and are struggling so much the women are happy to get a roof over their heads, let alone a few pennies for salary. I bet it was one of those. I bet it's why no one knows her."

"Wouldn't her employers send out an alarm over her disappearance?"

Mable shook her head. "You think they bring them to the country legally? They sneak them here with their contacts, to avoid immigration. They're not likely to pipe up and volunteer that they've broken the law."

"Wow," Seldom said, for lack of anything else. That solved the problem of who the girls were, but not of why they were being killed. "Does Boots think the air force is behind their deaths?"

"He hasn't really said," Mable said then, cupping her hands around her mouth yelled, "Child, put down that stone and do not bash your brother in the head." She rolled her eyes to Seldom. "Violent tendencies, that one. Don't know where she gets it."

Seldom could probably guess. "Do you like working for the Montgomerys?"

"Oh, yeah. They're nice and fairly reasonable, really generous. I get a bonus every Christmas I manage to keep the children alive. So far, so good." Five-year-old Daniel crawled up in her lap, crying, and poked his thumb in his mouth. Mable cuddled him close and kissed his head. "Hungry, baby?" He nodded and she moved to hand him a cracker.

Seldom waited to speak again until he ran off and joined the others. "Do you ever feel afraid of Mr. Montgomery?"

Mable laughed. "No, why would I? He's as gentle as a lamb."

"He's never tried anything inappropriate on you, even when he was drunk?"

Mable's expression turned serious. She reached over, took Seldom's hand, and gave it a squeeze. "Not all employers are like yours, Seldom. You can come to me, if you ever need help, and I'll do my best for you. Boots knows people. One call and Mr. Pierce won't bother you any-more."

"Mr. Pierce doesn't bother me now," Seldom said, frowning. She appreciated Mable's offer of support, but it left her with more questions than answers. How did Boots seemingly have such reliable contacts that they'd be able to handle Andrew? And why did Mable seem bent on believing that Andrew was bad? Most importantly, was he?

"Why so many questions?" Mable asked.

"Have you ever noticed that when a man tells you not to do something, it makes you want to do it more?" Seldom countered. Maybe it was a generational thing. Maybe the women of this time were as sweet and deferential as Callum and Andrew pretended they were.

Mable laughed. "Child, half the things in my life were done because some man told me not to. Boots has gotten so sneaky about it that now he tries to tell me the opposite thing to try and get me to do the thing he actually wants."

"Does it work?"

Mable gave her a saucy little smile. "Only when I let it."

Seldom smiled in return. "Mable, I think you and I are going to get along mighty fine."

27

The next morning, Andrew had more bruises, more scraped knuckles. He winced when he leaned forward to hug the children. Briefly, Seldom wondered if he was Batman. Had the story started with a grain of truth, a wealthy socialite who fights crime by night? But try as she might she couldn't picture Andrew doing anything to help the riffraff. He seemed too fatalistic, as if he believed the working class brought whatever ills befell them on themselves, by virtue of being born poor. Why, then, did he sneak out at night and return home in the morning battered?

"And why are you staring at me this morning, Miss Murphy?" he asked, his probing blue eyes assessing Seldom as relentlessly as hers assessed him. Unlike her, he seemed to approve of what he found.

"Were you injured, sir?" she asked, trying and failing to sound innocent.

"It's sir now, is it?" he asked.

"I am ever so deferential," she replied.

He laughed and winced when his puffy lip pulled taut. "For a deferential wench, you hold a firm certainty that your question needs an answer."

She waited him out, maintaining eye contact until he waved his hand dismissively. "I ran into the wall in the night while searching for the commode. Blasted dim hallways."

"It's odd how often your clumsiness coincides with your secret midnight rendezvous," she noted.

"I have insomnia. Sometimes I like to go for a drive when I can't sleep," he said.

"I don't believe you," Seldom said.

"I don't care," he replied, reaching for his coffee with a wince.

"Did you know that some of your cohorts hire illegal workers from Eastern Europe," she said.

"Are you trying to tell me people break the rules to get what they want?" He faked a gasp. "Shocking."

"Have you ever done that?" she asked.

"Absolutely not. I'm a stickler for the law," he said.

"Interesting, because your son told me two nannies ago the woman spoke gibberish. All they could understand was her name, Kalina."

"Yes, the gibberish was quite off putting. Turns out she was mad, I had to let her go," Andrew said.

"Mathew said her favorite food was cabbage, cabbage for every meal," Seldom continued. "Isn't Kalina a Polish name?"

Andrew set down his coffee with a sigh. "What is your point here, Seldom?"

"What really happened to her?" Seldom said.

"What always happens to women like that? She disappeared," he said.

"She disappeared?"

"She disappeared."

"And you made no move to find her?"

"Why would I? She eased back into the teeming masses of Five Points. They have their reasons for disappearing. It's part of the risk of taking on an illegal, the knowledge they can be gone at any moment."

"It didn't occur to you she might have been injured, might have been abducted or murdered?"

"Why would it?" he countered. "Do you think I concern myself that much with the private lives of my staff? She left a void, and I filled it. The end. Would you like to tell me the point of this assignation?" He pinched the bridge of his nose between his fingers, wincing again when he touched a bruise.

"No point," she said.

"You're not spying for your beau, asking questions to relay my answers to him?"

"I am expressly forbidden from interfering in Callum's case," Seldom said. The order still stung, as did the imperious way he'd handed it down.

Perversely, Andrew smiled. "Ah, I see. It's like that, is it? I was married for five years, and it took exactly five minutes to learn not to tell my wife what to do."

She wanted to ask what his wife died from, but she wasn't so gauche. She wondered, though. Whenever the staff spoke of her, it was in whispers. If she had lived, she would have been a year older than Seldom. What could cause such a young woman to die so prematurely?

"You're staring at me," Andrew said.

"I'd imagine a lot of people stare at you," Seldom blurted and had immediate regrets. It sounded flirtatious, when in fact she'd meant it the opposite. Andrew was a decidedly handsome man whose commanding presence demanded attention. Briefly, she was reminded of Christian. He'd held court in the center of the restaurant, drawing the admiring and curious gazes of everyone in the dining room. What she now realized was that Christian's attempts to be imposing had been carefully calculated and manufactured. He had likely studied which seat in the restaurant would put him in the spotlight, he had made a point of using everyone's names, of exuding maximum charm and appeal. Andrew did that naturally. When he wanted, he could be extremely charismatic, could likely get his way with a smile. But, like Christian, it was best not to cross him. When provoked, his amiable nature could disappear in an instant, leaving ugliness behind. She'd seen glimpses of it on the occasions they'd disagreed. The taste had been enough to convince her she never wanted to see the full effect.

"Cold?" Andrew asked, and Seldom realized she'd shivered.

"No," she said and turned away. She gathered the children and began the journey to the public library. On the way, they passed a street corner where a boy about Mathew's age was shouting out the day's headlines.

"Mass murderer stalks the city, mass murderer stalks the city," he screamed, causing the children to stare it him in wide-eyed wonder. Seldom stopped, fished in her velvet coin purse, and bought one of his papers. When they reached the library, the children began to roam, selecting their books, while she sat at an oversized oak table and started to read that morning's article.

The city has a secret. One of its own is roaming the streets at night, preying on poor, working class women. Bodies are piling up, four in Manhattan and three in Montauk. No one has come forward to claim the women, leaving police to wring their hands in dismay.

Seldom tried and failed to imagine Callum wringing his hands in dismay. It was easier to imagine him popping his knuckles before punching this reporter in the face. The article had obviously been written with an eye toward sensationalism. *New York PM Daily*, was the title of the paper. Seldom had never heard of it, possibly with good reason. They had included a picture of one of the dead women from Manhattan, the first one Callum found. She was covered by a sheet and only her feet were visible, but still. She was about to close the paper in disgust when she leaned in for a closer look.

Something was familiar about the shoes, something distinctive. When Seldom first started with the Pierces Daisy had clattered across the room wearing too-big high heels.

"Where did you get those?" Seldom has asked laughing as the little girl wobbled and toddled.

"They were our mother's shoes, and she's not allowed to play with them," Mathew had answered, giving his sister a severe frown that made her cry. Janet, one of the surly maids, had seconded his assessment. After some tricky negotiations and a lot of hugs and kisses, Seldom had wrested the shoes away from Daisy and given them to Janet to return to the former Mrs. Pierce's closet. Wrenching them off Daisy's feet had given her an up close and personal view of the shoes; they were definitely the same make as the ones in the picture. She remembered because the leather stitching had looked hand sewn and expensive.

She stared into space, forcing herself to take a deep breath and swallow. A lot of people probably had those shoes. Maybe they were the Nikes of the 1940's, a brand so popular they had become ubiquitous. There was absolutely zero correlation between the shoes in the picture and the shoes in her employer's dead wife's closet. Was there? And if so, what could it be?

She wanted to call Callum and tell him what she knew, to ask him about the shoes. But of course she couldn't. He'd been adamant that she didn't get involved in any way. But she did know someone who could clear up the mystery of the shoes, someone with a keen eye for fashion who would be able to lay to rest at least one piece of the riddle.

When Mathew and Daisy presented her with their book selections, she gave them a beaming smile. "How would you two like to pay Mrs. O'Rourke a visit again?"

They clapped their ready agreement, begging her to take them now. Mathew was keen on scoring another piece of apple cake, but Seldom had another idea.

"We'll bake her a treat to take and go tomorrow, how does that sound?"

They were amenable to that idea, and for Seldom it was a necessity. She'd need to go home and find a way to get the shoe, and she'd have to do it without getting caught.

28

"Seldom, what a pleasant surprise," Mrs. O'Rourke said the next afternoon when they showed up on her doorstep. "And my favorite little visitors," she added, giving Daisy and Mathew a hug.

"We made you dis," Daisy proudly announced, jutting the cake they'd baked into her hands.

"Wonderful. Should we go and cut ourselves a piece, do you think?"

Daisy and Mathew nodded their enthusiastic assent and followed Mrs. O'Rourke as she turned and led them toward the kitchen.

"I'm sorry, you just missed Callum," Mrs. O'Rourke said as she set down the cake and turned on the water for coffee. Seldom helped herself to plates and a knife and set about cutting the cake while the older woman arranged their coffee.

"I'm here to see you, as it turns out," Seldom replied. She knew Callum's schedule well by now, had waited until after the time when he normally left for work.

"Oh? How lovely," Mrs. O'Rourke said. "Anything in particular?"

"Yes, but," she eyed the children, "the little pitchers."

"Ah," Mrs. O'Rourke said, nodding sagely. They made pleasant small talk while they ate their treat, and then Mrs. O'Rourke turned on a radio program for the children while she and Seldom retreated back into the kitchen.

"How can I help you?" Mrs. O'Rourke asked.

"I was wondering if you could tell me about this shoe," Seldom said, withdrawing it from her bag. She held it out to the older woman who took it and inspected it. Mrs. O'Rourke had been a seamstress for years, taking in odd jobs for the wealthy whenever they arose. She didn't make clothes for them, but she handled small or emergency jobs, last minute tailoring or repairs. That, combined with innate curiosity, had given her a vast knowledge about clothing and shoes.

"Oh, my," Mrs. O'Rourke said with something like reverence as she handled the shoe, turning it over and over as she made her inspection. "This is a very well-made shoe. The leather is extremely high quality, the stitching and piecing exquisite. It's handmade by an Italian manufacturer on Fifth Avenue. See the little symbol there?"

"So it's not mass produced, then."

"Oh, no, not at all. These shoes are individually crafted for extremely wealthy individuals. They're sculpted to fit each foot. I'd wager no two are alike."

"Hmm," Seldom said, staring thoughtfully at the shoe, a quavering sensation in her belly.

"I take it that's not the news you hoped to hear," Mrs. O'Rourke said.

"It's not so far from what I expected, but it does lead me to a new quandary," Seldom said. She told Mrs. O'Rourke about the dead girl who was wearing the shoes in the photo, about how Callum had warned her away from involving herself in his investigation.

"If I'm understanding you correctly, you hadn't gone out searching for the shoe. You saw the shoe in the picture and recognized it, is that correct?"

"Yes," Seldom said.

"Well, then, I don't see how that's involving yourself. It's merely being intelligent and observant," Mrs. O'Rourke declared.

"Is that how Callum will see it?" Seldom asked.

"You have a point there," Mrs. O'Rourke said, her smile wry. "There is another way to go about it."

"What's that?" Seldom said, eager for any solution.

"Do you have the paper in question with you?"

Seldom pulled it from her bag and handed it over. Mrs. O'Rourke took it and set it on the table, comparing the picture with the shoe still in her hand. "It's a definite match, I'd say. Leave the paper with me. I'll point out the shoe to Callum tomorrow and tell him what I know about it being a one of a kind. It's possible someone else may have noted the same thing and already pointed it out. Either way, he won't take it badly coming from me. Except for the fact that he'll believe I bought this paper, which is something I wouldn't do because of their harsh stance on the police. But I could tell him I wanted to keep abreast of what they were saying. In any case, I'm not certain how much help it will be."

"What makes you say that?" Seldom asked.

"These shoes, they'd cost more than a year's wages for someone like us. If the victim is, as you suspect, an Eastern European servant, there's no way she would have bought them, meaning they've likely been stolen."

"They might have been a gift," Seldom said.

"That's an awfully extravagant gift," Mrs. O'Rourke mused.

"If someone wanted to keep her silent about something, it might have taken a lot of money," Seldom said.

"Interesting. But, as Callum or my husband would tell us, it's all conjecture without any proof."

"If we give him this, maybe he can find some," Seldom said. "Do you mind if I leave Callum a note?"

"Help yourself, dear," Mrs. O'Rourke said, her eyes fastened on the paper as she read the salacious article. Seldom took a piece of paper and pen from the phone stand and dashed off a message.

Hi, Handsome. I hope your week is going well. She paused, dithering about how to sign it. She was going to go with her standard *XO*, but worried maybe it wasn't a thing now. What if he had no idea what the letters meant? She certainly wasn't going to sign it "love." It might be a different era, but that didn't mean she wanted to be the one to define their relationship or say important words first. In the end she decided on an ambiguous little heart, along with her name. She carried it into his bedroom and laid it on his pillow, pausing to stare at a picture on the nightstand. She picked it up for closer inspection.

A much younger Callum stared back at her, his arm around a girl who stared up at him in adoration. Seldom might guess it to be his sister, except that Mrs. O'Rourke had told her Rose was a brunette, like her. The woman in the picture was blond. Who was she, and what had happened to her? They hadn't discussed their past relationships much, beyond saying nothing had ever worked out. Why hadn't it worked with this woman who so obviously adored him? Was she still in his life? Had she married someone else? Did he pine for her?

Realizing she was heading toward a crazy spiral of jealousy and desperation, she forced herself to set the picture down and walk out of his room. Whoever the woman was, he wasn't with her now, that much was certain. Callum wasn't the sort of man to two-time anyone. Maybe she was dead or maybe they'd broken up. Maybe *she* was the love of his life, the reason he seemed to pull back from Seldom every time they got too close, the reason words of endearment had to be wrenched so painfully from his heart. Maybe that was why Seldom was here, to help Callum open his heart and learn to let others in, to heal him for some future love.

She wrinkled her nose. She wasn't quite altruistic enough to relish the thought that she was a placeholder for some other woman, past, present, or future.

Mrs. O'Rourke compelled them to stay for supper so it was much later than Seldom intended when they set off for home. No cabs would swerve for her. Bitterly, she thought that she never had any trouble getting a taxi when she set out from Andrew's posh Upper East neighborhood. It was only in the O'Rourke's dicier Chelsea neighborhood that no one would stop for a woman and two children.

"Looks like it's the subway for us," Seldom said cheerfully to her two charges.

"I don't want to take the subway," Mathew said. His imperious tone was reminiscent of his father.

"Me neever," Daisy added.

Me neither, Seldom silently agreed. "Come on, guys, it'll be fun. I'll tell you a story while we ride, okay?"

Reluctantly, they trailed beside her toward the station. Seldom felt tense and on edge. Worse, she felt as if someone's eyes were on her. When she checked, though, the street behind them was empty of people.

Because they're all in this subway station, Seldom thought as they made their way down the stairs. She held tightly to the children, always anxious that one of them might slip away and get lost. Other people with children, presumably their mothers, seemingly had no such anxieties and let their kids run unabated. Maybe it was the time she was from, an era of sunscreen, helmets, and seatbelts, or maybe it was because she was new to caregiving. Whatever the reason, she couldn't seem to tamp down her irrational fears that something would happen to the children if she wasn't with them, if she took her eyes off them, if she allowed them to engage in unsupervised play. Even Andrew had commented on it.

You're a mother hen, aren't you? he'd said when she insisted on sitting at the edge of the water, touching distance of the kids as they played at the beach.

Perhaps it was simply that Seldom was acting like what she'd always wished for—someone who cared enough to be overprotective.

The train was coming. Seldom could hear it, could almost see it. She could definitely feel it as everyone jostled forward, jockeying for their turn to load up. Somehow the three of them had ended up at the front of the platform. She was glad, thankful they'd be able to get in first and try to get a seat. There was no way Mathew and Daisy would consent to standing the entire way home.

The train was almost upon them when someone nudged Seldom hard in the back, causing her to stumble forward. One foot edged over the platform and she began to lose her balance. Abruptly, she let go of the children, not wanting to drag them with her as she fell. Her arms had just begun to windmill when a heavy hand reached out and clamped onto her shoulder, dragging her back.

She turned to face her rescuer, heart thumping wildly, and blinked in shock at his familiar face. "Boots."

He grinned at her, his perpetually ruddy cheeks making him look more cheerful, jolly almost. "Whoa there, honey. You almost took a header. You okay?"

"Someone bumped me," she said, looking wildly around. "Did you see who?"

The train made its noisy arrival, drowning out her words. Boots stood close by and herded their little party onto the train, elbowing people away when they got too close. Seldom sat and he crouched in front of her, still in possession of one of her hands. She double checked to make sure Mathew and Daisy were seated on either side of her. They were, seemingly unaware of her near tragedy.

"Someone bumped me," she repeated.

"I don't doubt it. People get crazy when it's time to go home. He pressed his palm to her cheek, comfortingly, as a mother might a child. "You okay? Want me to see you the rest of the way home? We have the same stop, you know." She glanced around at the crowded interior of the subway car. People were eyeing them, disapprovingly, she thought. To the outside observer it probably looked like a tender romantic moment, him kneeling in front of her, his palm pressed to her face.

She sat back slightly, easing out of his reach, and took a breath. "No, but thank you so much, Boots. I think I'm fine now. I was careless, too close to the edge. Rookie mistake."

"Don't worry about it, kid. Could happen to anyone." He stood, knees popping. "I'll be right over there attached to that strap. You call if you need anything, okay? Old Boots will take care of you."

"Thank you," she said, giving him an appreciative smile. He gave her a friendly one in return and went to take his place near the far wall.

"Seldom, I believe you promised us a story," Mathew said, quirking his eyebrow at her, daring her to go back on her word.

"So I did," Seldom said. She drew in one more shaky breath and began telling them the story of the Avengers. Not being creative enough to come up with stories on her own, she had begun blatantly plagiarizing popular stories from her day. Daisy's favorite was *Frozen*, but Mathew had an affinity for heroes. Seldom caught sight of Boots eyeing her with concern. She gave him what she hoped was a reassuring smile, trying not to think what might have happened if he hadn't been there to rescue her. *What do you know? Turns out I have a thing for heroes, too,* she thought and began to tell Mathew the engrossing saga of Iron Man.

29

Seldom put the children to bed. She wanted nothing more than to collapse into her own bed, but there was one more task that awaited her. She needed to return Hillary Pierce's fancy Italian shoe to its closet in her room, a task that was harder than it should have been. Seemingly someone was always roaming the hallways upstairs, whether a maid, the butler, or Arthur. Seldom had barely been able to swipe it in the first place, had sweated like a popsicle in a furnace until the task was completed. Now, as she began to contemplate returning it, she began to perspire again.

Now or never, she told herself when the hallway was finally clear. Clutching the shoe to her chest, she darted into Hillary's room, opened the closet, aligned the shoe perfectly beside its mate, and closed the closet again. Somehow she knew if she was caught in this room, she'd be let go. No one would believe she was slipping in to return something; they would think she was there to steal.

She turned and began tiptoeing toward the door when, to her horror, the handle began to turn. Like a runner stealing home, she darted for the bed and slid under it, sustaining painful carpet burns on her forearm and knees, praying she hadn't put a run in her stockings. With effort, she held her breath, forcing herself to go still and silent as a pair of men's shoes advanced into the room. They walked to the closet, opened the door, and stood surveying something. After a few beats, two hands reached down and began loading shoes into an oversized bag, the very shoes Seldom had just returned to their rightful place. When the bag was loaded, whoever it was turned and began heading toward the door again. And then he paused. Slowly, he walked around the bed, pausing again, this time mere inches from Seldom's head. He sat. The bed bowed so low it nearly touched Seldom's temple. He shuffled something. A few seconds later she heard the flick of a lighter and then the smell of cigarette smoke drifted down, choking her.

It was Andrew's brand of cigarette, and Andrew's shoes she saw, four inches from her face. Above, she heard the deep inhale of nicotine, a slight pause as he held it in his lungs, the shaky exhale when he let it out. *He's nervous,* Seldom thought. *And so am I.* What could she possibly say if he caught her there? Then again, what was he doing there, and why was he taking his wife's shoes?

After what felt like a long time, long enough to have smoked the entire cigarette, he stubbed it out on the bedside, stood, and left the room. Seldom waited a long time, barely daring to breathe. At last when she heard the front door open and a car start, she eased from beneath the bed, poked her head into the hallway, and darted to her room.

Once there, she leaned against the door, heart hammering. Why had Andrew taken the shoes? *You know why,* a little voice said. There was only one possible explanation for why he would have taken them on the same day the same shoes appeared in the newspaper on a dead woman's body. Whatever she wanted to believe about her boss and his activities, there was no way around this one fact: Andrew had just hidden evidence that tied him to a dead woman. She needed to call Callum, but what could she say? She wasn't even supposed to know about the shoes. Instinctively she knew that, while he might be glad for the information, he wouldn't be glad she was the one who gave it to him. Somehow this case felt like a line between them, like the definition of all their differences. He was an old-fashioned manly man who insisted on being in charge. Seldom was a modern woman, the captain of her own fate, under the tyranny of no one. To toe over that line might destroy whatever was brewing between them. On the other hand, she couldn't very well *not* tell him, could she?

I need more information. If she could go to him with everything she knew at once, it might go over better. More than that, it would assuage her roaring curiosity over Andrew's activities.

Easing away from the door, she made herself open it and walk down the stairs. After two adrenaline spikes in one day, her legs felt shaky and weak, but she was determined. And she felt better now that she had a plan.

She picked up the phone and dialed Mable. "Do you know anyone who has a car and might be willing to let me borrow it for an evening?" she asked with no preamble. She and Mable were new friends, but they had the potential to become close. It was better Mable understand Seldom's single-minded determination up front so she knew what she was getting into.

"Johnny Light Feet has a car, but he might want something in return for letting you borrow it," Mable said coyly.

"I told you I'm seeing someone," Seldom said.

"Tell me who. I know everybody."

"Callum O'Rourke," Seldom said.

"I don't know him," Mable said and Seldom laughed. "I'll call Johnny and let you know. He might let you off with saving him a dance next time you see him."

"Now that's a price I'm willing to pay," Seldom agreed and hung up. A few minutes later Mable called back and it was all set. Tomorrow night she'd have the means to spy on her boss. She only hoped he'd provide her with the opportunity.

The next morning was Sunday, Seldom's day off. Callum phoned early, as soon as Mass was over.

"How's about a date, pretty girl?"

"What did you have in mind, Copper?" she asked.

"Wait and see, kid," he said. An hour later she was in his car driving through Manhattan.

"Everything's closed," she noted.

"Blue laws," he said.

"What's that?"

"Everything is closed on Sundays. Except the movies. They changed that when I was a kid. The church wasn't happy. It's still a touchy subject with Ma, so don't bring it up, for future reference," he said.

"Duly noted. What do you do if you need something on a Sunday?"

"Get it on Saturday."

"But what if it's an emergency?"

"Then you go to the emergency room. What could you need to purchase so badly that it becomes an emergency?" he asked.

"Chocolate."

"If you need chocolate that badly, you have bigger problems," he said, his glance darting to her. "Why are you so far away again?"

"I forgot." She eased closer and he patted her knee.

"Wonder how long it will take for this to become the new habit," he mused.

"I think you're trying to reprogram me in all the ways," she said, only half joking.

"No," he said seriously. They stopped at a light and he picked up her hand, brushing his lips on her knuckles. "You are very much to my liking, exactly as you are."

"Does that mean I can drive sometimes?" she asked.

The light turned green. He dropped her hand and faced forward. "No."

She laughed. "You're all talk."

"You think so?" he countered.

She gazed out the window, unwilling to answer. He wasn't all talk, not by a lot. She wished he would talk more, specifically about his feelings. He was a show-don't-tell type of guy, stark contrast to every man she knew. In the intervening decades between them, men had gotten in touch with their emotions. Seldom had no idea what to do with a man who wasn't. She was torn between not wanting to cast him into her generation's mold and desperately wanting to understand what was going on inside him. How was she supposed to know if he didn't tell her? By observation and osmosis? Her last boyfriend kept a podcast where he detailed all of their dates and his daily emotional state. If she wanted to know how he was feeling about her, or anything really, all she had to do was download his latest episode. Contrast that with Callum who, despite being free with quippy endearments, held absolutely everything in check.

They arrived at the park. Callum opened the door for Seldom and then opened the trunk, withdrawing a basket and blanket.

"You packed us a picnic?" she said.

He smiled at her, but otherwise didn't answer.

"What's in it?" she said, trotting to keep up with his long strides.

"Wait and see," he said.

"Did your mother do it?" she said. Preparing food was women's work. Try as she might, the mental image of Callum laboriously making a lunch for them wouldn't form. It had to have been his mother. Right? She shouldn't be disappointed by that. The thought was what counted, after all. But it lost something as she thought of Mrs. O'Rourke being the one to prepare their food, though she doubtless would have done it with love.

While Seldom would have meandered a bit, searching for the perfect spot, Callum marched forward with purpose, stopped under the shade of a maple tree, and unfurled his blanket. He held her hand while she sat down, a gallant notion she otherwise wouldn't have considered. It was nice not to have to wobble precariously as she attempted to settle gracefully while wearing heels. When had men stopped thinking of things like that? She was sorry for everyone else in her generation who had to do without because it actually *was* helpful to have someone help her with her coat and steer her around muddy puddles. She'd been here only a few weeks, but already four different men had given up their seats for her on the subway, and two others had volunteered to hail cabs for her when she was out shopping. If only there were a way to keep her independence and their manners, life would be just about perfect.

Callum folded himself lithely beside her and reached for the basket, placing it between them. He eyed her, smiling. She had no idea what that look meant, but it made her heart beat faster in response.

"Are you ready?" he asked.

She nodded, smiling in anticipation of she knew not what. He lifted the lid of the basket and began setting out items. Seldom waited to inspect them until he was finished, and then she gasped. Before her sat a bevy of French pastries, so perfect they looked as if they'd just come from a patisserie. Additionally, he had procured chicken salad, some pungent cheese with a wax coating, cornichon pickles, and a bunch of plump purple grapes.

"Where did these come from?" Seldom breathed, picking up a croissant to admire its perfect lamination.

"I scouted around, until I found what I wanted and bought them yesterday. I spent some time in France and the memories weren't altogether unpleasant, mostly because of the food. Something told me you would approve." His eyes looked almost shy when he asked, "Do you approve?"

Carefully, she set the croissant aside and dusted her hands before cupping his face and kissing him soundly. He reached for her, resting his hands on her waist as he returned her kiss. Eventually they remembered they were in Central Park and eased apart.

"Thank you for this, Callum. It's spectacular."

"You're welcome," he said, reaching out to swipe what she imaged to be a smudge of red lipstick from beneath her bottom lip. "How's life in the castle? Did my interview cause you any problems with your boss?"

"No, he's acted normally," she said, her insides twisting with guilt over what she was holding back. Should she tell him about the shoes or not?

"You're never going to believe this," he said, interrupting her anxious thoughts.

"What?"

"Ma helped me out on a case."

Don't choke, don't choke, don't choke. Seldom forced herself to swallow her bite of grape before speaking. "How so?"

"One of the dead girls was wearing this hoity-toity shoe. Ma caught sight of it in the paper and led me to its maker. It's saved me a ton of legwork. Might have solved the case, even, if I can ever get in to see the guy who made it and get him to talk to me."

"So, you're thankful for you mother's help, then," she said, nibbling a bite of croissant.

"Of course I am. I mean, I wouldn't want her to go sticking her nose in or put herself in danger, but when it's a coincidence, I won't say no," he shrugged and took a bite of his chicken salad.

"Mm, hm, mm, hm, right, right, right," Seldom muttered, staring at the éclair without really seeing it.

"What's the matter?" he asked.

"Nothing. Why?"

"You seem a little preoccupied," he said.

"Do I? Maybe it's because I'm busy trying to figure out if this baker used a poolish for her croissants," she said, holding a croissant aloft to stare at its underside.

"It could be those gibberish words, but maybe it's something else."

She blinked at him, feeling caught and guilty all over again. "What else?"

He set down his sandwich with a sigh. "You left that little note in my room which, by the way, totally adorbs, if I'm using that word correctly?"

"Yes, and you're more adorbs for trying," she said.

He grinned at that and continued. "I know you saw the picture on my nightstand."

He thought she was jealous. She hastened to interrupt. "Callum, you don't have to explain anything to me. We're practically thirty. Obviously there were people in our lives before each other."

He tipped his head at her. "Who specifically was in your life?"

"Lots of people, I suppose. I've been at this dating thing a long time," she said. Her life was so normal to her. In comparison to seemingly everyone else, she'd had fewer dating partners. But here, when one seemed to find one and be done, she probably looked like the Mata Hari.

"And there's been no one special, in all that time," he said.

"I suppose it depends on the definition." Absently she picked up a grape and examined it.

"For a girl who says she likes to talk about everything, you're being awfully cagey right now," he said. "Let's start at the beginning. Tell me about the first boy who stole your heart."

From his tone, it was hard to tell if he was being flippant or sincere. But his gentle and probing gaze was fastened on her in a way that made her believe his curiosity was genuine.

"A boy named Xavier. I was fifteen, a late bloomer. Love made no sense to me, outside of literary settings, which is shocking, given my environment."

"What does that mean?"

"After my dad left, my mom's life became an endless parade of men. Usually girls in that kind of setting don't fare so well. But I put a lot of thick barriers in place." It seemed to Seldom she'd been born with the propensity to keep everyone at arm's length, but maybe the habits developed so early she didn't remember not having them. Had there been a time when she wasn't cynical and self-protective? It seemed unlikely.

"How did Xavier manage to get around them?" Was it her imagination, or did he sound like someone who was looking for pointers?

"The same way it always happened—with words. He told me I was the girl of his dreams, there was no one like me, we were meant to be, all the usual suspects. I fell and fell hard. And then I imagine he said the same things to the girl he cheated on me with."

Callum clicked his tongue. "Faithless."

"And yet it took me five years to get over him. I dated casually in that time, nobody got an in, until Dallas with the podcast."

"What is a podcast?"

She explained it to him and he stared at her, horrified. "This person, I can't in good conscience call him a man, recorded himself talking about your private relationship for other people to hear?"

"Yes, but in his defense, he only had about twenty subscribers."

"Is that why you broke up with him? Because of the massive breach of trust?"

"No, he broke up with me, something I learned by listening to podcast episode thirty one titled, 'Why We Broke Up.' Apparently I was too immersed in my career and 'unavailable to meet his deepest emotional needs.'" She finished speaking and Callum continued to stare at her, brows lowered, mouth open slightly, a mixture of shock and revulsion. Seldom couldn't help it, she started to giggle. How must it sound to this man who had spent five years fighting a war on another continent to hear about a man who recorded himself weeping because Seldom was too busy with the opening of her business to immediately return his calls? Should she add that Xavier was a vegan who spent two hundred dollars a month getting facials and ended each podcast with "virtual hugs and kisses for his peeps?" No, information like that might make his brain explode. Then she felt bad because Dallas had a good heart, deep down. His only crime had been being as messed up as Seldom was, but in drastically different ways.

"Huh," Callum finally said, tipping his head to study her.

"He was a nice guy," she added lamely. "Really sweet and thoughtful. He was better at keeping track of all the little milestones than I was."

"What milestones?"

"First date, how long we'd been together, things like that."

"How long were you together?"

"Two years."

"Two years?" he exclaimed. "It must have been serious."

"Not really. I was, as he said, emotionally unavailable. The bakery consumed me. I worked round the clock trying to get it off the ground. There was always so much to do." At the time it had felt natural to devote herself to the opening. But now, in retrospect and with some distance, she wondered why she had done it. The bakery was gone, ripped away like a used bandage, and what did she have to show for it? Josh was the only thing that stuck out to her, the only part of her former life she mourned. She had become a cliché of everyone with a near-death experience, belatedly learning that it's only ever the people in life who matter, not the successes, not even the security. She had wanted the bakery because it represented stability, something all her own no one could take away from her. And now that it had been taken away from her, she was still okay. There was something freeing and powerful in that, in realizing that it hadn't been all the hard work she'd put into her business but something inside her heart that gave her the security and stability she'd always longed for.

"That's a pretty smile," Callum said, taking her hand and giving it a squeeze.

"I'm happy, I guess," she said, squeezing his hand in return. "Are you happy?"

"I guess I never thought about it," he said.

"You've never wondered if you're happy?"

He shook his head. "Maybe that was something I thought about before the war. I honestly don't remember. For a while, it was enough to be alive. So many other people weren't. How could you ask for more? Since I've been back..." He trailed off, staring into the middle distance.

"What?" she prompted in whisper, unwilling to break the spell that was allowing her this glimpse into his heart.

"I suppose it's felt a little like waking up from a long sleep in an unknown place. You don't quite know what to do with yourself, so you just keep doing the things you did before, hoping someday everything will feel all right again. That it will go back to normal, whatever normal is." He scanned the park, his eyes lingering on the couples, the families. "Everyone else seems to have accomplished it, to have moved on and forgotten. And I..." He pulled himself back and gave his shoulders a little shake, as if he could physically pull himself from wherever he'd been. "I probably sound like your fella with the radio program, huh?"

"Not even a little," Seldom said. Dallas had once spent an entire podcast detailing an encounter he'd had with a bully in third grade, trying to determine if that was why he always felt inadequate in high school basketball tryouts. Hearing Callum try and articulate in some small part the horrors of war and the toll they'd taken on him wasn't even in the same realm. Dallas had liked words, too. He had loved to hear reassurances from Seldom, that he was worthy, that he was loved, that he was necessary and vital and wonderful and all the other things she could think of to tell him. But words meant nothing to Callum, so she edged closer, erasing the space between them, and slipped her arms around his waist, hugging him, trying to convey to him with her arms all the things he needed to hear—that he was safe, that someday everything would feel okay again, that she was here for him, if he needed or wanted her.

He returned her hug, enveloping her in his strong arms, holding her tight and kissing the top of her head. "You're good medicine, kid," he whispered at last.

It was only much later, after he'd brought her home and kissed her goodbye, that Seldom realized they never got around to talking about the woman in the picture or anyone from Callum's past.

30

Now or never, Seldom silently urged her boss. Not only did she have Johnny Light Feet's car for this one night, but it was also her day off. Janet the maid was watching the children. If Andrew was ever going to sneak off to one of his mystery rendezvous, the kind that left him with a swollen face and bloody knuckles, tonight should be the night. There was also the fact that all of his outings had matched up with the death of a girl, but she wouldn't let herself think about that. She would instinctively *know* if he was a murderer, wouldn't she? You had to be able to sense that about a person, didn't you? She had sensed something off about Christian. It would stand to reason the same thing would happen with Andrew, unless he was a better actor. Or her love for his children had blindsided her. Okay, it was probably naïve to think she could tell by looking if someone was a killer. Either way, she had to find out what Andrew was up to, if only to assuage her overblown curiosity, to say nothing of her desire to help Callum.

Finally at nearly midnight, the door opened and closed. Seldom bolted out of her bed, already fully clothed, and sprinted silently down the stairs. She eased out of the kitchen and stopped short behind a Canadian hemlock, watching Andrew as his car emerged from the garage and slid into the night. Johnny Light Feet's car was parked at the end of the block. Her heart palpitated with the dread of losing the chase before it began, but it was as close as she could park the car without drawing too much notice.

When she finally reached it, she easily caught sight of Andrew, a few paces ahead of her on streets that, by modern New York standards, were almost comically bare.

He drove for a long time, until he reached Harlem. *What is he up to?* Seldom's curiosity increased along with the miles. She was no longer thinking of Callum and his case, merely quenching her own nosiness. Why was her millionaire boss, doubtless a billionaire in Twenty-First Century terms, driving around Harlem at midnight on a Sunday?

At last he parked, exited his car, and walked confidently forward to an unmarked door. Without knocking, he opened the door, walked through, and disappeared. Seldom found street parking a block away, something else that would have been miraculous by modern standards, and followed, pausing outside the unmarked door, hand outstretched on the knob.

Did she really want to do this? She had the feeling there was no going back, that whatever she might learn about Andrew had the potential to change both of their lives, and not for the better. Taking a deep breath for courage, she turned the knob and stepped inside.

Seldom entered the dark, windowless building and leaned against the door, allowing her eyes to adjust to the darkness. Something about it was familiar, and then she realized it was eerily similar to the place Christian had stashed her, dark, damp, closed off from the outside world. Panic crept up her throat, threatening to cut off her air. She struggled for a breath, and then another, forcing the panic back down. She hadn't been brought here against her will; she wasn't handcuffed to anything. This wasn't the same.

Her eyes began to adjust to the darkness and she could pick out dim shapes, bags, chairs, awkward lumps of who knows what. None of them were moving, however, and that was a good thing. Whatever this place was, it wasn't filled with people waiting to accost her.

She eased forward one tentative step at a time. As she advanced further into the space, she began to distinguish faint sounds, something more than the rush of water through pipes, the groans and clicks of old electrical connections. The first sound was the insistent smack of flesh on flesh. The second sound was an intermittent groan. Less often there was a whoop of triumph, possibly even joy.

Intrigue mixed with curiosity and fear. Seldom's mind couldn't assign a mental image to the noises. None of them seemed to belong together. If someone was being beaten, why was it accompanied by so much exuberance?

The sounds grew louder as she edged farther into the building, and now the smells began. Sweat, so much sweat. And something salty, a pungent brine that made her stomach knot with an unnamed primal dread. *Blood.* She didn't know how she knew what the smell was, only that she was certain. Someone had bled in this room, might be bleeding now.

She came to a doorway and stopped, the sounds and smells comingling now so that it felt like someone was standing beside her, shouting in her ear, confusing her senses. All she had to do was take one step forward, and her questions would be answered. Against all the warning voices inside her telling her to run away, Seldom took the last step, her hand gripping the doorway for support as her head slowly poked around its interior.

She froze, allowing the scene to assimilate itself because it didn't make sense. Two men stood in the center of the room, attempting to pulverize each other with their fists. A handful of other men stood around them, urging them on. Seldom searched for Andrew among them, certain he was involved in some kind of illegal betting ring. He wasn't among the spectators, though. He stood in the center of the circle, fists raised in defense. And then he caught sight of Seldom, momentarily dropping his fists, allowing his opponent's fist to connect with his face in a mighty way. She watched, spellbound, as his nose burst into a fountain of blood, and then she turned and fled, running back the way she came, bumping hard into everything in her path this time.

She burst through the doors and blinked. The lighting wasn't as harsh as the glare of modern LED streetlamps, but it was still a drastic change from the darkness of the building.

Her feet sped toward the car, mindless of the rest of her now, until she arrived and realized she had tossed the keys haphazardly into her purse. She began sorting through the mess of useless items in her bag, fingers numb and shaky in her haste. Finally, her hand latched onto the key. She withdrew it and reached for the handle of the car when an iron grip settled on her wrist.

Startled, her gaze darted to the livid face of Andrew Pierce, blood oozing unabated from his swollen nose. Even in the darkness his eyes snapped rage and fire.

"Whose car is this?" he asked, his voice raspy with suppressed anger.

Seldom didn't say anything; she couldn't. It was all she could to keep standing on legs that wobbled. His grip tightened painfully on her wrist, squeezing until she thought it might snap off in his hand. "J-Johnny Light Feet." The name wouldn't, couldn't mean anything to him, except apparently it did. He glanced over her head, causing her to realize someone else was there. *At least there will be witnesses to my demise,* she thought.

"Take this car to Johnny Light Feet." He reached in his pocket, withdrew a twenty dollar bill, and handed it to the man who, Seldom now realized, was black. "Tell him Seldom sends her thanks."

The unknown man pried the key from Seldom's grasp and drove away in Johnny's car, leaving only Andrew and Seldom and awkwardness behind. It didn't last long. He gripped her bicep and frog marched her to his car where he tossed her roughly into the passenger seat before slamming the door and going to his own side.

"Do you..." she began.

"No," he snapped.

"But I..."

"We are not discussing this. Stop asking," he said.

Seldom faced him. Blood was still trickling from his nose. She fished in her purse and withdrew a handkerchief, feeling oddly reluctant to stain it with his blood. It couldn't be helped, though. She slid closer, reached up, and staunched the bleeding, plugging his nose with her pretty lace kerchief. "You should know that when men tell me not to do things, I tend to do the opposite. Rest assured we *will* talk about this, if not now then twenty minutes or twenty days from now."

He gave his head a hard shake, enough to convey his displeasure, not enough to dislodge her hand from his nose. They rode in silence the rest of the way to Manhattan. Seldom kept up the pressure on his nose. As the miles passed, she could feel his anger recede, leaving in its place a kind of resigned exhaustion. By the time he parked in the garage, he was limp. He rested his head on the seat behind him. Seldom dropped her hand from his nose, checking to see that the blood on her kerchief was no longer fresh.

"I think the bleeding has stopped," she said softly.

He gave her a little nod, eyes still closed.

"If you don't want to talk about Fight Club, then let's talk about the shoes."

Slowly, painfully, his eyes wrenched open and he stared at her. "What shoes?"

"The shoes you got rid of from your wife's room. The same shoes the dead girl was wearing."

She wondered if he would try to deny it, but he didn't. "How did you know about that?"

Now it was her turn to remain silent.

He blew out a breath but otherwise didn't talk.

"The police are going to find out," she said.

"Because you're going to tell them?" he asked.

"No, because it doesn't take a genius to put two and two together. Callum already knows who manufactured the shoes. It's only a matter of time until he tracks them to you. So tell me, Andrew, why was a dead woman wearing your wife's shoes?"

"They weren't my wife's shoes," he said softly, scrubbing a hand tiredly over his forehead. "They were her own shoes, bought by me."

"Kalina?" Seldom asked.

"I assume so, unless she gave the shoes to someone."

"What happened?"

"Exactly what I told you. She left, disappeared, went back to the docks where she came from."

"But you were involved with her." A statement, not a question.

He stared at the wheel for so long she thought maybe he wouldn't answer. At last he did. "Yes."

"While your wife was alive?"

He looked at her then, frowning fiercely. "I am many things, Seldom. An adulterer isn't one of them. Hillary and I weren't a love match, but I still respected our vows."

"What happened to her, to Hillary?"

"Hillary was like a butterfly. Society was everything to her. She was pretty and lively but, like a butterfly, delicate and fragile. Having Mathew took something out of her, and then Daisy followed two years later. It was as if the light had been snuffed out of her. I could see her trying to rally for my sake, for their sake, but she couldn't. One day I walked in and found her... she had tried to..." he drew in a shaky breath. "She didn't succeed that day, but it put her on a path of weakness and ill health that would eventually lead to her death. She got consumption. Her body couldn't fight it, and she died."

"How soon after her death did Kalina come along?" Her tone was softer now, more sympathetic.

"Six months. As you can imagine, I was in a bit of a state. Two young children, no wife, war raging. Kalina was bright and pretty, new and young. She was away from home. We were both lonely."

"Why did it end?"

"An ending was always inevitable. What was I to do, marry my illegal Polish immigrant governess? Set her up as mistress of all this?" He motioned around them which, at the moment, only encompassed the dark interior of the car and garage. "I broke it off, cruelly and with brutal honesty because I told her the truth, that she was a servant, would never be anything other than a servant. She ran away in the night, never to be heard from again until that blasted picture in the paper." He patted his chest, in search of cigarettes that weren't there. Giving up in defeat, he gripped the wheel, hands shaking.

Seldom was quiet a few minutes, digesting all he'd said. There was a lot in there that was his fault, his callousness in breaking things off, in sending her away. On the other hand, he had been a victim of cruel circumstance as well. His wife had tried to take her life, eventually died, left him the clueless father of two small children. She could feel his loneliness and desperation like a physical thing. Kalina must have felt like a lifeline, in more ways than one. And then there was the war.

She reached over, pried one of his hands off the steering wheel, and clasped it firmly, trapping it between both her hands, physically imbuing him with calm and comfort, the same way she had tried to do to Callum that afternoon when she hugged him. The war had ravaged the country, even those who hadn't fought it with guns. "Tell me about the fight," she commanded in a tone that would brook no resistance. Either he sensed that or he was out of arguments because he took a breath and complied.

"My time at Yale was the highlight of my life."

"Weren't you at Yale during the height of the Depression?" she asked.

"What's your point, Seldom?" His tone was dry, infused with a trace of its former wry amusement.

"Nothing, Andrew, continue."

"So young, carefree, and adventurous. I boxed there, but everyone did. It was the thing. And then, before I knew it, I was married and a father and a businessman, and then a widower, and I just...wanted it all back again. The freedom, the innocence, the *fun*."

"Do you think on some level this is because you didn't go to war when so many other men did?" she asked gently.

He paused. "Maybe, perhaps," he said softly.

"You know, Andrew, I would submit that success is not measured by how you fight, but what you have that's worth fighting for. You don't have to go to war to be a worthy man. You've already done it by being a good father."

"You think I'm a good father?" he asked, darting her a glance so quick he winced and touched his injured nose with his free hand.

"I think you're as good as you can be for the time you're living in," she said.

He laughed. "I'll take it, I suppose." He stared at her and then the hand that wasn't holding hers eased slowly toward her face, landing softly on her cheek, cupping it. He shifted. Seldom let go of his hand and slid to the far side of the car, pressing herself against the door.

"We should go, I think."

They stared at each other, silence and tension thick and heavy between them. He gave a slight nod and opened his door. Seldom didn't even consider waiting for him to open hers. She pushed it open and stepped out, taking a deep breath that smelled of gasoline and motor oil. What had almost happened there? *He was going to kiss you,* a little voice said. Seldom had no time or inclination to wonder if that was something she wanted because, more than anything, she wouldn't hurt Callum that way. Thoughts of Callum returned her to their earlier conversation. They stepped out of the darkness of the barn together, standing side by side in the dim moonlight. Seldom faced Andrew who peered down at her, his face fully guarded now.

"You should call your lawyer and tell him everything because they're going to come for you," she said.

"And what will you do, when that happens?" he asked.

"I'll keep watch of Daisy and Mathew, try to lessen the impact on them."

"And when your copper friend accuses me of murder, what will you say?"

"That despite all evidence to the contrary, I don't think you're a killer. Not that it will matter. My opinion doesn't much matter to him in that arena."

"I wouldn't be so certain about that. I think everything about you matters to him." He started to take a step away, but she tugged him back.

"The night of the party, is this the reason all the servants were afraid of you?"

"I suppose so. I broke the cardinal rule, comingled our worlds. Those men know things about me, and I know things about them."

"I thought it was because I was dancing with Jonny Light Feet, because of Mable and Boots."

He shook his head, and they started to walk again, side by side companionably. "From all I know, Johnny Light Feet is a good guy. Boots, on the other hand..."

"What's wrong with Boots?"

"Remember we talked about all that gin I drank during prohibition?"

"Yes."

"Who do you think got it for me?"

"Boots? But isn't he younger than you?"

"He couldn't have been more than fourteen, but he was the best rumrunner any of us knew. The intervening years haven't changed him much, from what I understand. You'd do best to keep your distance from that one."

She thought of Boots, of how he had rescued her when she almost fell off the subway platform. Or had he? Boots was the closest person nearby. Had he rescued her, or had he pushed her?

They had reached the house now. They stopped short and faced each other. "I told you mine, Seldom, now tell me yours. I know you're not from Canada. Where did you come from?" His finger tapped her shoulder tattoo again.

Seldom took a breath and let it out in a rush of words. "From almost eighty years in the future. Callum found me chained to a pipe after a guy kidnapped me and tried to do the same that's been done to those girls. I have no idea how I wound up here, but in my world it's almost eighty years in the future."

He stared at her, blinking once, twice, three times, and then he laughed, loud and sharp. "All right, keep your secrets, you bonkers dame." With a final pat to the top of her head, he turned and walked away, laughing silently all the way up the stairs.

31

The next morning Callum called. "I think you should come home," he said after a pleasant preamble. And though he tried to keep the tension out of his voice, Seldom heard it.

"Why?"

"Because."

"Need a better reason, Copper," she said.

"Because I miss you," he said.

"Need a realer reason," she amended.

He blew out a breath. "Things in this case are ratcheting up. Obviously someone in the world you're in is a player. I'd feel better if you were here instead of there."

She paused a beat, sifting the words. In her time, men didn't normally want things from her without an ulterior motive. She couldn't imagine what his could be in this case, minus a genuine concern for her safety. Having her in his house would be an extra burden, an extra mouth to feed. The only possible benefit he could gain from it would be the assurance of her safety. The realization made her stomach twist because she had never meant that much to anybody, not even her own family.

"I can't leave Daisy and Mathew." If Andrew was about to be arrested, they'd need her more than ever.

"They'll be all right," Callum said.

"Will they? I'm not so sure." There were plenty of people in their world, maids, a cook, creepy, overbearing Arthur, and other servants. But no one seemed to pay particular attention to them, not even their father. It probably wasn't a stretch to say that Seldom was projecting her own painful childhood onto them and trying to make up the difference.

"What are you doing today? I'll come see you," he said.

"I'm taking the kids to Mable's to swim." She had only agreed after assuring herself that the Montgomerys were gone for the day. She did not want a second encounter with Giles, even if they were the only people for miles with a private pool.

"I'll give you a ride."

It was on the tip of her tongue to tell him that Mable only lived five blocks away, whereas he was across town. But Callum was a doer. He was worried about her, and he needed to take care of her. Surely she could give up an ounce of independence for that, couldn't she?

"All right," she agreed.

"Good, be there in a bit." She could hear the smile in his voice and smiled in return.

He was still smiling when he arrived. Seldom stepped outside the servant's entrance to greet him and he picked her up, holding her so tight against his chest her feet came off the floor.

"Hiya, kid," he whispered, his breath warm on her ear.

"Hiya, Copper," she returned. He set her down and she pressed his cheeks with her palms. "You're stressed."

"What makes you think that?"

"Maybe I can tell by the tone of your voice, or maybe it's the fact that you navigated forty minutes of traffic to drive us five blocks."

"I'm fine," he said.

"You can talk to me," Seldom said. A little line of worry or frustration worked its way between her brows. Callum used his thumb to smooth it away.

"It's just work stuff, sweet. Not worth the bother of words."

"What is worth the bother of words, in your world?" she asked, her tone somewhere between wryness and exasperation.

"If I find an answer to that, you'll be the first to know," he said.

Daisy poked her head out the door, grasped his hand, and began tugging it with urgency.

"Mr. Callum."

He knelt on one knee in front of her. "Yes, Miss Daisy?"

"We're going to go swimming," she said solemnly.

"That's very lucky," he said.

"Yes," Daisy agreed. "My swimsuit is blue and Seldom's is red."

"I bet you both look beautiful," Callum said.

Daisy nodded. "We do. Father said so."

"Did he now?" Callum asked, standing to regard Seldom with a raised eyebrow.

"Not to me," Seldom said.

"No, he said it to me and Mathew. He said Seldom is our prettiest nanny, prettier even than Kalina, though I don't remember her."

Seldom could see the name "Kalina" wash over Callum like a bucket of ice water, could almost see the moment he made the connection between his dead victim and her boss. His eyes, momentarily frozen on Daisy, released their hold and traveled to Seldom.

"You need to come home with me," he said, an urgent whisper.

She shook her head.

"Seldom, there are things you don't know."

"There are things you don't know," she countered.

That gave him pause. "What things?" Mathew eased out to join them. They looked down at the children together.

"Everyone ready?" Seldom asked. The children heard the falsely cheery note and weren't buying it. Mathew was especially leery. When Seldom reached out to squeeze his shoulders in a one-armed hug, he let her.

They trooped to Callum's car, waiting until he held the doors for Seldom and Daisy. Before Seldom could ease in, he caught her hand. "What things?" he whispered, taking a step closer.

She glanced at the children sitting placidly in the back seat. "It's not him," she whispered.

"I have evidence," he said.

"Your evidence is wrong," she said.

"How do you know?"

"Because he told me."

"And you believe him?"

"I do," she said.

"Why?" he asked.

She thought of the suppressed emotion in Andrew's voice, her belief that, buried somewhere deep inside, he was a good man, possibly even an honest man. "Because in all the time I've spent with him, he never made me feel the way Christian made me feel in the first five minutes."

"Maybe he's better at hiding it, or..." he trailed off, glancing away.

"Or what?"

"Or maybe you have different reasons for wanting to believe him."

She let that sit a minute. "Are you jealous of my boss, Callum?"

"You tell me. Should I be?"

They stared at each other, the moment broken only when Mathew poked his head out the window. "We're hot."

"Coming," Seldom said. She pulled her hand out of Callum's grasp and slid inside the vehicle. They made the short drive to the Montgomery's house in silence. Seldom's first instinct was to open her own door and walk away, but she stayed seated, allowing Callum to open the door for her and take her hand to help her out. He kept her hand as he opened Daisy's door, allowing the children to precede them up the walk.

"I've never considered myself the jealous kind," Callum whispered. "As it turns out, I never cared enough to be jealous before."

They reached the door. Mable wrenched it open and blinked at Callum with a smile of surprise. "You must be Callum," she said, her grin widening.

Callum smiled in return. "You must be Mable." He let go of Seldom to shake Mable's hand.

"Would you like to stay a while?" Mable offered.

"I'd love to, but I have to get to work. Some other time, perhaps, thank you."

Mable gave him a little nod and turned to Seldom. "Why don't I take the kids for a minute so you can say goodbye?"

"Thanks, Mable, I'd appreciate it," Seldom said. They waited until she disappeared with the children and then faced each other.

"There is nothing between me and Andrew. I'm not even certain we could be considered friends. He's my boss, nothing more."

"I've seen the way he looks at you. Trust me when I say he'd like to be much more."

"He's never said as much to me, never said he likes me. Never told me he wants to be more than friends or made any declaration whatsoever. Then again, neither have you," she said.

"I'm here, aren't I? That seems like a pretty bold declaration," he said, clearly uncomfortable with the conversational shift.

Seldom stepped slightly closer and rested her palms on his chest. "I know you're a man of action who doesn't put much stock in words, and I've tried to make my deeds match up to that. But, Callum, I need some words from you from time to time."

"Which words?" he whispered, resting his hands on her hips.

"All of them, I think." She stood on her toes, brushed her lips to his, and reached for the door.

"Seldom," he said softly. She paused and turned to face him. "Please be careful. I...would be very upset if something happened to you."

"It's not Shakespeare, but it's a start," she said. She kissed her finger, touched it to his cheek, and let herself in the house.

<h1 style="text-align:center">32</h1>

"Well, well, well." Mable waited to speak until Seldom and the children were safely settled in the pool.

"What?" Seldom said, suppressing a smile.

"Got yourself a fine one, didn't you? I can see why you've been hiding him."

"I haven't been hiding him," Seldom said.

"You should. My lands, child, that boy's face could talk a nun into giving up her habit. Where on earth did you encounter a man so fine?"

"He helped me out when I got into some trouble," Seldom said.

Mable's brows rose. "Loan shark?"

"Police officer."

Mable's mouth puckered into an unspoken "O."

"You don't approve?" Seldom guessed.

"No, I do. It's just," she twisted the skirt of her bathing suit between her fingers, "Boots had some trouble with the law a while back. I guess he's taught me to be leery."

"I heard Boots used to be a rumrunner," Seldom chanced, her tone purposely light.

"We all make mistakes when we're young, I guess," Mable said uncomfortably. "That's why we're so thankful for Mr. Montgomery. He doesn't seem to care about Boots's past or the color of my skin."

"Why is that, do you suppose?" Seldom asked.

"He's a good man," Mable said, more than a little defensively.

219

"He kissed and groped me the night of the party. And *that's* why I didn't come back," Seldom said and now it was her voice that held a challenge. Would Mable deny it? Call her a liar? How far did her loyalty to her employer go?

"He'd likely been drinking," Mable said calmly.

"That doesn't make it okay. A man never has the right to put his hands on you, if you don't want them there. It doesn't matter if you're a woman or a servant or have what he believes to be the wrong color of skin. Your body is your private property, not anyone else's."

Mable stared at her a few beats and then burst out laughing. "Where did you come up with that? Sounds like the pamphlets the communists handed out on street corners during the war. Are you a communist?"

"No." She shook her head. "I don't understand the incongruity here. On the one hand men treat women like priceless treasures. They open doors, they give up chairs, the walk on the street side and willingly defend honor. On the other hand they treat women like possessions or mindless artifacts to add to their collections, whose bodies were invented only for their pleasure."

"What's it like where you're from?" Mable asked.

Seldom rubbed her eyes wearily and regretted it when she blinked what felt like pure chlorine. "The opposite, I suppose. Manners have gone the way of the dinosaur, but women have autonomy over their bodies." She thought of the graphic sex on display everywhere she turned in her time, of the way women's bodies and sex were used to sell everything from food to jewelry. "Or maybe not. I don't know. Technically I guess we're supposed to be empowered, but most days it doesn't much feel like it." The whole conversation was making her depressed. She thought of Andrew, of the way he had chastised her for her reaction to Giles Montgomery. He had embarrassed her, made her angry. On the other hand, he had gotten her out of harm's way. And Giles hadn't retaliated, as Andrew said he might. Was it because he thought Andrew had punished her already? Had that been Andrew's aim all along, to make Giles believe he was handling it so he didn't have to?

And then there was Callum who had said he would physically insert himself to defend her honor, a cozy thought on the night she was assaulted, but did she really want that? Two men beating each other senseless for the benefit of which of them could lay claim to her? "Did you ever notice that the older you get, the grayer life becomes? Remember when you were a kid and everything was all black and white?"

"It's always black and white to me," Mable said, holding her dark arm next to Seldom's pale one.

"I guess I'm making a fuss over nothing," Seldom said, feeling chastised. She had gone back in time nearly eighty years, and she was still complaining over first world problems. Had she learned nothing from being here the last few weeks? Why did she keep trying to pigeonhole everything into her worldview instead of the other way around? She was no better than the missionary who went to a foreign land, ignored all their culture and beliefs, demanded the new world conform to his Americanized way of life, and then wondered why he had no converts. Of course she was going to keep getting the same results if she kept making the same demands. Just because she was the same didn't mean everything else was. The world didn't revolve around her. She was not the star of every play, the heroine in every act. She took a deep breath. "I want to know about you. Tell me what your life has been like, from the beginning until now."

Mable complied and Seldom made a concerted effort to listen, really listen, with no thought to how the story affected her or wonder what she might do in a similar situation. *It's not about you,* she told herself, something her Millennial mindset would likely need to hear a few more times before it sunk in. Mable's father died when she was young, leaving her mother with six children and no money. Mable had gone to school through eighth grade, until she had to drop out to get a fulltime job. She had started life at one of the factories, hated it, and—with determination and perseverance—pushed her way into service for another wealthy family until she became the Montgomery's governess at age eighteen, beginning as soon as their first baby came home from the hospital seven years ago.

"Had you ever taken care of a baby before?" Seldom asked.

Mable shook her head. "I had no idea what to do with her. I was terrified, but my mother was on standby to answer lots of questions. And I learned by doing, like with everything.

"Mable, you're amazing," Seldom said sincerely. Mable didn't reply, but her cheeks flushed slightly. She was like Callum, like everyone Seldom had met here; she did because it had to be done, never bothering to ask if it made her happy or fulfilled. It was likely the first time anyone had ever said such a thing to her, had called out her bravery for essentially becoming an adult at fourteen and taking care of herself all the years since. Their lives weren't so different, except Seldom had allowed herself to dwell on all the accompanying emotions—the resentment of having been born into a family that didn't want her, the unfairness of having only herself to depend on, the frustration and loneliness of being on her own. Like Callum, Mable was a doer and while that might not make them the psychological picture of good health, it also made them pleasant to be around. Complaining wasn't in their nature. In Seldom's time, complaining was an art form, and when she allowed herself, she could be a master.

"You got awful quiet," Mable noted.

"My mind is on overload," Seldom said. It occurred to her that Mable might offer Seldom insight into Callum's mind. "Do you ever tell Boots you love him?"

Mable grimaced. "Why would I do that?"

Seldom laughed. "Maybe because you do."

Mable shook her head. "He already knows. What's the point of being mushy about it?"

"Maybe he doesn't know. Maybe he's been wondering all this time. Maybe he needs some assurance of where he stands with you."

"Are we still talking about Boots?"

Seldom sighed. "Callum's very different from every other man I've known or dated."

"Be honest, isn't that what makes him special?" Mable guessed.

Was it? In Callum, had she found the missing ingredient everyone else seemed to lack? "I think so."

"Then why do you keep trying to change him? Just appreciate him for how he is," Mable said.

"You give good advice, Mable," Seldom said. "I'm going to come to you with all my problems. Fair warning: there are a lot of them, and most of them don't exist outside my own head."

"Child, how'd you get to be such a mess?"

"It didn't happen overnight. Believe me, it's taken a lot of years of obsessive self-involvement," Seldom said. Mable laughed. "Did you just giggle? I didn't know you had it in you."

"I think it's you; you bring out the worst in me," Mable said.

"You've been a grownup even longer than I have. I think you're overdue for a bit of giggling," Seldom said. "Mable, did you know Kalina?"

The smile fled. "Oh, I knew her."

"You didn't like her?"

Mable shook her head, lips set in a grim line.

"Why not?"

"Because it was obvious from the start she came here intent on scoring an American husband. And the first person she set her sights on was Boots."

"Really? Did they...did he and she..." she trailed off awkwardly, unable to find the best way to ask someone if her longtime boyfriend cheated.

"No, but not for lack of trying on her part. When it became obvious Boots wasn't interested, she set her sights on bigger fish."

Did Mable know about Kalina and Andrew? Did everyone know? Before she could blurt the truth, she caught herself. "Who?"

Mable leaned in to whisper. "Mr. Montgomery."

Seldom gasped. "No. Did it work?"

Mable shrugged. "I don't know. Things were sketchy and tense there for a while, between the Mr. and Mrs. Kalina stopped coming around, and then she disappeared altogether so," she shrugged, "problem solved."

Seldom shuddered, thinking how finally the problem had been solved. Poor Kalina. Poor Andrew. Poor everybody. "Kalina was the dead girl in the paper. Callum thinks Andrew killed her."

"I could see that," Mable said solemnly.

"Mable, he didn't," Seldom exclaimed. "I know you don't like Andrew, but murder, really?"

"It has nothing to do with liking and everything to do with fearing. Would Mr. Pierce's name be the first I thought of when I heard the word murder? No. But do I think him capable? Yes."

"It could be anyone," Seldom said, though that likely wasn't true. Given that the two murder scenes were Manhattan and Montauk, it had to have been someone in the manor-bred world. And the cross section of those people with the people who knew Kalina was very small. "It had to have been someone who knew her though, right?"

Mable lifted one eyebrow as if to say, *Mm-hmm, like your boss.*

"Well, well, well, you ladies seem like you're having fun." Giles Montgomery stood at the edge of the pool, towering over them. How long had he been there? How much had he heard? Mable seemed to be asking herself the same question because she wouldn't make eye contact with anyone.

"Yes, sir," she said meekly.

Seldom didn't say anything. She wondered if he would give her the heebie-jeebies even if he had never attacked her. She kept her focus on Daisy and Mathew, fully believing that if she ignored him, he'd go away. That wasn't to be, however.

"Seldom, may I have a word?"

It was on the tip of her tongue to tell him no when Mable took the decision out of her hands. "It's time for the children to have a snack anyway," she said, rounding them up. Seldom tried to toss her an accusing glance, but Mable studiously avoided eye contact. Soon she departed with the children, leaving Seldom and Giles Montgomery together. Worse, Seldom was wearing a swimsuit and below him in the pool, clearly at a disadvantage. *Why did I come here? Swimming is not worth it.*

He knelt beside her. "Seldom, please allow me to apologize for my behavior at the party. I'd had too much to drink, and I was out of line."

What was she supposed to say? That she absolved him? She didn't.

He had used his greater height and weight and position of authority to terrify and assault her. Drunk or not, it was the worst sort of thing to do to another person. On the other hand, she felt like the horrible tension would keep mounting unless she gave him something.

"I accept your apology," she said, still not looking at him.

"Thank you," he said meekly. He was still kneeling by the side of the pool. Even though she wasn't looking at him, she could tell he was staring at her. "You're a very beautiful woman."

She didn't answer, didn't turn to look at him, didn't do anything except continue to stare straight ahead, frozen, waiting for it to be over because she knew what was coming next. His hand reached out, but then he froze, hovering a few centimeters away from her shoulder. The hand hung suspended for a dreadful moment, and then withdrew.

"Yes, well," he said. He stood, made a show of brushing himself off—to get rid of the contamination of being near her?—and then turned and walked toward the house.

She waited a full minute until she was certain he was gone and then got out of the pool, dried herself off, and put on her cover up.

Mable returned a minute later with the children, smiling at something one of them said.

"How could you leave me alone with him?" Seldom hissed, and Mable's smile fled.

"He wanted to apologize," Mable said. "Didn't he?"

"He did, but…" How could she articulate the feeling Giles gave her when she didn't understand it herself? "We have to go."

Mathew and Daisy started to complain. Part of their whining was due to being tired, furthering her resolve to leave.

"Don't go," Mable pled. "Look, I'm sorry, but what could I do? He's my boss."

That part was true enough. And it was clear that Mable thought Seldom was blowing things out of proportion, even though this time she was certain she wasn't. If given the chance, she had no doubt Giles would try to grope her again, or maybe worse. "I really have to go." She wanted, no, *needed* to put distance between herself and the man who paid Mable's bills.

"All right," Mable said, clearly remorseful over the entire situation. "Let me get Boots to drive you."

"I can get a cab," Seldom said. She would volunteer to walk, but the children were already sleepy. It was doubtful she'd be able to drag them all the way home in their present condition.

"If Mr. Montgomery is here, then Boots has nothing to do. I insist. Stay right there. I'll go find him and bring him back." She pointed a finger at Seldom as if she were an errant dog and then disappeared. With nothing left to do, Seldom sat down to wait.

33

Boots arrived smiling. "Hullo, Seldom."

"Hullo, Boots. Thanks for doing this."

"No trouble. You kids ready?"

She nodded and herded Daisy and Mathew together. They thanked Mable and headed to the car. By the time Boots got the car turned around, they were asleep.

"They always light that fast?" Boots whispered.

"Yes. For a while I thought maybe they had some kind of vitamin deficiency, but now I've realized they just really love to sleep in cars," Seldom said. She glanced at Boots in her peripheral. He still had a vague smile on his face. That, combined with his perpetually ruddy cheeks, gave him a jovial appearance. He was a thinner, darker haired Santa. "Mable said you knew Kalina."

He whistled softly. "There's a name I haven't heard a bit. I'm surprised she told you about her. Those two were like two cats with their tails tied together. Made for some awkward moments when the Pierces and Montgomerys got together, I'll say that."

"Did the Pierces and Montgomerys get together often?" Seldom asked.

"Yes, ma'am."

"I didn't think Giles and Andrew were friends." If he thought it was odd that she used their employers' first names, he didn't show it.

"I'll tell you, Seldom. Their world is not our world. Their rules are not our rules. They don't have to like each other to play in the same pool, you get me?"

"It's a very odd world," she agreed.

"It's more than odd. It's dangerous." They stopped in front of the house. He turned to face her. "Have a care with your boss. He's not a man to be trifled with, something Kalina found out the hard way."

"You mean because he fired her."

He held her gaze. "What else could I mean?"

"You don't think, I mean, Andrew wouldn't, couldn't...He's not *physically* dangerous."

"If you say so," he said. "Why the questions about Kalina?"

"Haven't you ever been curious about your predecessor?"

"I didn't have one. I'm Mr. Montgomery's first chauffer," he said.

"You must have been very young when you started," she said.

"Sixteen," he said proudly.

Had he still been a rumrunner back then? Or was that when he went clean? She stared at him, pondering. He stared back, clearly amused by her inspection. "You puzzle me, Boots."

"I think Mable would say the same." He glanced to the back seat. "You ready to take these lunkheads inside?"

"Don't trouble yourself. I can wake them."

"Hey, now, my girl is a governess too, remember? I know how it is when Betsy and Daniel conk out. Mable'd rather do anything than to risk waking them. I'll take him, you take her." He hefted himself from the car before she could protest, not that she wanted to. He was right; if she woke them before they'd had their full nap, they'd be beyond cranky. Boots took Mathew while Seldom took Daisy. Janet opened the door for them, tsk'ing in disapproval again. Boots followed Seldom upstairs, tucked Mathew into his bed and held the door while Seldom tucked Daisy into hers.

"Thanks, Boots," Seldom said. They were paused in front of her door. The scene, so reminiscent of the one she'd shared with Callum, made her yearn for him with an almost physical pain in her stomach.

"No problem," he said. He took a step and paused, turning back.

"Mable likes you a lot, so I'm going to tell you this. Don't ask anymore questions. You might not like the answers you find."

"I never find any answers," she said.

"Good. Keep it that way." He put his hat on, tipped it to her, and headed down the stairs.

Later that night, Andrew once again demanded their attendance at supper. "Does Father usually request you this often?" Seldom asked Mathew. When he shrugged, she realized she was trying to find life answers to large questions from a six year old and let it go.

Once in the dining room, Seldom had no idea why Andrew wanted them there. Visibly anxious and withdrawn, he sat silent and sullen, alternately forcing a few bites of food and smoking an endless chain of cigarettes.

"Those are really bad for you," Seldom couldn't resist telling him. "And for the children." She waved her hand pointedly at his second hand smoke.

He smiled, a mixture of wryness and relief, as if he'd been waiting and hoping for a distraction. "You must be fun at parties."

"Only the ones where no one is smoking," she said.

"I take it no one smokes in Canada," he said, clearly mocking now.

"I wouldn't know."

"Oh, that's right. You're a magic fairy from the future. Did you cast a spell to get back here?"

"No, I got kidnapped and chained to a pipe," she said, watching him carefully to note his reaction. Either there was none or he was very good at hiding it.

"Ah, right. Lucky for you your copper happened to be in the right place at the right time for a rescue," Andrew said. "He's very earnest."

"Yes, he is," Seldom agreed. "It's refreshing to be with someone honest for a change."

"How very wholesome. I bet he always drinks his milk and washes behind his ears," Andrew said, stubbing out his third cigarette. Or was it his fourth? Seldom had lost count.

"Is there a reason you're so intent on putrefying your lungs tonight?" she asked.

"A better question is why don't I do it on all the other nights," he said, taking a bite before reaching for another cigarette.

"I'm not sure it's good for the children to watch you attempt to…" she trailed off, not willing to say "kill yourself" in front of Daisy and Mathew.

"They're my children. I can do what I want with them," he said.

"Not as long as I'm here."

"Then don't be here. What's keeping you? You said you were leaving. So leave."

Daisy started to cry and Mathew looked at her with big eyes. "You're leaving Seldom?"

Seldom narrowed her eyes at Andrew as she pulled Daisy into her lap. He looked away, taking a deep draw from the cigarette in his hand. "No one is leaving right now. Father and I are talking about something else. Finish your supper, and I'll read more from *The Wizard of Oz*, before bed." She smoothed her hand down Daisy's head, kissing her crown.

"You don't allow yourself to be an easy target," Andrew said.

"No," Seldom said evenly. He wasn't better than her; she wouldn't allow him to convince her otherwise. They might not have an equal amount of money, but they *were* equals. If there was one thing she was glad to bring into this time from her own, it was that—the inerrant belief that her life held as much value and promise as anyone else's.

"Good," Andrew said, holding her gaze before the butler interrupted, genuflecting his way to the head of the table like a broken bobble head.

"Pardon the interruption, sir, but an officer O'Rourke would like to speak with you.

"Tell him no," Andrew said, his gaze returning challengingly to Seldom.

But it wasn't Seldom who spoke next. "I'm sorry to say this time it's not an option," Callum said, entering the room flanked by two other officers in uniform.

34

❦

Seldom was exhausted. After seeing their father leave with Callum and the two officers, the children were understandably upset. It had taken four chapters of *The Wizard of Oz* to get them to go to sleep. Even though Callum hadn't cuffed Andrew, had kept it light and friendly for the sake of the kids, they had picked up on the palpable tension in the room. How could they not? The room had crackled with it.

"And if I refuse?" Andrew had asked after Callum made his entrance.

Callum motioned to the two officers on either side of him.

Andrew's eyes landed on his children and then on Seldom. "You know the truth," he said, and Seldom had felt caught, trapped, pinned down. Andrew knew he was asking her to choose sides in front of Callum, but she couldn't lie. She gave him a little nod.

"Well, then," he said. He stood and put on his suit jacket, straightening his cuffs before the butler supplied him with his fedora. And now it was Callum's turn to look at Seldom, his lips twisted in annoyance. She wrinkled her nose at him, displaying her own annoyance—with him, with Andrew, with men in general. His lips quirked into a smile, and he tossed her a little wink. She rolled her eyes, but she was smiling a little now too and they were okay, she thought. If not now, they would be after they had a chance to delve into it, after he realized he had the wrong man.

Now Seldom lay in her bed, staring at the ceiling, spent but unable to go to sleep. What if Callum never realized he had the wrong man? On

231

the other hand, what if he didn't have the wrong man? What if her odd loyalty to Andrew had blinded her to the fact that he had killed Kalina, had killed those other girls? When she looked at the facts, things looked bad. He had a house in Manhattan and one in Montauk, giving him access to both crime scenes. He'd had a personal relationship with Kalina, one of the dead women. Who were the other women and had he known them, too? He had a habit of disappearing and returning bruised and bloody. She knew he boxed, but what if that was part of his cover, a way to explain away the wounds caused by the women he attacked?

Seldom tried to be detached, to view the evidence with a cool and clear mind, but it was impossible because her feelings kept getting in the way. Andrew drove her crazy. He was annoyingly pompous, a privileged jerk of the first order. But he wasn't a murderer. She had seen too many flashes of tenderness with the kids, moments of kindness with the staff to believe otherwise. He was many, many things, most of them bad, but murderer was not on the list.

For now all she could do was have faith that the truth would out. She believed Andrew was innocent, and she believed Callum was a good officer. Surely the two things would comingle into a positive outcome. And if not, Andrew's lawyer would surely be able to get him off. After all, he hadn't officially been arrested. This was merely the next step, a formal interview. Perhaps in the course of the interview, Callum would learn something that would either lead him in another direction or disqualify Andrew from the suspect list completely. Of course they would probably talk about the shoes, the expensive ones Andrew had made for Kalina. And they would talk about the bruises. Andrew still had a faintly purple eye and swollen nose. And they would talk about Andrew's home in Montauk, his proximity to both murder scenes, his strange midnight disappearances.

Seldom flung an arm over her eyes. Without the benefit of a gut feeling that he was innocent, Andrew's prospects looked horrible. No two ways about it, he looked guilty. The only thing that would get him off at this point would be another murder while he was in custody, proof positive it couldn't have been him. Seldom couldn't hope for that, however. She wouldn't wish death and dismemberment on another woman for the sake of proving her boss's innocence.

That was her last coherent thought before she drifted to sleep, and her first one when she was jolted awake by a rough hand covering her mouth.

35

If Seldom thought things were tense at the house, she would have revised her opinion once she was in the car with only Callum and Andrew as passengers. *That* was tense, so tense that, if they were facing each other, it was likely one of them would have taken a swing at the other.

"Some girl, Seldom," Andrew said, throwing down the gauntlet. He reached in his inside pocket and paused. "Mind if I smoke?"

"Yes."

"Why?"

"I've recently given it up," Callum said.

Andrew snorted a laugh. "I can only imagine why."

Callum didn't reply.

"You know she thinks she's from the future," Andrew said mildly.

"She told you that?" Callum asked.

Andrew smiled, enjoying his displeasure. "We're close, Seldom and I." He glanced over to see how this was received. Callum's face was impassive, but on the steering wheel, his knuckles were white. Andrew's smile deepened. "Doesn't it concern you over her mental state?"

"No," Callum said.

"Why not? A straight-edged copper like you, you'd think you'd be a little more worried about taking up with someone who's bonkers."

"No more worried than a high-profile stockbroker like you," Callum countered.

"Ah, but there's the rub. Seldom's not my girl; she's yours."

"Glad to hear you say so," Callum said.

"Were you worried?

Callum didn't answer.

"Because clearly Seldom and I have a certain, ah, bond."

"Maybe she'll visit you in Sing Sing," Callum said, tossing him a wicked grin of his own.

Andrew clucked his tongue. "And she thinks you're so sweet. Where did she come from, really?"

Callum didn't answer.

"Interesting."

"How is silence interesting?" Callum wondered.

"Because it almost seems like you believe her."

"What's your explanation for her? Have you ever encountered any-one else like her?"

"No, there's only one Seldom," Andrew said softly. "But what she's saying, it's not possible. It's more likely she escaped from some institu-tion somewhere."

"If you really believed that, would you trust her with your children?"

Andrew shrugged one shoulder. "Good help is hard to find these days."

"Unless you try Poland," Callum said, shooting him another look.

Andrew whistled. "Was that part of the interview or merely a low blow?"

"A statement of fact. I don't get you, Pierce. You have all the money in the world, and you hire an illegal."

"It was the war," Andrew said, rubbing his face tiredly. "Nothing was as it should have been."

"You can say that again," Callum agreed softly.

"Why should you complain? You got to play the hero," Andrew said with thinly veiled bitterness.

They reached a stoplight and faced each other, heads tilted as they made their inspection. For the first time, each of them was on the edge of grasping that they had both been shaped by the war, in vastly different ways. Then the light changed and the thoughts skittered away before either of them could latch onto anything definite. All that was left was a vague feeling of unease, as if their preconceived notions of each other had been upended, leaving uncertainty in the wake.

They reached the station. Andrew was led to an interview room and offered coffee and water. Usually suspects were made to wait a while, to make them sweat and squirm and stew. But Andrew wasn't the type to do any of those things. Callum sat across from him, tossing his pen and legal pad onto the oak desk between them.

"I suppose it goes without saying that your forthright cooperation in this matter would be much appreciated, Mr. Pierce."

"May as well call me Andrew. Seldom does."

"Seldom is not going to be part of this interview," Callum said.

"How can she not be? She's part of everything else," Andrew said.

"How so?"

"Seldom was the one who found the body in Montauk. The one who confronted me about Kalina and her shoes. The one who spied on me, discovered me in the middle of a boxing match I'd preferred to have kept quiet."

It took all of Callum's training to keep his face impassive. Seldom hadn't mentioned that she'd confronted Andrew, that she'd spied on him, that she knew about the boxing. He felt like she was living an entire other life, keeping secrets, keeping vital things from him. *Was* there something between her and Andrew? Why else would she keep his secrets? *Why do you keep yours,* a little voice asked, but he pushed it away. It was totally different. He kept things from Seldom because he didn't want to burden her. The same couldn't be true in reverse because he was strong enough to handle whatever she dished out.

Andrew must have taken his silence as encouragement because he continued. "I'm honestly surprised you haven't confronted me before now."

"Why?"

"After what happened at the party."

Callum shouldn't ask, he knew that. Clearly Andrew Pierce was trying to throw him off kilter, to get the upper hand. But he knew something happened at the party to upset Seldom, and she hadn't told him about it. "What happened at the party?"

"Seldom entered the main house and went upstairs to soothe Daisy. I was keeping an eye out for her return when I noticed the party's host, Giles Montgomery, slip away. I went upstairs and saw him on Seldom, saw him groping her like an animal."

Beneath the table, Callum's hands balled. He forced himself to swallow past a lump of bile. "And what did you do?"

Andrew laughed a little. "Nothing, there was no need. Seldom took care of it herself, incapacitated him with her knee and bashed him good in the ears. Did you teach her that?"

"No, I'm guessing life taught her that." He felt sick, thinking of Seldom in that position, remembering the way she'd trembled and cried in his embrace at the beach. He thought it was in reaction to finding the dead girl. But now... He wished he could go back, could keep her in his arms and carry her home and continue to hold her for as long as it took to forget. Not just Giles Montgomery, but all the people who'd hurt her and done her wrong.

With effort, he took a deep breath and pulled himself back to his job. Later he would find Seldom, would force her out of Pierce's world by any means necessary, even if it meant bringing Daisy and Mathew home with her for the time being. For now, he had a job to do.

"You seemed to have prescient knowledge of what Giles Montgomery intended. Had you ever seen him do that to someone else?"

Now it was Andrew's turn to go silent and look away. "Kalina," he said, a choked whisper.

"Did she fight back the way Seldom did?"

He shook his head. "She was just standing there. At the time, I took that as acquiescence. Not until I saw it happen to Seldom did I understand it was merely shock."

"How did you know it wasn't acceptance on her part?" Callum asked.

"Because they were wearing the same expression. I didn't realize until I saw it on Seldom."

"What was the expression?"

"Terror, horror, revulsion. When I saw it on Kalina, I thought it was guilt because she'd been caught cheating on me with Giles." He blew out a breath. "I wasn't in the best place." He tapped his head. "My wife had died only a few months previous. The children were small, the war was going."

"What happened? With Kalina, I mean." He knew what state Seldom had been in after. He forced the mental image away and made himself focus on Andrew.

"I sent her away. I said some things, harsh, horrible things about her being for sale to the highest bidder, about her being cheap and worthless. She went to bed crying. The next morning she was gone."

"Did you try to find her?"

"No."

"Why not?"

"The ending was fairly definitive, O'Rourke. If you'd ever had a bad breakup with a girl, I think you'd understand."

"Four years after her disappearance, her body was located at a construction sight that got shut down because of the war. Judging by the condition of the body, it's estimated she was killed as soon as she went missing."

Andrew blanched. "I didn't know that. I thought..."

"What did you think?" Callum prompted. He leaned back, pressing the blunt tip of the pen under his chin.

"I thought she ran away, back to the docks, back to where she came from. And then somehow she crossed paths with the killer more recently, when she was discovered. It never occurred to me she didn't make it home." He reached into his pocket, took a cigarette, and twirled it absently between his fingers. His upper lip was sweating, as was his forehead. He did nothing to dab them, instead allowing the sweat to drip into his eyes, causing them to water and burn. At least he told himself it was sweat.

"Let's say for a moment I believe you. You had a horrible blowup with the woman, thought she went back home, and put her out of your mind. Knowing what you know now, what do you think happened to her? Who do you think killed her?"

Now he did remove his handkerchief and dab his face, pressing it to his eyes a moment before he cleared his throat and answered. "I don't know. She knew everyone I knew."

"Did she have trouble with anyone else?"

"There was some kerfuffle with Mable and Boots, but I never heard what it was. Kalina was brusque and blunt. None of the other staff liked her, thought she was inappropriate." He smiled a bit. "Turns out I have a type."

Callum knocked on the table between them. "Focus."

"I don't know what you want me to say here, O'Rourke. It could have been anyone. We attended parties and functions with all the same people we still do, and they're all the same people who go to Montauk. It could be anyone, a couple of hundred staff members, give or take."

"What makes you so sure it's someone in the servant class?"

Andrew gave him a look. "Be serious. How could it be anyone else?"

"I thought you were blowing smoke the day you said that, but you really mean it, don't you? That it must be someone lower born?"

"Yes," Andrew said with complete conviction.

"Why?"

"Because someone of my standing has too much to lose. The risk would never be worth the reward."

"You're speaking as if it's the act of a rational man," Callum said. "You can't conflate the sane with the insane. I'm poor, but I would never kill someone. It's not about where someone comes from; it's about what they do with it."

Andrew rolled his eyes. "Now you sound like Seldom."

"I'll take that as the compliment it should be," Callum said. He ran a weary hand over his face. As much as he hated to admit it, he believed Andrew Pierce. His shock when he learned Kalina was murdered four years ago was too real, as were the tears he hastily tried to hide. Seldom might never let him live this down, not to mention that he was back to square one with zero suspects. On the other hand, there was one other person who had reason to harm Kalina that night.

"Tell me more about Giles Montgomery," he directed, reaching for his pen and paper again.

36

It was amazing how rapidly one could go from dead asleep to dead awake. When one hand pressed on Seldom's mouth and another on her windpipe, she thought soon she might be merely dead. But then the voice spoke, a croaky whisper near her ear.

"Make a noise, and I'll slit Daisy's throat. Come along willingly and she'll be safe."

She sat up, put her feet on the floor, and reached for her shoes.

"Leave them," the voice whispered. She could only see a dim outline, but she could smell him and the overwhelming smell of fear sweat made her stomach churn.

"I'm not going barefoot," she said.

There was an annoyed exhale then, "Fine."

She slid into her shoes and stood, wishing for more than her thin cotton nightgown. He took one of her arms and began frog marching her toward the hallway. As soon as they reached the dim lights there, her captor was revealed.

"Boots," she breathed.

He didn't react, didn't turn her way or flinch at his name. Seldom stopped short, ready to protest, ready to fight. He used what was in his hand to tap softly on Daisy's door. The sound of the knife plinking on the door was too soft to wake the sleeping girl, but it was enough to make Seldom's feet move again, a reminder of his promise, a promise she had no doubt he'd make good on. She welded her lips together and pressed on, stumbling as Boots tugged her toward the stairs.

She held onto the hope that someone might peek out of a doorway, go to the kitchen for a glass of water. But, no. No one stirred. Boots kept hold of her arm as he herded her to his car, tucked a block away on a side street. She studied him as the car roared to life and he eased onto the street.

"I don't suppose it would do any good to ask where we're going or why you've taken me," Seldom said.

Boots gave a longsuffering sigh. "A mix of reasons."

"Because I was asking about Kalina?"

"That's one of them," he said.

"So you were involved with her."

He snickered. "Are you nuts? Mable would have my hide."

Seldom sat back frowning in confusion. "That day on the subway. You pushed me?"

He nodded.

"But then you pulled me back again. Why?"

He gave another sigh. "What can I say, Seldom? You conflict me."

"So, what, now you've decided to kill me for real?"

"Kill you? I'm not going to kill you. I'd never be able to look Mable in the eye again. She likes you. That's why I couldn't do it the first time when I was supposed to. No, I'm just the delivery mechanism." The car came to an abrupt halt. Seldom looked around and realized they were at his house, at Mable's house, at Giles' Montgomery's house. The fear that had so far been absent made a crashing arrival, flooding her body with a surge of adrenaline. *Run*, it told her. But too late. Boots was already opening the door and hauling her out.

"If you couldn't kill me, I have serious doubts that you'd kill Daisy," Seldom said.

Boots's cool gaze settled on her with a chilling little smile. "I didn't say I couldn't kill you; I said I didn't want to. As for the kid, she's just a kid. They don't feel things the way adults do."

"What? That's..." her outraged exclamation was stifled by his hand over her mouth.

"Enough, Seldom. We're going to be very quiet walking through the house. Not a peep, right? Because right now I'm in a good mood. Take my word that you don't want to see me angry."

She nodded her agreement and he dropped his hand, using it instead to grab her arm and urge her forward. To her further surprise, he opened the front door of the house and led her through a long hallway toward a door the back of the house. She had assumed that like her, Mable had a room near the children, but then a door off the main hallway started to open. Boots gave Seldom a hard shove, sending her flying into the wall. He had time to toss her one warning glance before Mable opened her door all the way.

"Boots," she said in sleepy surprise. "I thought I heard a noise."

"Sorry, Baby, that was me. Mr. Montgomery sent me out for some seltzer water to calm his stomach." His body was lodged firmly in her doorway, blocking her line of vision. Seldom hugged the wall, contemplating her options. Boots wouldn't hurt Mable, of that she was certain. But Mable wasn't her concern at the moment. Daisy was. She would never forgive herself if the little girl was harmed because of her, and she didn't doubt Boots would keep his word and make good on his promise. There was a sort of calculating viciousness in him she hadn't recognized before, a certain street sense that espoused an eye for an eye retribution.

"Oh," Mable said. Was it Seldom's imagination that she still sounded suspicious? Maybe she thought Boots was cheating on her. Slowly, careful not to draw any undue attention to herself, she slipped out of her shoes and, using her foot, eased them up against the wall outside Mable's door. Maybe it wouldn't do any good. Maybe by the time Mable found them it would be too late. Or, worst of all, maybe when she found them, she wouldn't care enough to do anything about them. Remembering how deferential Mable had been to Giles almost made her put the shoes back on. But for the moment it was the only hope she had. Mable would recognize her shoes. In this time period, they were one of a kind. What she did with the knowledge would be up to her.

Boots kissed Mable goodbye and closed the door, practically shoving her inside it. If it were Seldom, alarm bells would be blaring over his behavior, but maybe it was normal for him. Maybe Mable wouldn't think anything of it.

They resumed their march down the long hallway. The plush rug runner was soft and lush under Seldom's bare feet, sharp contrast to the cold panic now pervading every pore of her body. They stopped outside a door. Boots opened it. Seldom saw only darkness inside, a deep, foreboding chasm that sent a shudder through her. Whatever happened, she did not want to go in there. Boot's knuckle ground into her back, alerting her to the fact that she had no choice. She took a step forward, swallowing down a wave of panic that threatened to choke her.

Keep your wits. Stay with it. Use what you have. Fight, fight, fight.

A set of stairs loomed before her, a dim light at the end of the dark stair tunnel. Seldom put her hand out and grabbed the bar, but part of her was tempted to fling herself down them. They wouldn't be able to hurt her if she was already hurt, would they? The rational part of her brain quickly pointed out all the flaws in that logic—that she might break her neck and die, that she might incapacitate herself, putting herself further into their reach, that she might hurt herself horribly and they wouldn't care, would carry on with their plan regardless. She gripped the bar tighter as if to save herself from the temptation of falling on purpose.

The stairs, unlike the carpet above, were rough and dusty on her tender feet. She was glad for that bit of roughness. It gave her a focus and an outlet. At this point, she was willing to latch on to anything as a reprieve from the encroaching terror. She remembered how it had been with Christian, how much he seemed to thrive on her fear. *Not this time.* Whatever was at the end of those stairs, she wouldn't let her fear show, wouldn't give them the satisfaction.

When she reached the bottom of the stairs and saw Giles Montgomery waiting for her, she faltered, almost gave in and revised her opinion on the fear. His face wore an expression of what was probably supposed to be a smile, but was instead a kind of taut grimace, far more terrifying than his usual condescending sneer.

"Ah, Seldom," he said softly, pleasantly, as if she'd popped in for an unexpected visit. Boots took Seldom's arm, handed it to his boss, and took a step back.

"Need anything else from me, Boss?"

"Not at the moment, no. Thank you, Boots. Afterwards I'll require your services again, of course," he said, giving him a nod. Seldom couldn't stop herself from turning to watch Boots ascend back up the stairs. Would he notice her shoes outside Mable's room and take them? She hoped not. Even though he was the one who'd brought her here, she experienced a pang at watching him go. After all, the evil you know is always better than the evil you don't.

Speaking of evil, she thought, turning to face Giles Montgomery once more. "Handy system you two have," she said, striding to keep her tone even.

"Isn't it, though?" Giles asked, showing his teeth this time when he smiled. His canines flashed and Seldom was reminded of a hyena. He might be smiling but, like a hyena, he was lethal.

For the first time she looked around the basement and took in her surroundings. There was a surgical table set up, much like a field hospital in a war zone. There was a tray of instruments. And like a war zone, they were spotted with blood and tissue. Giles was watching her watch the room. For that reason, she pushed back her revulsion and kept her expression neutral. "What do you do if your wife or kids come down here?"

"They don't," he said happily. "They're very obedient, my family."

The way he stressed the word "obedient" made it clear it was of great value to him. "Are you sure? Because if my husband told me not to poke my nose somewhere, it would be the first place I poked."

"Aren't I lucky that Jillian doesn't have your," he paused and let his eyes roam over her, "temperament."

"Is that what this is?" She motioned to the room. "Retribution for some girl who hurt you? What did your mommy do to you, Giles? Lock you in the attic and beat you with wire hangers?"

"Ha," he said, actually said the word "ha" instead of laughing it. "How delightfully absurd you are. No, my mother was as dull and sullen as my wife, caring only about parties and our standing in the community." He sighed. "I'm afraid I've always had to look elsewhere for entertainment."

"Come on, someone had to have warped you. No one becomes a full on psycho for the fun of it. Was it your dad?" His eyes remained amused, impassive. "A former nanny?" The eyes narrowed slightly. Seldom laughed. "That's it, isn't it? You had a crazy nanny, some Victorian throwback who drowned you in castor oil and scrubbed your back with eggshells or something, and now you're taking retribution on all the nannies of the world." She spread her arms, encompassing the macabre workroom around them.

"No one did anything to me. I am my own man. I always have been."

"You didn't go to the war, did you?" She had the feeling that if it was a tender spot for Andrew, it would be a tender spot for Giles as well. Whereas with Andrew the sensitivity made her want to hug and reassure him, with Giles, it made her want to poke at it. "While everyone else was off fighting for freedom, proving their worth, you were here, piddling with girls, overpowering them, making them afraid. You're no better than that kid who tears the wings off of flies."

His face was mutinous and mottled red. He backhanded her hard across the cheek. Tears leapt to her eyes. She pushed them back in again and forced a laugh. "You're, what, six inches taller than me? Outweigh me by at least seventy pounds? Big man, Giles. Big, big man."

Enraged now, he grabbed her wrist and gave it a hard yank, dragging her to the table. *What now?* Seldom thought. She'd clearly gotten a reaction from him, but what was the point of that if it only accelerated his timeline? "Did all the other women reject you, too? Kalina and the others?"

"Don't speak her name," Giles hissed. He tossed her toward the table, shoved her down and began manacling her wrists.

"Kalina, Kalina, Kalina," she said, and he slapped her again.

She was making it worse, but she couldn't seem to stop herself. After being petrified with fear by Christian, she felt the almost obsessive need not to give Giles the same sort of power over her. When his hands shook slightly while tightening the straps on her wrists, she felt she was succeeding, at least in part. He would likely kill her; it didn't have to be easy for him.

"Poor Giles, unfit for the war, unable to get a woman on his own merit. I bet Jillian had to be made to marry you, too. How much money changed hands for that pairing? You guys have separate bedrooms, don't you? I bet she locks her door at night. I know I would."

He turned his back on her and began noisily arranging instruments.

"You're so textbook," Seldom continued. "Weak, puny, emasculated. The only way you can gain an ounce of control, to make yourself feel good, is by literally tying a woman up and making her suffer. Wow. Stereotype much, Giles?"

He put a mask over her face, the kind used to deliver ether. Seldom tried not to let her relief show. *Bring it,* she thought, desperately glad for the chance to escape into unconsciousness. But there was no comforting hiss of gas. Giles' leering face leaned closer.

"Oh, you thought I was going to knock you out? Cute. This mask doesn't deliver relief; it merely catches your screams. Can't have you waking the household." He tapped the mask that now felt as if it was suffocating her. Seldom forced herself not to gasp or struggle, to take low and deep breaths of what was likely recycled air. Maybe the lack of oxygen would make her pass out long before he had his fun.

Giles held up a wicked looking scalpel. "I usually do this at the end, but your impassioned little speech has changed me, Seldom. I've seen the light. I'm going to change up my whole routine." He thumped his hand over his heart. By his sarcastic tone, she knew he was lying. He might change the order he did things, but everything else would be the same. When he began dragging heavy buckets to the table, she knew they were to catch her blood, the blood he was going to leech from her body before or after he cut off her hands. Which would come first, the leeching or the amputation?

He picked up her wrist and made a show of inspecting it before touching his lips gently to the tender inside. *That* was what made Seldom shudder and try to draw away. Right now the looming threat of pain was much easier to grasp than the lover like ministrations he was performing.

"You don't like that?" Giles asked, now giddy with delight at her discomfort. He stuck out his tongue and licked her arm, from elbow to wrist, watching closely for any reaction. Seldom forced her eyes to be still, not to react. Behind the mask, she stuck out her tongue. And for some reason, that made her giggle.

Giles did not like the giggle. His smile fled. He dropped her arm, set down the scalpel, and reached for something resembling a machete. *It would have to be big to chop through bone, wouldn't it?* Seldom mused, trying to school her features again. She wanted to scream. More than that, she wanted to deprive Giles of any pleasure, so she kept her mouth firmly closed, withdrawing her tongue and settling her lips into a grim press of expectancy. *Let's do it,* she thought. Giles picked up her hand and positioned it on the table. He raised the weapon high like an axe. Seldom didn't want to watch, but it was as if her body refused to cooperate. She stared in horrified fascination as the arc of the knife swept toward her wrist and then, before it could touch her, away and across the room. Giles went with it, tossed like a rag doll against the far wall.

"Hiya, kid. We've got to stop meeting like this."

37

Callum loomed over her, a tentative half smile on his face.

"Callum?" she tried to say, but the mask was still choking her. He reached out and plucked it off her face. She sucked air greedily a few beats while he worked on unfastening her wrists. Across the room, Giles had been subdued by two officers, the same two officers who had come to Andrew's house only a few hours ago. Callum finished unbuckling her wrists and leaned over her again.

"Your face," he whispered, reaching out to brush soft fingers on her cheeks.

"It's fine," she said, though it wasn't exactly true. Her cheek was starting to swell. Her nose and eyes stung. But compared to what it might have been, what it might now be, it was nothing. "What are you doing here?"

"Got a call from Mable at the precinct. Sharp girl, Mable. Said probably it was nothing, but she found your shoes outside her door. And sharp girl, you, for thinking of it. My girl." He leaned in and kissed her cheek tenderly. She slid her arms around him and clung for just a second, still not wanting to give too much away in front of Giles who was doubtless watching.

He let her go and helped her sit up. Giles was in handcuffs now, watching them with a snarling sneer. "How touching," he said, trying hard to regain some of his former frosty superiority.

"How textbook," she said, forcing boredom into her tone and expression.

"Man, you are some kind of stupid," Callum said, adding insult to injury as he looked around the basement. "What kind of dummy has his death studio in his own house? With your money, you could have set up someplace we'd never find. And you do it *here*." He shook his head as if to say, *rich people are crazy*, which was probably what he was thinking. He was holding Seldom's hand, she realized. Their fingers were laced together and his thumb was making soothing passes over hers. She squeezed his hand, ridiculously glad for his solid and reassuring presence. If not for her, he would likely be working the room, gathering evidence, making notes. For now he was here, hovering protectively by her side, offering quiet care and comfort He squeezed back and then eased his arm around her.

"Ready to go upstairs, babydoll?"

She nodded. He kept his arm around her, shepherding her toward the top of the stairs where Mable stood waiting, nervously wringing her hands.

"Oh," she said when she caught sight of Seldom. And then she flung herself at Seldom, weeping. "Oh, Seldom."

Seldom hugged her tightly. "It's okay, I'm okay."

"But Boots," Mable wailed.

It wasn't ideal to comfort someone over the fact that her boyfriend turned out to be the paid assistant of a serial killer, but friendship duty called. And Mable *had* called Callum. She could have ignored the shoes, might even have taken the further step and hidden them. So Seldom rubbed her back and made soothing shushing noises until Mable had herself under some semblance of control.

"I saw her," Mable muttered, wiping her eyes with the handkerchief Callum proffered.

"Who?" Seldom asked, easing her away so she could hear her better.

"Kalina. That night, all those years ago, the night she disappeared. I saw her in the hallway. I thought...I thought she and Boots. But then I realized he wouldn't do that, so I thought she and Mr. Montgomery.

And I hated her for it. But it turns out they brought her here to...to..." Her glance darted toward the basement and she dissolved into tears all over again. "To think I might have stopped it, have stopped him, *them*." Now she began to wail as everything mixed together, guilt, recrimination, horror, fear.

"Mable, you couldn't know. No one would think that about their boss," Seldom said, tossing Callum a look over Mable's head. *Though some of us are right*, her look said.

He rolled his eyes, but he was smiling. "You'll be glad to know he's back home, though how glad is still a question I'd like to have answered."

Now it was her turn to roll her eyes. They led Mable to the kitchen where Callum began to question her gently, writing down answers on his trusty legal pad. The only girl she had any inkling of was Kalina, and then Seldom. Suspicious of Boots's odd behavior, she had stepped into the hallway after his retreat, only to stumble on Seldom's shoes.

"At first I thought you and Boots...but then I realized you wouldn't." She motioned to Callum as if his presence explained Seldom's inability to cheat with Boots. "So I realized it must be something else. And then I remembered what you said about Kalina being killed." She shuddered. "How could he, Seldom? How could he?"

Understanding a woman's heart, Seldom realized she was talking about Boots and not Giles. "Because Giles gave him a place, a job, a purpose. He went from a hapless street kid to a chauffer for one of the most powerful men in Manhattan. And he's loyal. And despite what he did, he really loves you, Mable. He told me so. He did a bad thing, a series of them, but he really loves you. Don't doubt that part."

"I'll be too busy doubting everything else," Mable said. She rubbed a weary hand over her face. "What am I going to tell the children?" Of course it would fall to her to tell them something. It wasn't like their mother would bother.

"You'll think of something, and you'll do it gently and lovingly because that's who you are," Seldom said, reaching out to rest her hand on Mable's forearm.

Mable nodded. "Yes," she agreed, drawing herself up slightly. "I'd best go check on them. If you're done with me here," she added to Callum.

He gave her a nod. She handed him his kerchief and nodded to them before turning to plod silently from the room. Seldom watched her go, sullen and worried.

"Seldom," Callum said softly. She turned to face him with a smile that soon faded at the intensity of his expression. "You scared me. I never drove so fast in my life, and then we reached that basement and saw you." He pressed his lips together and shook his head hard, trying to stop the words, to force everything back inside where he kept it.

"Callum," she said gently. She smoothed her thumb on his lips and leaned forward, pressing her lips to his. He kissed her in return, intently, almost roughly while his arms reached out and cinched her to his chest, melding her body to his. The kiss ended and they rested their foreheads together, breathing hard.

"I need to check on the children," she whispered.

He nodded. "Come home," he pled.

"I'll try," she said. She kissed his cheek and hugged his neck. He hugged her in return and then stood, took her hand, and drove her five blocks away to the Pierce mansion.

Andrew sat on the stairs when she entered, an unlit cigarette twirling between his fingers. At first sight of Seldom, he dashed to his feet and tossed the cigarette away.

"You're all right," he said, both a statement and a question.

She nodded.

"I was..." he broke off, looking away. "I was worried, Seldom."

She eased forward and hugged him, sliding her arms around his waist and resting her head on his chest. She wondered when he was last hugged, if he ever had been. His wife likely hadn't been a hugger, and neither had his mother. His arms slid around her tentatively and then tightened as he rested his head on hers.

"Are you really okay?" he whispered.

"I am," she said, she let him go and stepped away. "Try to get some sleep. We'll talk in the morning."

He touched his finger to her cheek. "I think that's supposed to be my line."

She smiled. "We should both sleep. Your children wake early."

"I'll take the first shift tomorrow. You try to sleep in."

"Thank you, I'll try," she said, though she knew it would be impossible. It was likely she might never sleep again, thanks to the nightmares Giles Montgomery would likely cause her for years to come.

But as soon as she made her nightly ablutions and crawled between the sheets, she was lost in a deep and dreamless sleep.

38

The next morning when Seldom went downstairs to the kitchen, Mrs. Walsh greeted her. "Himself's got thoose childrens in the dining room."

"Thank you, Mrs. Walsh." Seldom turned toward the dining room and paused. "Where are you from?"

Mrs. Walsh regarded her with narrowed eyes. "A little boot of ever'where. And where be ye from?"

"The same," Seldom said. They shared a smile and Seldom continued on her way.

"Seldom," Daisy exclaimed on sight of her, propelling herself into her arms. "Where were you this morning? Father said we weren't allowed to wake you." She allowed herself a little pout before tossing her father a look to see if he'd call her on it.

"I had a late night, and father was very kind to let me sleep in this morning," Seldom said, hugging her tightly for longer than necessary. What if Boots had hurt her? She kissed both of her cheeks before setting her down.

"Children, run along and play while Seldom and I have a chat," Andrew commanded. The kids turned and ran off without a protest. Seldom watched them go with a fond smile. She had no idea when she took the job how attached to them she would become. "How are you this morning?"

"I'm well," Seldom said, unfurling her napkin before placing it in her lap. "And you?"

He shrugged one shoulder. "A bit restive." There was something new in his look, something kind. "I suppose you'll go back to your copper now."

She gave a light nod. "I think it's time. And as a replacement, I'd like to suggest Mable. I don't know if she'll want to leave her current post, but if I were her, I would. She's wonderful with the children, loving but not too much. The kids already know and like her. I think it would be a good fit. I can talk to her, plead the case, if you like."

"I'd appreciate that, thank you. And what of you? What will you do?"

"I don't know," Seldom said. "If I'm going to stay here, I'm going to have to find a career, a real one."

There was a heavy pause before he spoke again. "We could try wife, if you like." Seldom glanced up sharply. Andrew stared at her with his usual wry amusement. Behind it there was something else, something almost vulnerable. Seldom was having one of those moments where she had a foot in either world, now and in the future as it could play out. She could picture it, the two of them together. They wouldn't pull their punches with each other. Maybe in time their foundering friendship would give way to love. There was a certain undeniable attraction there. But someday that attraction would likely burn itself out, would give way to resentment on both their parts, him because she could never be of the manor-born set, her because he could never love her with the wholeheartedness she craved. Even if there was no Callum, Seldom thought it unlikely there could ever be an Andrew for her. If she had been born out of time, so had he. He would do better in 2020 when he could indulge his innate self-centeredness and entitlement. She could picture him at Coachella or cruising on a yacht in the south of France, partying with the Jenners and Biebers of the world. It was his bad luck that he'd been born in a decade when selfless commitment to duty was the fashion.

"That's a wonderful offer, but I'm convinced we'd kill each other, probably sooner rather than later."

"Yes, but think of what a fun death," he said, his gaze falling to her lips.

"Where I'm from..."

"....Canada?" he interrupted sarcastically.

"Shh, Andrew, we're having a moment here. Where I'm from, men and women can be friends."

"Ah, so not from Earth, then. I suspected as much," he said.

"Take it or leave it, Andrew, the offer's on the table," she said.

"It would seem I have no choice, seeing as how my children can't seem to live without you."

Giving up on the bounds of social propriety altogether, she stood and erased the space between them, pressing her palms to his cheeks. "There's good in you, no matter how hard you might try to snuff it out, you big phony. Don't give up on it. Your kids adore you, and they need you. Continue to be the hero they deserve." She kissed his forehead and dropped her hands.

He reached up and brushed at her hair, pushing it away from her face as he studied her. "You're quite odd, improper in a way that should be off-putting. By all rights I should loathe you. But I don't." Slowly, tentatively, he eased forward and kissed her cheek, pausing to linger a few beats before pulling away.

Seldom resumed her seat and put her napkin once again in her lap.

Andrew observed her in silence a minute before he spoke again. "Before you go, you should know I've been garnishing your wages."

"Why?"

"I've made some investments on your behalf. You've done quite well for yourself, for a witch."

She blinked at him, lashes fluttering rapidly as she thought. "Can I bequeath the stocks to someone?"

"Are you actively planning your death?" he asked.

"Death or disappearance, it never hurts to be prepared," she said.

"Yes, you can do that. I take it you want me to add your officer's name as beneficiary."

She shook her head. "Not him. His mother." Callum didn't need her money, and he wouldn't want it. Mrs. O'Rourke, on the other hand, would do marvelous things with a heavy dose of financial independence.

"Very well." He observed her eating for a few more minutes before he spoke again. "What does being friends with a woman entail exactly?"

"We could meet for lunch or dinner sometime, with or without the kids," she suggested.

"Would your copper be okay with that?"

She smiled. "That's the beauty of having an independent spirit. It doesn't much matter."

"Very well," he repeated, sounding more satisfied this time.

"Of course there's always the possibility that I won't be here much longer," she added.

"And where will you go?"

"Back to where I came from." She held up a finger. "Don't say Canada."

"The future?" he said, one eyebrow held aloft to convey maximum sarcasm.

"Yes." She held his gaze unblinking. He was the first to do so, blinking rapidly as he assessed her.

"Huh."

She had the feeling that, while he didn't quite believe her, he didn't *not* believe her, either. Much like Callum, he seemed to be aiming for some sort of middle ground his mind could accept.

"At the very least, you're never dull, Seldom," he mused.

"I aim to please," she said.

"If that were true, this conversation would have had an entirely different outcome," he said, tipping his cup to her.

Laughing, she raised hers and tapped it to his before taking a sip. "Cheers, Andrew."

"Cheers, Seldom." He poured another coffee and she finished her meal in pleasant, companionable silence.

39

Mrs. O'Rourke fussed over her. It had been so long since Seldom had a mother figure do that—never, in fact—that she indulged in hearty enjoyment, receiving as many hugs and exclamations of delight over Seldom's safe reappearance as the woman could dole, which turned out to be a lot.

"Our poor girl," Mrs. O'Rourke said for possibly the eighteenth time as she stood beside Seldom and petted her hair.

"I'm okay, Mrs. O'Rourke," Seldom assured her with a smile, secretly indulging in the loving affection.

"Ma, please," Callum snapped. "You're hogging her." Then he bundled Seldom up and pulled her into his lap, snuggling her close, not seeming to care that his mother was standing nearby smiling in what Seldom could only hope was approval.

For the first couple of days, it was heavenly. And then the old familiar restlessness began to set in. What was she going to *do*? Neither Callum nor Mrs. O'Rourke seemed to mind that she had no job and no life plan. Neither seemed to feel that her presence was an undue burden, that she was an interloper who sucked up all their resources. But from her earliest memories, Seldom had always felt like she had to earn her keep to earn people's love, beginning with her own parents and continuing through the present day. She'd never felt confident that she would be loved by virtue of being herself, but only because of what she brought to the table. At present she brought nothing to the table.

"That's not true. You help Ma with the dishes and the cleaning and the laundry and her mending," Callum pointed out.

"Yes, but she doesn't actually *need* my help. Your mother is a marvel with the energy of a toddler," Seldom said, almost sullenly. It wasn't Mrs. O'Rourke's fault that she was so ridiculously energetic and efficient as to render Seldom even more useless.

"Babydoll, you've got to relax," Callum said absently. The majority of his attention was taken up by a baseball game being broadcast on the radio.

If she was regressing into old habits, she wasn't alone. Callum, now that he had her secured back under his roof, was once again retreating into the shell he'd created for himself. Seldom had no doubts that he cared for her. He proved it in all the ways he took care of her, in the kind way he talked to her and asked about her day, her interests, her life. The problem, as she saw it, was his inability to reciprocate on those conversations. He told her glancing details but kept everything else bottled up inside. Worse, she could see him settling in for the long haul, could picture decades from now in this same house, in their same spots on the couch, his mother in the chair beside them.

Callum: *How was your day, doll?*

Seldom: *Good. How was yours?*

Callum: *Good. *reaches for the radio and turns it on**

That was how it would play out for all of eternity, until they bought a TV, and then he would watch instead of listen.

"Callum," she said one night as they sat at the table nursing cups of after supper coffee his mother had made for them.

"Yes?" Callum said, dunking his cookie in his coffee, a thing he did every night. It was kind of adorable, as were most things about him. She shook her head, working to keep her focus.

"We need to talk."

He froze in the universal way men had every time those words were uttered. "About what?"

"Us."

"Do we? I thought things were going fine." She watched his Adam's apple bob convulsively with panic and could practically hear what he was thinking. *Abort, abort, abort.* His eyes darted for escape. Finding none, they resettled pleadingly on Seldom.

"Things are going well," she assured him.

"Then why do we need to talk about them?" he asked.

"Because we do. Because you keep so much of yourself bottled away from me. That's no way to start a life, if that's what we're doing here." She wasn't sure. Sometimes it seemed like they were a foregone conclusion. Other times, like now, she wondered. If he cared about her, how could he feel this much panic over the thought of a conversation? Was he frightened of commitment? Of love? Of her? Not having an answer to the questions made them weightier. Even if she had some understanding of what she dealing with, she might know better how to approach it. With gentleness? By barging in and knocking down his barriers? She had no idea. The not knowing was making her crazy.

"Come on, Seldom. You know how it is between us."

"Do I? Because I think I do, but you've never said."

"Look, I'm no dummy. I know you were upset when you asked me if I'd go with you and I said I couldn't answer."

Something to Seldom's right caught her attention. She turned and saw her bakery, once again sparkling on the other side of the wall as if there were a glass divider instead of solid plaster. She returned her attention to Callum, trying to keep the pleading out of her expression. She had sworn never again to twist his arm or beg for his affection. *Now or never,* she silently tried to communicate.

"The thing is, I did that before. I said goodbye to my mom and sister and went across the ocean, convinced I'd never come back. The looks on their faces. I'm not sure I could do that to Ma again, Seldom, not even for you."

She reached out and clasped his hand. "I get that, Callum, I really do. It's not that you didn't say you'd come with me. It's that you've never once asked me to stay." She stood and cupped his face in her hands, much as she had done to Andrew. Except this time she kissed him, sweetly, lingeringly, sadly. "Goodbye, Callum O'Rourke. Have a good life. You deserve it."

"What," he began, but didn't get to finish before Seldom stood and walked toward the wall, toward home.

She stepped through the wall as if stepping through a doorway, but once she was inside the bakery, the light dimmed. It was barely dawn, the sky still a watery shade of gray. Someone unbolted the lock. Seldom turned expectantly to Josh, waiting for his shocked reaction.

"Hey, boss. What's up?"

She blinked at him. "Aren't you surprised to see me?"

He turned to make sure she was talking to him. "No, should I be? You're always here first. I used to believe you lived here, like some kind of flour fairy."

"Josh, didn't you miss me?"

He chuckled. "Of course I did, but it usually takes longer than nine hours before I curl into a ball and weep. What's up, Seldom?"

"What day is it?"

"Thursday."

"Thursday what?"

"Thursday, Ma'am?"

"Which Thursday?"

"June eighth."

"That can't be possible. I was there for almost three months." She put her hand to her head. Josh strode forward and gripped her biceps, peering intently into her face.

"You're starting to worry me here. Seriously, are you okay?"

She grasped his shirt for support and stared up into his face. "I had a date last night, right?"

"Yes. It was a bust and you texted me after." He pulled his phone from his pocket, swiped it, and showed her their correspondence.

"And that was really last night?"

He nodded and pressed his palm to her forehead. "Seldom, clue me in."

She swallowed hard and took a deep breath. "Flip the sign, Josh, we're taking the day off."

"Now I know something is wrong," he said, his tone turning from amused to worried. "Seldom, what is going on?"

"Call the police for me, he took my phone. I'll explain as best I can while we wait." Unable to support herself any longer, she sank to a heap in the middle of the floor, resting her head on her knees while Josh flipped the sign and dialed 911.

40

The police came, and they didn't believe her. Not that she told them the part about traveling through time; she wasn't insane. Or, at the very least, she wasn't willing to let anyone know she was insane. Maybe someday she'd tell Josh. For now he seemed to think the drugs Christian gave her had left her confused. The part he found most unbelievable was how she'd managed to get away. She had no good explanation for that one, either. How could she when she couldn't tell anyone about Callum?

"I don't know," she said for the tenth time to the detective taking her statement. She had taken him to the building where Christian had held her, still a warehouse as it was when she emerged in 1946. They had tracked down the owners, gone inside the building, and saw nothing suspicious. No handcuffs, no medical instruments, no evidence that Seldom had ever been there. Her phone was gone, but she used her laptop to try and pull up Christian's dating profile, but it was gone, too. Her ace in the hole was the emails they'd exchanged, but those were also gone, wiped from her computer as if they'd never existed.

"But I told Josh I had a date," she told the detective. Josh was with her, as he had been since he found her in the bakery a few hours previous.

"Did you ever see the guy?" the detective asked Josh.

"No," Josh drawled. "But Seldom doesn't lie. If she says the guy kidnapped her, then it happened." He laid a protective arm around her shoulder, giving it an encouraging squeeze.

"Uh-huh," the detective said, clearly not buying her story.

Seldom sighed. "Look, why would I lie about this?"

"You tell me."

"There is no reason," she said.

"Publicity?" he tried.

"This is not the kind of publicity I want, believe me. Why would I want anyone to look at me the way you're now looking at me?"

"How'd you get free?"

She pinched the bridge of her nose. "I don't...I can't explain it. Maybe he didn't make the cuffs tight, I don't know. But it was real. It was all so real." She was including her time traveling journey in that statement. It had been real, hadn't it? But if so, how did she explain the fact that she had gone back in time for nearly three months and only been gone a few hours?

"Uh-huh," the detective said.

"Please stop saying that," she pled.

"Look, girly, I believe you've had a hard time in one way or another. Get some rest, and give us a call if anything else turns up." He eyed Josh, giving him a heads up nod as if to say, *Can you take care of this crazy, insane person?*

Josh gave him a nod in return. *Yep, got it covered.*

Keeping his arm around Seldom, he took her home, made her a cup of tea, and tucked her into her bed. Then he lay down beside her and stretched out.

"You don't have to stay," she said.

"You want me to go?" he asked.

"No," she said.

"Well, then. Get some sleep, boss. I'm going to do the same. This might be our only day off for ages. Think of it like a vacation." He ended on a yawn. His blinks grew sleepy and he closed his eyes. A minute later he was out. Seldom studied him, thinking he reminded her of someone. At last she realized it was Mathew. They both had that little boy way about them, all sweetness and innocence. Thoughts of Mathew sent a stabbing pain through her midsection. She missed her babies. And Andrew. And Mable. And Mrs. O'Rourke. And *him.* Scooting closer to Josh to try and siphon any comfort he might provide, she finally fell asleep.

When she woke, Josh was still there. They ordered takeout and watched a movie while they ate. "You should go," she said.

"Is that really what you want?" he asked.

"No," she answered honestly and they watched another movie.

Josh stayed that night and the next and *then* she was ready to face life alone. She threw herself into work with renewed vigor, working increasingly longer hours, hoping to get back to normal again. She had settled back into her life as if she'd never left it—mostly because apparently she hadn't. But inside everything was different.

For one thing she felt a near-crippling dependence on Josh she didn't understand. Always before Seldom had been the grownup in charge. Josh was only twenty one, still a baby. She was his boss, in charge in every way that mattered. But now she found herself hovering in his periphery, trying to soak up whatever he offered. Lucky for her, he offered a lot. He was a hugger, an affectionate sweetheart who never crossed the line into inappropriate or creepy. He seemed ready and able to provide whatever Seldom needed. At the moment, she needed a lot.

Work also didn't hold the same charm. Not so long ago it had been her life, her all-consuming passion, her ever waking thought. And now it was just...work. She longed for a purpose and a passion outside her job, but nothing came to mind. So she kept working, kept trudging along, hoping something would magically click, that somehow life would return to the way it once was. Or, at the very least, a new path would present itself.

Two weeks after her return, a bike messenger entered the bakery and handed Seldom an envelope. She signed for it and gave him a cupcake for his trouble. He didn't look like the type of person who indulged in cupcakes, but that was merely proof he needed one.

She tore open the cardboard package. A letter fell out, her name spelled in shaky scrawl along the front. Abandoning her post in favor of curiosity, she eased into the back room and started to read.

Heya, Dollface. (That's a throwback. I haven't called anyone that since you left.)

Turns out you were wrong. I never found anyone I liked better than you. I've been a confirmed bachelor all these years, and I blame you for all the rumors that's caused.

But it also turns out you were right. About a lot. The sixties were rough for an old cop like me. (You could have warned me about JFK. I met him twice and shook his hand; that one still hurts.)

Turns out you were right about forgiveness. It's easier for an old man with a lot of years to admit these things. Eventually I let go and learned to forgive the Italians, the Germans, and even the Japanese. (You were right about the technology, too. Never thought I would have bought that VCR in the eighties, but the darn thing still works to this day. It's practically unbreakable.)

You were right that it helps to talk about things. That one took me a long time to figure out. I saw a lot in the war, Seldom. It left scars, some too big and too deep to give a name to. But I wish I had tried. Maybe then I could have told you that I loved you, that I loved you from the moment I saw you and never stopped all these years later. Maybe then I would have begged you to stay. Maybe we would have had a life together and children. At least I should have tried. I'm sorry I didn't. And you were right when you said maybe we were meant for each other, that we shared a special connection. I never found it with anyone else, not even close. I hope you do because a good woman is a terrible thing to waste. I should know—I did it with you.

You were right that they eventually tore down my house. When the developer came calling, his offer was too sweet to pass up. I took the money with a thought of going to Florida, but in the end I couldn't leave New York. Now all that money sits in an account, gathering dust. So I'm giving it to you, with instructions to be delivered on a date when I know you'll be there.

Make a good life with it, sweetness; live, love, have joy. Because I was right, too. What's the use in having a life if not to make it worthwhile?

Always Yours, Callum.

Seldom was surprised she could see the check through her tears, but there it was, made out to her in the amount of seven hundred thousand dollars. She held it in one hand, the letter in the other. And that was how Josh found her when he finally went to the back to check on her.

"Seldom?" He was using the new tone, the tender one that now made it seem as if he was the grownup in their friendship. "Are you okay?"

She shook her head. "I think I've made a terrible mistake, Joshy."

He pulled her into a hug. She rested her head on his chest and had a good cry. "Want me to make you a cup of tea?" he asked, smoothing his hand up and down her back.

She laughed and eased away. "You think tea cures everything."

"It's because I'm British," he said.

"Yes, you are," she said, reaching up to pinch his cheek. He was adorable, and it wasn't bias that made her think so. He had developed quite a following among a group of young girls who came in ostensibly for cupcakes but actually for him. "Don't you miss your family, Josh? You never talk about them."

"You're my family," he said simply. She had no tea kettle at the bakery, so he microwaved water for her tea, reaching for a bag from his private stash.

"True, but you're so far away from everyone else, and you're so young. It pains me."

He smiled vaguely as he dunked her tea. "I'm not so far from home. Half my family is from here. My grandmother was American."

"I didn't know that," she said.

He nodded. "This neighborhood, actually. In fact, I never told you this, but the reason I came into the bakery that first day was because this was her house. Not the bakery, I mean. It used to be an old brownstone..."

"With red geraniums on the front stoop," Seldom whispered.

He laughed. "I don't know about that."

"What was her name?" Seldom said, gripping both his wrists in hers so that he winced.

"Rose Pevenzy, but her maiden name was..."

"O'Rourke," Seldom supplied.

Josh smiled. "That's right. How did you know? Did you do research on this property?"

She nodded and swallowed hard. "Do you know anything about her brother, Callum?"

"A lot, actually. I'm named after him."

Her blinks were coming fast and furious. "Callum J. O'Rourke. Joshua."

He nodded. "Obviously you've heard of him."

She nodded. "Tell me what you know, please. Is he...is he still alive?"

He laughed lightly. "No, he'd be a hundred. He lived to be ninety something. I never met him, but I wish I had, being that he was famous and all. Well, sort of."

"He...he was famous?"

"Well, yeah, didn't that come up in your research?"

She shook her head.

"He was the commissioner, of course."

Her smile was ridiculously wide. "He made commissioner?"

"Yes, for a record fifteen years. And then there was that whole thing with 9-11."

She gripped him harder. "What thing?" *Please don't say he died in the towers.* So many people had died that day. Somehow she couldn't stand it if Callum was one of them.

"He was 81 when it happened, but he put on a uniform and went to work, searching the rubble, standing at attention when they pulled out any of the officers. It was a big story, made the papers. I heard they're thinking of doing a movie about it. In fact it was why I wanted to come to America." He blushed faintly, whether with pride or at having been found to be secretly sentimental, she didn't know.

"That sounds about right," Seldom said softly. "You look like him, I see it now." She pressed her hands to his cheeks, beaming with affection.

"You're the weirdest boss a guy could ask for," Josh said, leaning in to kiss her on the forehead.

"I really love you, Josh, just so we're clear. You're the closest thing to family I've got here. I just wanted you to know, in case there was any doubt."

He pulled her into yet another hug, squeezing her tightly. "I love you, too, Seldom. And I already told you you're family. You're like my, hmm, what? Too young to be my mum, too nice to be my sister."

"Aunt?" she tried.

"Yes, you're like my cool, young, favorite aunt."

"You're my very favorite nephew," she said, squeezing him in return. "And I'm giving you a bonus."

He laughed. "Why?"

"For all the reasons I just said. I want you to get a better apartment, somewhere closer, preferably without rats and roaches."

"Sounds too posh," he said.

"That's because you haven't seen how big your bonus is," she said, Callum's check still clutched in her hand. Josh was his rightful heir, his namesake and nephew. Seldom didn't feel right about keeping everything for herself.

"Okay," Josh agreed, laughing. His tone made it clear he thought she was still suffering some kind of mental break, but Seldom had never been more certain of her mental clarity. It had been real, all of it. Christian, Giles, Andrew, the children, and Callum. *Callum.* Her heart wrung thinking of him, holding his letter, remembering. At least she had this little piece of him to hold onto, this boy who was already so much a part of her life. She would be thankful for that, would be thankful for everything.

"You can go back out. I'm going to be okay now."

He let her go and peered into her face. "Will you really?"

She nodded and held up her right hand. "I solemnly swear."

"Good, because I'm worried about you."

"I'm going to be okay," she told him, and she meant it. Today was the first day of the rest of her life. She planned to make the best of it for all the days she had left.

41

Things did get better for Seldom after that, and not just because she had a lot of money. The painful tightness in her chest eased, a direct result of Callum's letter. He had lived a good life. He had done it without her, but he had done it. And he was real, so very real that when she Googled him, she received dozens of hits along with a series of pictures. Young Callum, middle aged Callum, elderly Callum. She read the story from 9-11, could almost see him shuffling down to ground zero. Despite his age, he would have been a commanding presence, would have inspired his fellow officers. She was so proud of him. Her biggest regret was that she would never get the chance to tell him. It was unfair that he had been able to leave her a letter and she couldn't do the same in return.

Eventually life returned to normal in all the ways. Seldom began working regular hours again, stopped pushing herself as some type of punishment, stopped looking for a way out. For the foreseeable future, the bakery was her life. She had loved it once; someday she would likely learn to love it again. In the meantime there were her customers and Josh. She didn't have to fake her enthusiasm for them.

She gave Josh fifty thousand dollars. He cried and said he couldn't accept it. She cried and said aunts always gave gifts for birthdays and Christmases and she was making good for all the ones she'd missed. He laughed and said she was crazy. She laughed and said she agreed but he was taking the money nonetheless. Currently he was enmeshed in a hunt for a new apartment that was as daunting as apartment hunting in Manhattan always was.

In all the excitement, she had forgotten to take down her dating profile. Since her return three more men had responded, asking her to meet. She said no to all of them and removed her profile. Maybe in time she would be ready to try again, or maybe she would meet someone organically, the way it was supposed to be. Either way, she was done trying to force things that weren't meant to be, at least for the moment.

She let herself into the bakery as the first hazy rays of dawn began to steal over the horizon, trying not to think about how the bakery had looked the same on the day she returned. It was too painful to remember what she had walked away from. She returned her keys to her purse, took a step further inside, and stopped short.

"Well, well, well. Seldom. Missed me?"

Christian stood in the middle of the room. His face was in shadow, but she had memorized his voice, apparently, because she had no trouble recognizing it when he spoke.

"No. What are you doing here?"

"I missed you."

She stood surveying him in shock, hands on hips. Out of everything that had happened to her, Christian had seemed the most like a dream, or rather a nightmare. For a while, she had convinced herself he hadn't been real. "How did you get rid of the emails you sent me?"

He shook his head, smiling as if it amused him that this would be the question she chose to focus on. "It was a simple little hack; a kindergartener could have done it. Couldn't have you running to the police, could I?"

She almost told him it hadn't mattered because they hadn't believed her anyway. Instead she said, almost conversationally, "Why are you here?"

"We have some unfinished business, you and I."

"No, we don't. Go away."

He laughed and strode toward her, standing too close so she was forced either to crane her neck or take a step away. She chose to stand her ground and look up.

"Look at you, still so perfect. You complete the picture, Seldom. You were exactly what I was looking for, but you had to go and mess it up. I would love to know how you got away," he said. His hand reached out to touch her face. She batted it away. He reared back to smack her. She put her arm up defensively and kneed him in the groin. As he doubled over, he grabbed a fistful of her hair and brought her with him. They struggled back and forth. Seldom dropped her purse to use both hands. Christian grabbed her around the neck and began to squeeze. She used her legs to try and push him away. He moved away so rapidly that at first she thought she had succeeded in pushing him. And then she realized he'd been pulled away.

For a second, he and Callum stood eye to eye, and then Callum clocked him, his fist hitting Christian's temple with such force that he dropped to the ground like a crumpled piece of paper.

"Exactly how many men have tried to kill you?" Callum asked, shaking out his fist.

"That was the same as the first one," she said, staring at him in disbelief. "What are you doing here?"

"I have no idea. I got home from work, sat down to eat my supper, looked up, and saw this guy pawing you."

"You're here," she said.

"Yes, I'm here."

"No, you're *here*, here in my bakery, here in my year."

"Oh." The word puffed out of him, leaving his mouth frozen in a little ring of surprise.

"I guess I should call the police," she said, but it came out like a question.

Callum nodded. She bent and retrieved her new phone from the purse. She called 911, gave them the information, and disconnected. The awkward silence returned. "So, this is my phone." She held it aloft for his inspection. He took it from her and turned it over, making a cursory inspection.

"Mesmerizing," he said. He tossed the phone onto the counter and reached for her with both hands, kissing her. She kissed him in return, standing on her toes to get closer. When that wasn't close enough to suit either of them, he picked her up.

"I missed you so much," she said, resting her forehead on his chin.

He laughed lightly. "It's only been a few hours, kid." She eased back so she could see his face. "But I missed you, too," he hastily added. "Seldom, I shouldn't have let you go, should have asked you to stay. I don't know why it's so hard for me to say things sometimes, but I want to be with you. Please let's be clear on that."

She thought of the letter he'd sent her, of how much the war had messed him up and left scars. "Callum, all I want is for you to let me in." She tapped his heart. "Please don't shut me out."

"I'll try," he promised. "I can't promise I'll succeed, but I'll try."

"I missed you so much," she said again. "What day is it?"

"The same day you left, sweet girl. The worst day in the world."

"But it's not. It's been weeks again, and when I got back here, it was the same day."

"Must be that pesky space-time continuum," Callum said, and she laughed.

"Seldom?" Josh had entered unaware. He now stood a couple of feet away, his gaze bouncing from the unconscious man on the floor to the stranger now canoodling his boss.

"Josh," Seldom exclaimed, leaving Callum to hug him. "This is Josh." She gave Josh a mom hug, pressing his arms to his sides.

"Yes, I see," Callum said coolly, and she laughed.

"Josh *Pevenzy*. He's named for his great uncle, isn't that something?"

Callum blinked at her before returning his gaze to Josh, much warmer now. "Is he? Well, isn't that something."

"And who might you be, stranger no one has explained," Josh said, his tone as cool as Callum's had been.

"I'm Seldom's," he glanced at her, "what's the word, doll?"

"Boyfriend," she supplied.

"Well that's news. Clue a bloke in, why don't you," Josh said, squirming free of her grasp to squeeze her shoulders.

"It's been a bit complicated, sort of a long distance thing," Seldom said. She let go of Josh and eased back to Callum, needing to touch him again, to make sure he was still real, still there. He put his arm around her and kissed the top of her head, apparently needing the same reassurance.

"And who's this?" Josh asked, toeing Christian.

"This is Christian."

"He came back?" Josh asked. She would love him forever for not saying, *He was real?* instead.

"Apparently he needed closure," Seldom said.

"Huh, so do I," Josh said and kicked him hard in the ribs.

"I like this kid," Callum said.

"I knew you would. Peas in a pod, you two. It's almost as if you're cut from the same cloth," she said, her gaze bouncing back and forth between them. Side by side they looked startlingly alike. She wasn't sure how she hadn't seen it before. She had thought Josh reminded her of Mathew, but she was wrong. He was a younger, softer Callum. She wasn't sure if Josh was what Callum could have been if the war had never come or if Callum was what Josh would someday become when he grew up and matured. Either way, she adored them both.

Two uniformed officers arrived, followed by a detective.

"I'm Harry Tanaka," the detective said, staring hard at Christian on the floor. He was just beginning to stir.

"You're Jap...anese," Callum said.

Now the detective stared hard at him. "Nothing gets by you, kid. That a problem?"

"No. I knew a lot of Japanese people once," Callum said, still staring like Harry Tanaka was the fascinating thing in this scenario, and not a man who stepped from 1946.

"Small world, me too," Detective Tanaka said before kneeling next to Christian and tapping his chest with a pen. "What we got here?"

"He attacked my girl," Callum supplied.

The detective looked up at him, squinting. "Your girl? You own her? And why you dressed like that." He waved to Callum's suit, topped by the fedora he had either forgotten to take off when he returned from work or inexplicably grabbed on his way out.

"We're into vintage," Seldom said, motioning to her swing dress. "Right down to the lingo. This guy attacked me before. I made a report."

"That so?" Harry said.

"Yes. Your other detective was less than impressed," Seldom said with some bitterness. The other officer had made her feel crazy.

"Takes a lot to impress an NYPD detective," Mr. Tanaka said.

"That's true," Callum agreed.

"I think he was trying to copycat a serial killer," Seldom said.

"You do, do you?" the detective said, deadpan. He stood, knees cracking, and put a hand to his back, wincing. "What makes you say so, see it on one of those CSI shows?"

"No, I saw it in person. Last time he chained me to a pipe and set out a tray of medical instruments. Have you ever heard of Giles Montgomery?"

The detective squinted, thinking.

"Mass murderer from the forties," Callum supplied. "Chopped up eight girls."

"Eight? I thought it was six," Seldom said.

"We, I mean they, cracked him. Sang like a little bird, wept like a baby and confessed to each one."

"That the guy that took the hands?" Mr. Tanaka said.

"One and the same," Callum agreed.

"Geez," he eyed Christian again, with more interest this time. "What makes you think this moron was trying to do the same?"

"He targeted me, I think because I look like this," Seldom said, motioning to her dress again. "It all seemed the same, felt the same." She shuddered. Callum gave her shoulders a bracing squeeze. On her other side, Josh reached out and did the same to her hand.

For the second time since her return, she closed the shop. This time she sent Josh home, wishing him luck on his fruitless apartment hunt.

"Nice to meet you," Josh said to Callum, holding out his hand. "Sorry, in all the confusion I didn't catch a name."

"Callum," he said, shaking Josh's hand in return.

"That's...that's odd," Josh said, glancing back and forth between Callum and Seldom. "That was my uncle's first name."

"Small world," Callum said.

"The smallest," Seldom agreed.

"Call if you need anything," Josh said, giving Seldom a sideways hug, his eyes still on Callum.

"She's in good hands," Callum said, somewhere between amused and territorial.

"Hmm," Josh said, easing backwards out of the bakery, his eyes still on them.

"Seems like a good kid," Callum said, "emphasis on the kid."

"Yes, he is a good kid," Seldom agreed, "emphasis on the good."

A couple of hours later, the detectives were finished. "Are you going to be able to hold him for simple assault?" Callum asked, bringing up something Seldom hadn't considered. What would she do if Christian was released? Or, a better question, what would Christian do? Would he come back for her? Would he *keep* coming back for her?

"I'll tell you," Detective Tanaka said, taking a glance over his shoulder to make sure they weren't overheard, "there's been a couple of cases like what you said, girls drained of blood. We've managed to keep it out of the news so far. This might be the guy. Good news is he left some DNA at one of the scenes. If we can connect it to him and get all our ducks in a row, should be open and shut."

"Excellent," Callum said. He jutted forth his hand for the detective to shake. Mr. Tanaka stared at it, amused by what he considered an odd gesture. Seldom, on the other hand, was delighted. If he knew what a leap forward it was for Callum to do so, he'd have no qualms. Reluctantly, he stuck out his hand and the two men shook.

"Good cop," Callum commented after he was gone. Seldom hugged him, understanding it wasn't as casual an admission as it seemed.

"So," Seldom said when they were finally alone.

"So," Callum said, grinning.

"It would seem the time/space thing works to our advantage. You could probably stay here a while and no one would be the wiser about your absence," she said.

He glanced at the wall, still a wall, no other dimension available. "It seems I don't have a choice."

"And if you did?" she asked.

He brushed her cheek with his knuckle. "I'd stay, at least for a while."

Seldom clutched his shirt, doing a little dance of excitement. "There's so much to show you. I don't know where to begin."

Callum smiled. "I'm happy you're happy, kid. But all I care about here is you." He tipped her face and kissed her and it was a while before either of them thought of the outside world or the year or anything but each other.